MW01233433

Honor & Chivalry Among Vampires

Books 1 and 2 of the Elders of the Paper Flower Consortium

Written and Illustrated by Elizabeth Guizzetti

First Edition Novellas edited by Joe Dacy
Omnibus edited by Denise DeSio
Cover and Illustrations by Elizabeth Guizzetti

Omnibus Hardback ISBN: 978-1-950708-33-8
Omnibus Paperback ISBN: 978-1-950708-34-5
Omnibus Ebook ISBN: 978-1-950708-35-2

This book is dedicated to Dennis. I would walk into eternity with you.

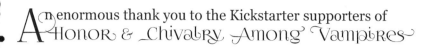

An enormous thank you to the Kickstarter supporters of
Honor & Chivalry Among Vampires

Angela Banks

Bess Turner

Brittnay King

Erik Sapp

Katie Cord & Tim Long

Gail Goodhand

Garret Lowe

Jerry & Sheila Guizzetti

Jennifer Brozek

Jennifer Dittrich

Katie Cord & Tim Long

Keith & Dawn Clement

Marie "Many Hats" Masterson

Mark "Grand PooBah" Monlux

Mary Alderdice

Raven Oak

Robert Woods Tienken

Stephanie Bissette-Roark

Vampy

Wendy Zaballos

Will

Liam Hemlock

I simply could not have put out this book without you!

Preface:

"Agata looked to be a woman in her thirties, her long chestnut braids went past her waist. Jakub might be a bit older, but not by much. Looking at the Shakespearean beard and mustache and midback curls, Laurence was glad he wasn't stuck with that much hair for eternity." --*Immortal House*

So here we are, Dear Readers,

After the success of the hardbacks of *The Vampires of the Paper Flower Consortium* and *Accident Among Vampires (Or What Would Dracula Do?)* I decided to re-release all the books as illustrated hardbacks. Now very few who collect hardbacks wants huge size difference between volumes so this book was created by combining *Honor Among Vampires* and *Chivalry Among Vampires* together. There are some minor changes from the two novellas. I noticed a few sentences that were in a strange order and that led to having this edition re-proofread. There was also the prologue problem. *Honor* did not have a prologue; *Chivalry* did. Good news. *Honor* has one now!

There was a lot of research for the two novellas. The word "viteji" is a Moldavian cavalry solider, most often noble born, heavily armed and armored. This is Jakub's job in *Honor*. I considered using "le chevalier" which is the direct translation for knight, but I wanted it to be clear. Jakub is not looking to be a simple cavalry officer. He wants to be a knight and all that entails. Perhaps even more importantly, I mention the word: "chevalerie" which is the French word for chivalry, I knew it would get confusing. De Charny was a real person who wrote a treatise called *Livre de chevalerie*, (Book of Chivalry) and was considered, both then and now, one of France's greatest knights.

I researched Romanian vampire myths, the former and current culture, and Roman, Saxon, and Ottoman influences upon the Medieval Period. Using a historical map, I made up the county and town of Râuflor — though if it existed, it would lie on the northwestern part of historical Trotus. By its description, the county lay in the Carpathians and needed to be close to ancient and 16th-century roads. I also had to research Roman, Saxon, and Ottoman influences upon the Medieval Period. I also had to do massive amounts of research on King Louis XII and France in 1510-1511.

The elephant in the room is Jakub and Agata both took vows which puts Jakub is in charge due to his gender. Compared to modern culture, Jakub and Agata's views on marriage are old-fashioned at best. However, I hoped I showed their views on marriage are nuanced and based on Moldavian marriage and divorce law and de Charny's views. So how do I write about a couple whose marriage can last for centuries? By writing about a marriage filled with mutual respect, love, and trust. Do they make mistakes? Of course.

I also think we tend to view the past with a microscopic lens; that is, we see what we want to see and our own cultural viewpoint.

It's incredible how many people assume people in the Middle Ages did not bathe and have questioned me on that topic after *Honor Among Vampires*.

I have so much gratitude for my Kickstarter supporters. I also want to thank Joe Dacy, who edited the novellas, and

Denise DeSio, who proofread this edition. I also want to thank my author buddies: N.D. Fessenden beta-read the novellas, Ashleigh Gauch listened to my fears about this storyline, Raven Oak and Jennifer Brozek who chatted with me multiple times about the premise of a multi-sub genre series of vampire family dramas.

And thanks to my husband, Dennis, who has supported me in all my writing.

And thank you, dear readers, I hope you enjoy it!

Honor
Among
Vampires

4 Bc

Prologue

The oracle, Phillipa, buckled the legatus's armor into place. Sweat coated her skin; the air stopped moving. She saw his death... and hers. "You will win the day, but if you... Come to my bed, or the man I love will die," she warned. "There will be endless nights."

"Is an assassin in camp?" Gaius asked.

"No. I don't know. I only see you die tonight and live again. Endless. I've foreseen endless." Phillipa held out his sword, which he accepted and buckled around his waist.

"Tonight? Not in battle, is there an accident?"

"Someone bites you! I see fangs...teeth...blood."

"Perhaps a boar? I'll send out a hunting party."

He was not listening. His mind was on the battle ahead. She grabbed his wrist. Gaius removed her hand. He kissed her. His lips tasted like the olive oil which cleansed and anointed his skin. He pressed his forehead to hers and gave her a winning smile. "The men must come first. However, if we have endless nights, plenty will be spent in your bed."

*

1509

Chapter 1

Agata Arturescu Vidraru composed a letter to her husband as she watched two of her five children outside her kitchen window. A great tactician, Jakub Petruescu Christian, had fought in several battles. In the seventeen years of their marriage, Jakub had been gone for nine in separate actions. She should feel pride. However, it had been almost four years since he last graced their home. Worse, Agata had not received a letter from him in seven months.

Just as his father had been, their current voivode was troubled by the never-ending invading forces of the Ottomans, Polish, Wallachian, among others, and broken alliances with those countries. Agata prayed each night for Moldavia's soldiers, but that did not stop her fear of plague or pox, which might afflict the army. Only God might know when her Jakub would return home.

Before her disquiet got the better of her, Agata reminded herself, "Snow came early last year; the new spring had just arrived. Jakub's fine. It's hard for letters to cross the mountains during the winter. One day, several letters arrive. If God is kind, my husband will deliver them himself."

Outside, their son, Artur, untied his sister's Mărțișor

from her tunic. A powerful talisman, the twisted white and red string ended in two tassels and held a silver charm. It seemed so universal. Red: the color of fire, blood, darkness, death, passion, and women. White: the color of ice, air, light, life, wisdom, and men.

"Tie it high this year!" Daciana demanded. "I don't want the goat to get it!"

Agata wrote:

Oh my beloved, how proud you would be of Artur. He has grown as taller than me over the past winter. His voice has lowered and is sprouting his first beard. After the ceremony, we moved him lived into the bachelor's quarters...

Agata went onto explain Artur's employment in the service of Jakub's brother, Count Mihai. He took guard duty with the other men, but he also counted the cows for Agata, studied their family's accounts, and had never lost even the most reticent heifer. Most importantly to Agata, he never lost patience with his youngest sister, the only child still at home. Like all four-year-olds, Daciana could be both loving, selfish, and taxing—often all at once.

"Your wish is my command."

Artur's sepia eyes, which he inherited from Agata, had a

haunting focus on his little sister's errand.

Any man would be proud to have such a son. His back was straight; his shirt and woolen coat hid his wiry muscles. Artur jumped onto a low branch. His dark hair was mussed; his tanned skin was made ruddy by the spring wind that blew the fragrance of the mountains into the valley.

Halfway up the apple tree, he called: "This high? Next to Mothers?"

"No. As high as yours." Daciana jumped around the tree; her black hair flying.

Artur climbed two more branches and tied the red and white string beside his own. The tassels fluttered in the breeze.

Agata sighed. While she and the servants had also tied their Mărțișors to the tree, only Artur and Daciana would tie theirs to the apple tree this year.

Her eldest, Irina, now sixteen, had married the spice merchant's eldest son and made a fine house on Merchant Street. As part of the marriage contract, her younger son, Petru, had received an apprenticeship with the spice merchant. No doubt, they would tie their Mărțișors to a tree in the center of town. Her middle daughter was in the grave; Little Daniela had not lived long enough to see the turning of a single year.

"We'll be strong all year!" Daciana shouted.

Artur lowered himself, careful not to land on his sister.

"Let's play Old Blind Woman!" Daciana said.

"I've guard duty," he said, pointing at the sundial.

"You never have time to play with me anymore." She pouted and wrapped her arms around his leg. "And Mama has to make bread today. Please."

He rested his hand on her head. "If you promise to stay out from underfoot, you can tag along and be a soldier today."

"Mama, I'm a soldier," she yelled toward the kitchen window.

Agata waved. "Listen to your brother and the other men."

Smiling, she returned to her letter.

She wrote how she was teaching Daciana her alphabet. Their youngest spelled out merchant signs around their town and could write cat, cow, goat, and dog on a wax tablet.

The sundial showed it was noon when Daciana dashed into the kitchen, jumping up and down with her eternal energy. "Mama, Auntie's coming!"

She ran out again; the kitchen door slammed in its frame. Agata set her writing supplies high on a shelf, rang for Cook, and went to greet her sister-in-law. They had bread to bake.

The count's towered castle situated on the hill on the east side of Râuflor also had a bread oven, but they used Agata's kitchen. While Count Mihai never minded paying for the flour or wood, he hated the mess, Cook's songs, women's talk, and the laughter of the children who stole bits of dough.

Tomorrow, as they did every Saturday, Agata and Gavrilla Musca Ricescu would pass loaves of bread to the peasant farmers, merchants, servants, soldiers, and priests as was their duty. Râuflor was not only the county seat and oversaw seven villages, but was the largest town in the area. Many farmers and hunters made the trip to collect their bread and buy and sell wares at the large market day. If the day was profitable, they might purchase goods at the row of permanent stores.

Gavrilla's footman helped the countess off the wagon.

Her servants unloaded the heavy bags of flour and carried them into the kitchen. Daciana bowed, then hugged the countess around her waist. Gavrilla picked her up and kissed her cheeks. She smoothed her linen le and fata once she set the child back on the ground. Daciana scampered back to Artur and the other soldiers, because of course, she was still on guard duty.

The women kissed each other on the cheeks.

Agata touched Gavrilla's plump belly carrying her fourth child. "And how is my little niece or nephew?"

"Kicking, but not as hard as my boys. It might be a girl this time." Gavrilla crossed herself. "I apologize for my lateness; Bogdan came to argue with my husband."

Agata had an icy feeling in her chest. She knew what Bogdan wanted. Though he shared a name with their Voivode, the parish priest's behavior was anything but princely. He had hinted Jakub had died in battle, and Agata might consider a husband who was home.

She was no fool. Bogdan did not have eyes for her. He desired her fine house and profitable dairy. Marrying his cousin's unprotected widow would be an honorable way to leave the priesthood, which he complained about to Mihai when he thought others weren't listening. Moreover, he had despised Jakub since they were boys. Agata did not like to think her husband had bullied his common-born cousin, but Bogdan's eyes alighted with joy at the thought of Jakub's demise.

Her hands felt clammy. She struggled to open the crock of maia. Cook took the jar away from her and opened it. The smell of yeast filled the kitchen.

"He feels I should take suitors," Agata said in a flat voice.

"Yes." Gavrilla sat on a wooden bench. She measured the water and thinned the maia.

"My husband will come home," Agata said.

"Of course, Jakub will come home," Gavrilla said. "The count will not consider otherwise."

"Perhaps, you ought to look for a daughter-in-law." Cook weighed the litrăs of flour for the first batch in a long wooden bowl. "You have a grown son. When Artur takes a wife, there'll be more babies in the house."

"My son will marry after he finishes his education, Cook," Agata said, careful not to speak too harshly. One should never talk sharply when baking bread. It spoils the rise.

"Move Irina and her man back into the house," Cook suggested, carefully measuring the thinned maia into the flour.

Agata stirred it with a wooden spoon until a loose dough formed. She placed a damp linen rag over the bowl and set the dough aside.

"Oh, Cook, Irina enjoys being mistress of her own house." Gavrilla prepared more maia with water for the next batch. "Please, we must continue our toils before night. It is the seventh day after the full moon, and the count has made a fine sacrifice for the Legatus, a yearling hogget with the fluffiest pure white wool."

"Continued blessings for our wise count and beautiful countess," Cook said.

Like every count whose county surrounded the nearby Carpathians (whether they be Wallachian or Moldavian), Mihai would leave one perfect ewe in the field on the ancient calendar. Or at least, that was what Agata had been told. She had only been to two counties. The one in which she was born and the one into which she married. During his life, her father also put out a sheep outside his township only it was the tenth night after the full moon. Nowadays, her younger brother bore the responsibility.

Though the counts paid their tributes and the peasants feared vampires, Agata did not believe in the myths of the old Roman Legatus, who lived in the crumbling Roman ruins on top of the highest mountain. She credited a family of brigands for using a well-told myth to keep themselves in relative comfort. Legends could be eternal. As the old saying went: some things were more lasting than bronze.

"Too bad, we can't sacrifice a priest who refuses the vows of poverty and looks at other men's wives," Cook said.

"Why would a vampire want an irritable old priest?" Gavrilla said. "His meat probably tastes as dry as twenty-year-old ram!"

The women looked at each other and laughed. The sound of joy lightened Agata's spirits.

"A donia," Gavrilla said.

"As Countess wishes." Cook improvised a happy song to help Agata forget her troubles and bless Gavrilla's coming child.

*

Agata moved about her home, preparing for the night. Her back was stiff from the long day's work. The smell of fresh bread followed every step as her soft leather shoes shuffled along the stone-tiled floor. Every step was lit with her candle.

Tomorrow, the sun would rise.

However, tonight, the waning moon was hidden by the deep clouds in the sky. Outside, the wind blew and rattled the leaded glass windows, which she checked and latched one by one. No doubt, the servants would whisper their superstitious stories as they held each other in the night.

Even if she spent all night in prayer, she would pine for Jakub. She hoped he was alive but feared her husband was dead. At thirty-two, Agata was still young enough to have a few more children if God would bring Jakub home.

She checked the nursery, which seemed eerily quiet. Only Daciana still nestled in her nurse's arms. The two were burrowed under a wool blanket and a heavy cow skin. The windows were already locked tight.

In silence, Agata padded out of the nursery.

The manservant, Florin, bowed his head. "The kitchen and buttery are locked up for the night, my lady, but your son is calling."

"Thank you."

Agata hurried down the stairs to the hall where Artur waited.

"Lady Mother, one of the first-year heifers suffers from calving—Robert requested your guidance."

"Yes, my son. I'm coming."

Though her back ached, she was grateful for the distraction. As it had been a day full of hard work, she was mostly dressed for such a venture. She removed her embroidered slippers and put on heavy boots. She pulled a cloak over her everyday cotton le and woolen fata. Her maramă, which covered her coiled black hair, was plain linen.

The manservant's hand trembled on the open door. "My lady, it is late. Be wary of the Legatus."

"I've my son to protect me, and the count put out a perfect sacrifice. Keep the house locked up tight," Agata said.

He inclined his head at her.

As the younger daughter of a Count and the wife of a Count's younger son, Agata could not be too safe when it came to money. Who knew when Jakub would return? Her own mother died in poverty because of the taxes and tithings-owed after Agata's father and elder brother died. With Jakub's blessing, Agata became a learned midwife and kept a profitable dairy. She could not afford to lose a cow and her calf. The cows were her children's inheritance. Artur and Petru were coming to the age where she would need to negotiate marriage—even if they did not marry immediately. She hoped Jakub would be home when that happened, but she knew his wishes on the matter.

Artur held her arm; Agata shivered in the cold air. They crossed the narrow path through the herb garden, where soft leaves brushed against her skirts as if to protect her from venturing into the night. The wind changed, and Agata inhaled the perfume of everlasting rosemary. Her other herbs and peppers had not bloomed yet.

With the great house behind her, Agata's eyes adjusted to the darkness as they picked their way across the meadow to the birthing barn. Her herdsman, Robert Robescue, waited for them.

The cow wrung her tail and tried to kick her stomach. She snorted and mooed weakly yet seemed restless.

"Shh, how's my good girl? I'll help you. Let us give her a

bit of fresh hay. How long has she been in labor?" Agata asked.

"She wasn't in labor after midmeal but didn't want to come in from the pasture tonight, Lady," the herdsman said.

Agata removed her cloak, rolled up her sleeves, and washed her hands with cold water and potash soap. She rubbed pressed oil onto her hands and arms.

She used more oil to feel the cow's cervix. She observed the calf's head and a frothy mouth and nostrils, but no hooves. The calf was straight on rather than leaning to its right. Worse, the cow's water had broken.

"She is dilated. The head is in the birth canal," Agata said.

"Will we lose her, Lady Mother?" Artur asked.

"She just needs a little help."

"Walk slow, Artur," Robert said. "New mothers can be skittery."

Agata reoiled her arm and waited for the next contraction. Once it passed, she pushed the calf into the correct position. She sang a donia to the cow and prayed—another contraction, then another.

Two hours later, she had a healthy mother and baby.

"Robert?" Agata called. No response.

"Artur?" She peeked out of the stall.

The men's frames leaned against the far wall asleep, next to several buckets of water and a bar of soap.

She thought about waking them, but instead, she washed the cow as the new mother licked her baby clean. Wet, but happy in her night's good work, she stole a moment to gaze upon her angelic son. She would not embarrass him by treating him like a boy in front of another man, but she felt a deep sadness that she would never embrace him like a boy again.

Outside, there was a low howl.

A chicken squawked from the coop. The cows in the main barn mooed in protest and fear.

"It is just an animal," Agata said but still felt the need to cross herself.

She decided once she was back inside, she would sleep in the nursery with Daciana.

Agata whispered a prayer. "Dear God, please return my husband to me. I miss him so much."

The priests said the most important thing a noblewoman could do was bear children for her husband and to produce cavalry officers for the Voivode's army that protected their country from generations of invaders. It was her duty and honor. So she added to the prayer. "If he returns, I'm still young enough to give him another child or two. Bless me with more children."

She shook Artur awake.

"What is it?" He asked, rubbing his eyes.

"A girl calf, my son. We've been fortunate tonight."

"And the mother?" Robert yawned.

"Both are doing well." Agata said, "It's late. Artur, did you plan on sleeping in the house tonight or going back to the bachelor's quarters?

"Robert, I can put you with the servants if you don't want to cross town under the darkness."

Another howl interrupted her words. This one sounded closer. Wolves never came in this close to the walled city.

She thought she heard a horse. *Jakub.*

Robert jumped to his feet. "Stay here, my lady."

He was just out of sight when he bellowed. The door to the birthing barn slammed shut.

"What is it?" Artur called.

Robert shouted an unintelligible reply. Another voice added to the deafening noise. Moos became brays of panic. Something hard hit the barn door. The door rattled. The entire barn trembled.

Agata held her cross tightly and said a prayer under her breath.

Artur grabbed Agata's wrist and pulled her behind him. He drew his short sword. "Mother, get back!"

The wooden door cracked. A board was ripped off the door. A massive arm silhouetted against the night sky. Another board broke.

"Who's there? I am armed," Artur warned.

The only answer was the door being ripped away.

An unseen force of wind and movement kicked up the hay. Artur unsheathed his sword.

Agata could only see a huge black mass as she was thrown away from her son. She screamed his name as a masculine battle cry filled the air. Artur shouted in return. There was a short clanging of metal. Then the sound of something fleshy hitting the barn wall, or perhaps a stall door.

Then silence.

Darkness was all around her.

"God, help us!"

The cow bleated in panic; the calf squealed. Hay rose in the sky as the cow kicked and bucked.

Hands clamped on Agata's shoulders and forced her away

from the cows, away from her fallen son. She was pushed against the wall. Her maramă was ripped from her head. Hands pulled her plaited, coiled hair. She screamed as two piercing blades ripped into her throat.

Agata slapped, scratched, and kicked her attacker, but he only buried the blades deeper. She could not see her son, only blackness. "Artur, Artur!"

"By rights, you're mine," a low husky voice whispered.

Agata felt as if she was being smothered by obscurity. Her mind grew woolly, and her arms fell to her sides.

Weakened, she could not breathe. Her fingertips grew cold, numb. She thought her heart would explode. She fell into darkness.

*

Chapter 2

Agata awoke against the wall of the barn; Florin and Cook stood over her. Their faces set in concern. Her skirt and shirt were covered in sticky blood and birthing liquid. She touched her bare head; her hair had been freed. A strange man had seen her hair. The fiend had touched it. Her throat and tongue were swollen with thirst. Her skirts were ripped. Her body felt torn. She must do nothing to expose her injuries, until she was sure.

"Cia?" she croaked.

"In the house, my lady." Cook found her maramă and handed it to her.

"My baby girl, my God, was she touched?" Agata covered her head.

"No, my lady. We were tucked safe in our beds until this morning when the household staff realized you were still in the barn."

Artur.

A cold feeling spread through her heart. "Artur? My son?"

"I don't see him," Florin said.

"Artur," she called.

He did not answer.

Though her throat felt like it was coated in dust, she called louder, "Artur!"

Using the wall and Cook as support, she rose to her feet. Her knees felt watery, but she stood as tall as she could.

In the birthing stall, her first-year heifer was on its side, breathing heavily. Shallow wounds covered her body. Beside her, the calf was crushed. She had lost a calf!

Agata licked her lips. Her throat ached, parched by dryness. Her tongue was cracked. Her mind screamed to press her lips to her sweet cow. If she could press her lips to her cow's wounds, the blood would banish this mad thirst.

Her mind flew to Saint Photina, the Samaritan woman who spoke to Jesus at the well. Photina suffered many tortures at the hand of Emperor Nero for her faith, eventually being tossed down a well. Jesus had told the woman if she drank from the well, she would always be thirsty, but if she drank the water he gave her, she would never thirst. Agata was a woman of God, a follower of Christ, yet she felt as if she drank from a well of corruption and sin. Her thirst would never slacken.

"Artur? Artur!"

In a daze, Agata wandered the barn, clutching Cook's arm. They found his sword on the ground first. Agata feared the worst. Yet, she discovered her son lying on his back in another stall, against the far wall, half-buried in dirty hay. He was bleeding from a wound on his arm and a gash across his brow.

"Artur!" She screamed.

He did not move. She pressed her ear against his chest. He was breathing. The fingers on his right hand were broken, and he had a lump on his head. She pulled her son to her chest and rocked him tightly. "My boy, my angel."

Artur's eyes fluttered open. "Ma, Mother? I wasn't able to stop them. I'm sorry."

Sobbing in relief, she said, "We're alive. We'll send a messenger to the magistrate.

"Where's Robert?"

"My lady, don't grieve, but your herdsman is dead," Cook said. "Outside. His throat has been ripped out."

Agata sobbed harder. With his uninjured hand, Artur helped her to her feet. His eyes full of tears that did not fall. "I'll wait for the mayor; you're overwrought." He lowered his voice, trying to sound like a man.

Agata told him. "I might need to defend my honor."

Artur straightened. He was his mother's son, but that did not give her comfort. "Mother! What does a woman know about anything? With my father in the world, I speak for this house."

"Yes, my son," she said. "Forgive me."

"There is nothing to forgive, you're overwrought. Take my mother to her woman," Artur ordered the servants.

What am I to tell Jakub? Will he believe me?

Divorce was legal, but Jakub's family would not suffer the loss of the family's honor. However, at this moment, Agata was the mistress of her house. She found her voice again. "And Florin will bring you a fresh cămaşa, pieptar and bandages to splint your fingers. You're covered in filth, my son."

He thanked her.

Agata held Cook's arm. She told herself not to look at the body. Yet when they passed Robert, his eyes stared at the endless sky and his throat was covered in dried blood.

While Artur waited for the mayor, Agata called for water

and went into her private chamber. Every wall was covered with thick tapestries of flowers, leaves, unicorns and symbols of astronomical power from several countries, proof of Jakub's devotion to her and the children.

Her arms were covered in scratches, and her body was torn by whatever the brute did to her. She had several bite marks, pairs of small puncture wounds. She tried to remember, but it had been so dark.

Dear God, please, let me not be pregnant.

If she was pregnant and Jakub was not here, her in-laws might accuse her of being an adulteress. Jakub's brother, Count Mihai, hated scandal above all. Perhaps she should provide betrothals for her younger children, especially Daciana, before her loss of honor was discovered.

She jumped at a knock on the door and covered her body with her sleeping coat. Her maid, Elana, came in with two buckets of steaming water which she poured into the tub. She sprinkled in rose petals.

"Are you badly injured?"

"I don't know." Tears crested her eyes and dripped down her cheeks. "I'm so sorry for Robert's death, yet so happy Artur lived. I feared he was dead too."

"As any mother would," Elana said. "Forgive me, but the guards want to know about the bread?"

She remembered the day. She was a lady of the county. People depended upon her.

"We'll distribute the bread as planned, but I must bathe," Agata said.

"As you wish, my lady," Elana said.

Agata wondered what her maid suspected, what her whole house suspected. Another servant brought in two more buckets. Her maid brought the final two. Agata touched the water. It was uncomfortably hot, but she climbed inside. The maid washed her face, her body, then left her to soak.

Knowing she only had minutes before the maid returned, she left the tub with a cup of soapy bathwater and opened her box of herbs. She seeped several bitter buttons.

Through the walls, she heard Daciana playing (and disobeying her nurse) who was trying to dress her appropriately. With her elder brothers and sister grown, she was often a lonely child with only adults for company.

Agata drank from the potion. She held down the sharp-smelling, soapy water as long as she could. She vomited in her chamber pot, prayed, and sobbed in silence.

She dressed in embroidered flax for the day, careful to ensure her costume was in order and proclaimed her station and her husband's great love. Her neck was covered in a high collar, a string of beads, and a Holy Cross. She combed and braided her hair and wrapped it in a snood. Agata carefully placed her veil and embroidered maramă. She covered her bruised hands with gloves.

Uninvited, male voices invaded her chamber from the window. Her fists squeezed the cold iron shutters as she spotted Artur and the manservant speaking to the magistrate and two deputies. The shutters were decoratively sculpted like leaves, but they felt like bars. Dishonored noblewomen were known to be walled into their homes, but she doubted Count Mihai would go to the expense. It would be cheaper to have her killed.

Trying to calm her nerves, she inhaled. The sweet and spicy perfume of her herb garden was absent. All she could smell was the vomit in her chamber pot and death. She gazed at the Mărțișors - talismans of strength- dangling from the apple tree; the tassels stirring in the wind. She must be strong for her children's sake.

Agata thought about calling down to the men, but she had a grown son to speak for her. He would decide to bring charges on behalf of his father — or not.

Their callous eyes stared up at her when they heard she was in the birthing barn. These were hard men. They knew the world. Even if Artur would not say the words: they must know she was raped. Yet, no one spoke of it. Perhaps, it was because if Jakub was dead on a battlefield, her rapist would not even be charged. Perhaps, if she was not pregnant, silence was better than scandal.

After they left, Agata went to speak to Artur. "What did you tell them, my son?"

"We were attacked and robbed last night. We were both injured, but our poor herdsman was murdered. Some peasants whispered the Legatus came down from the mountain, but the magistrate told me our assailants will be caught and hung for murder."

Injured? Tears splashed her cheeks. She was so furious; she could not look at her son in the eyes. Her assailant would be hung for murder. *Stop weeping! What good would it be for the count's sister-in-law to be embroiled in a scandal?*

"I'm sorry that you lost a friend, my beloved son, I know how you felt about Robert. Would you help calm an old woman today?"

"Of course, Mother, you have nothing to be frightened about, not anymore." He kissed her left cheek and then her right.

Daciana ran to Artur. "Our Countess is coming! I'm passing bread to the peasants, I'm passing bread to the peasants."

Her brother knelt and gave her a kiss on the cheek. "Are you coming with the soldiers?" she asked.

"Your brother has business to conduct today with your uncle," Agata said. "Are you ready to go? Here comes your noble aunt."

Gavrilla and her entourage approached the house. How would she face her? She was her dearest friend and sister-by-law, but she was still a Countess and must protect the county above all. Gavrilla was too intelligent not to know something was wrong.

Agata trembled.

"Perhaps you ought to stay home, my mother?" Artur said.

With more confidence than she felt, she put her quaking hands on her hips and stated, "And set idle tongues on me? No, my son, that will not do. The peasants need their Sunday bread."

*

Chapter 3

Agata walked beside Gavrilla along the fortified walls. Râuflor was the largest defended town in several counties, but today thick, stone walls provided no comfort. Several Guild towers were erected around the city by the Saxons to protect the town from the Turkish raids. The two soldiers walking in front of them seemed too young and inexperienced to offer protection. Daciana jumped, hopped, and skipped. She stopped to pluck a stray flower and handed it to Agata. Their servants and yoked oxen carried the baskets of bread. They passed the city gate carved with the words: 𝕲𝕺𝕯 𝕴𝕾 𝕷𝕺𝖁𝕰 and several solar crosses below. Every fruit-bearing tree bore Mărțișors.

Two peasant women moved out of the countess's path. One held an infant, who Agata had delivered, snug at her breast.

As they did every Saturday, she and Gavrilla set the wagon in the town square in the shade of the tallest tower. Nearby, peasant farmers set up their wares for market day.

Statues of Romulus and Remus stood at the door of the tower, above them was a carving of the giant wolf who suckled them. The clocktower was topped with the family signet to symbolize the accountability of the Town Council to the count who in turn was accountable to the Voivode. Beside the towers sat the gallows and a set of stocks. A woman and man sat clamped in irons. The sign above their head said: ᴄꟼɪᴇᴠᴇꙅ. They looked drawn and cold as if they had spent the night. *If the Legatus had come, wouldn't they be dead?*

I don't believe in the Legatus! She shuddered as she felt the deadly reminder of men's cruelty. *How many of my midwife sisters lost their lives in this square hung as witches?* Agata had lost her honor. If Jakub wanted a divorce, the count would not tolerate the scandal. She would be killed. Not hung publicly in a square, her death would be discreet.

Mihai would give Jakub a new wife before Agata's body went cold. The carved wooden porch and iron shutters would protect someone else from the rain. The new wife would remove Agata's tapestries and insist on new ones. She would change the carpet. She might paint over the flowers and fertility symbols which Agata's hand-painted on the row of tiles under the roof. Agata would slowly be erased.

"Are you all right, my sister?"

Agata coughed. Her tongue weighed a thousand drams. "I'm thirsty, my dear Countess."

Gavrilla snapped her fingers. A young soldier brought Agata a leather of watered wine. The wine did not quench her thirst, but she thanked him.

The sun stung her eyes. She drew her veil over her face. She could not look at the men as she passed loaves to each family. She did not know if one —or several— of them was Robert's murderer, Artur's assailant, her rapist.

Peasants whispered the Legatus of the Mountains had come down to feed on the populace last night. Several cows and pigs had gone missing. Artur and his mother were attacked. Robert was killed. She felt their eyes on her.

"What is it, dearest sister Agata?"

"Nothing, Countess, nothing."

Gavrilla made a sound under her breath to show she did not believe her.

"I would like to have more children when Jakub returns. If not for Daciana still at home, I might go mad."

"Perhaps, my dearest sister," Gavrilla said piously, "We ought to go to Church once we are finished. You've had a great shock and seem not yourself."

Agata could not stop the shiver which worked its way up her spine. Once Bogdan heard word of the attack, he would insist Jakub be told. He might write to him himself. Gleefully spilling Agata's dishonor to all the men under Jakub's command. They would know of her disgrace and Artur had not pressed charges. Agata must write to Jakub herself; she must tell him.

Yet, besides the church, there was no other structure in Râuflor that they could enter without causing excitement for the merchants or scorn of the town leaders. How narrow the path a noblewoman was allowed to walk.

All she said with a bowed head was: "As you wish, Countess."

A traveling minstrel walked out of the bar and through the rows of market booths, his bawdy song carried on the wind. How she wished he would shut up. Still, she knew he made his living traveling from town to town. She wondered if he had seen her younger brother and his family. *Were they well?* But she could not bring herself to speak to him.

The first peasants collected their bread with grubby hands and dirty clothing in burlap sacks. The wife told her, "Our family prays for you. It was with sorrow we hear you and Artur Jakubescu were injured, you must be wary of the old Legatus, my lady."

She thanked the family for their kindness. She was blessed for hers. The peasant family went to spend their small wealth on freshly churned butter, vegetables, honey, bundles of herbs and garlic in the rows of booths which filled the square.

Another family came forward. Their heartbeats seemed so loud over the sound of market day. Thirst drowned her thoughts. The sun was too bright. For the first time in her life, Agata hated Râuflor and all its inhabitants.

*

Agata and Gavrilla walked to the Kirchenburgen, the fortified Church on the hill. The thick stone walls were large enough to give sanctuary to the entire town, shepherds, hunters, and herdsman, but Agata felt no security.

Daciana skipped in front of the women. Her long black hair swung with her steps in the innocence of girlhood. Too soon, in a decade, perhaps, her hair would be coiled and covered when she became a married woman. Life seemed so transient, naive happiness so fleeting.

The soldiers followed them. Their noisy footsteps pounded on the cobbled stone roads.

Opposite the church was the main entrance to a serene cemetery. She wanted nothing more than to return to her father's county. She had an inexplicable and bizarre impulse to lie on the grave of her mother and sink into the earth, but she was in Jakub's county. The town of which she was born was only five villages to the north, down the main road, but it might be a thousand miles away. Agata had no cart to take her home. She had no horse — and did not know how to ride even if she did.

The women went inside the church. The stained glass dimmed the sunlight and Agata felt as if she could take a breath.

They passed a young novice who swept the stone floor. Incense tickled her nose but did not mask the smell of unwashed serfs sitting in the freshly-waxed wooden pews, speaking to one of the priests.

Besides the stations of the cross, every wall was covered in fresco, showing God's love through Jesus. Jesus handed out fish and bread, Jesus with children, Jesus with the bleeding woman, Agata made the sign of the cross and put alms into the poorbox. Gavrilla put her own charity into the box.

"Irina!" Daciana said behind Agata in a voice much too loud for Church.

Agata spun around to quiet her youngest daughter.

"Good day, Countess." Irina curtsied at Gavrilla first as was custom, but within moments — as the soldiers were outside — the women became a family again. Daciana embraced her sister, who picked her up and kissed her cheek. She curtsied at her mother and kissed her.

They moved into a private prayer room.

"My niece, you're more beautiful by the day," Gavrilla said.

"Thank you, Auntie."

Irina's lush raven hair was groomed in a married woman's

coil and covered as Agata's and Gavrilla's. People had always remarked her best feature was her entrancing eyes, the color of twilight: Jakub's eyes. She had his nose too. It was good for a girl to look so much like her father. The spice of Lexi's trade and Irina's herbal remedies infused into Irina's simply embroidered blouse and skirts.

Agata craved to hold Irina in her arms. Then, she desired her daughter's salty blood.

"Sister, is there more watered wine?" she whispered.

Gavrilla passed her the leather.

She wished to acknowledge her pain to sister-in-law and daughter so they might assure her, Jakub would not direct his wrath at her or at Artur who failed to protect her. He loved them too much. She could not bear his adoration or the dishonor she had brought into his house.

"I should think, Irina," Gavrilla said softly. "Your mother needs comfort today."

"Yes, Auntie," Irina said. "Artur sent word to us. Are you all right, Mother?"

"The knowledge my children are safe lightens my heart," Agata said.

"So, she is not all right." Gavrilla put a comforting arm around Agata.

"Right now, the peasants think the Legatus has come," Irina said. "But the sacrifice was not in the field this morning."

"I fear ... " Agata could not bring herself to say the words.

"Perhaps, my sister," Gavrilla said, "Irina should take Cia tonight. You're trying to be strong for your youngest, but there is no need. Let others care for you. Cia, we have a mission for you, a big girl mission."

Daciana answered with the utmost solemnness of a four-year-old. "Yes, my Auntie Countess?"

"Stand at the gate and say hello to anyone who approaches—even if it is a priest."

"Today, you're our strongest and best soldier." Irina handed her a small sheathed knife.

As she had seen Artur do, Daciana pressed her knife to her heart and bowed. Then she took her position.

Agata and Irina knelt at the prayer bench and lit a candle for Jakub together. They prayed for Jakub's return. Irina prayed for her mother's continued health and the return of her wellbeing. Gavrilla prayed for her beloved friend. Agata silently prayed for the ability to regain her honor. Her family's honor. She felt safe in the company of her daughter and sister-by-law.

Unfortunately, the comfortable family moment evaporated when behind them, in a voice much too loud for inside a Church, Daciana said, "Hello, Father Bogdan, my uncle."

The fragrance of a man who had washed in only aromatic smoke for days wafted into the prayer room. Agata thought that was strange. Bogdan regularly washed on Saturday to prepare himself for Sunday Mass. However, she did not smell just Bogdan's scent. She sensed dirty, fetid hay and the musk of animals upon him. *He must have spent the night anointing the sick or delivering last rites to some poor farmer.*

Ignoring Daciana, he bowed. "Countess. How may I be of service?"

"We light candles for my brother-in-law's safe return. We have no need of you at this time." Gavrilla waved him away.

Agata wished Gavrilla would take care around her daughters. Though Gavrilla was protected by the title Countess and Agata was a non-titled Count's daughter which offered some protection, her children were not protected by the nobility. They were commoners.

"Indeed, Countess, you may have no need of me," Father Bogdan said. "But I am sorry to hear of last night's horror, Lady Agata. This is why it is said a woman shouldn't be alone in the night. If you had a husband who was home every night, this wouldn't have happened."

Agata made the sign of the cross before turning to him.

"Thank you. But I wasn't alone. My son, Artur, was with me and our unlucky friend, Robert who cares for my herd. I thank God I have a healthy son to offer me comfort in these trials, my kinswomen and you, Father Bogdan."

The priest cast his eyes

31

upon her and stepped closer. His breath was sour with beer.

"Surely if a man can't protect his wife, she has grounds for divorce. A woman of your stature must have other suitors."

Feeling like a doe caught in a hunter's eyes, Agata did not move. She could not speak.

Gavrilla moved in front of her. "My sweet sister has no other suitors."

"The peasants say the Legatus has come down from the Mountains to court you," Father Bogdan said. "If he comes for you again tonight, a clear soul will at least allow you to sit at the feet of God. Might I take your confession?"

"Father Bogdan, while we appreciate your concern, if Agata wishes for confession, she will confess to our family priest. We came in to give alms and light candles for our beloved Jakub, not to quarrel with you.

"Leave my sweet sister in peace."

"Count Mihai will hear of your insurrection before God, Countess," Bogdan hissed.

"Please inform my husband you disturbed our prayers for his beloved brother. We might be only women, but there are three of us, we will agree that you interrupted us," Gavrilla said. "As might some young priest wanting to curry favor with the count."

Bogdan lowered his voice. "I still might give you absolution, my cousin's widow." Then he spun around, cassock flying.

Agata felt like all the air had been swept out of the room as Father Bogdan left the prayer room. She clasped herself around the stomach.

"Ignore that fool, Mama. He sought only hateful gossip about Papa," Irina whispered and hugged her about the shoulders.

Agata knew he wanted more. Bogdan wanted what was Jakub's. "I wish to leave this place," she whispered.

"Cia, do you want to sleep at my house tonight?" Irina said.

"Yes!"

"Perhaps Lexi will let Petru off a little early so you might play before the sunset," Irina said.

"You must behave for your sister and brother-in-law," Agata said. "And not be scared, because you'll see me at Mass in the morning, but I won't be able to be with you until midmeal."

"Don't worry, Mama, I'm your bravest solider," Daciana said. "You'll see."

Outside the church, Daciana put the knife in her belt and matched the soldiers' footfalls. As they escorted Irina home, the men quietly chuckled at the diminutive soldier in their midst.

Agata took a few moments to greet her younger son, Petru, her son-in-law, Lexi, and his father, Alexander, but was careful to not take too much of the men's time as the spice shop had many customers. Besides, no apprentice wanted to see his mother while at work.

✱

Chapter 4

Lying in her bed, Agata could not sleep. Parched with thirst, her stomach ached by the amount of water she consumed. Loneliness subsisted all around her. She rolled over and felt the cold place where Jakub should be. She squeezed the quilt to her chest. Nausea rose into her throat. *Dear God, let me not be with child. What if my attacker brought the plague to Râuflor? What if he brought a new disease of Venus?*

She wiped her eyes. "And I lost my calf. A calf that might have helped my boys find suitable brides. I can only pray for the heifer to regain her health."

Above, the servants argued. She did not remember the servants ever speaking so loudly. Did they want her to hear?

"The Legatus came to our town last night," a man said.

"Robert is dead, throat torn open and drained of blood. That's the mark of a strigoi," Another said. A woman?

Agata was pretty sure the last voice was Cook.

"I agree. Seven cows are missing. The heifer was badly injured. The calf is dead. Who else could do this except the Legatus?" Another answered.

"But if it was the Legatus, why didn't he take the count's sheep?" The first countered.

She caught more voices across the garden in the bachelor's quarters where Florin interrogated Artur.

"I barely saw our attacker," Artur growled, "But I will duel the first man who slanders my good mother."

The older men assured him that would not be necessary. They all agreed, never was a finer mistress than Lady Agata.

"No matter what happened," Florin said. "Our tongues will not wag."

Their protestations did not assure Agata since tongues were already wagging.

She slipped out of bed and covered herself in a robe. Her feet were cold on the stone floor. She reached for her door, but thinking better of it, she rang for her maid.

Elana's candle flame flickered as she opened her door. "My lady?"

"Come with me to the kitchen? Last night, I had such a fright, I fear going to the kitchens on my own, but I didn't eat enough at dinner. The attack and the ugliness with Father Bogdan weighs on my heart."

"Certainly, my lady," Elana said, "If you don't mind me saying so, it is unlucky to quarrel with a priest, the countess ought to be more careful. What if he puts the evil eye on you?"

"I fear thinking of such things," Agata said softly as she embraced herself and rubbed the ache from her arms. Though in reality, she feared Bogdan's loose tongue convincing Mihai that he be permitted to marry her and take her house more than the possibility of the evil eye.

Elana put an arm out. Agata allowed herself to be comforted by the other woman's closeness. Her stomach cramped in hunger. The scent of Elana's flesh made Agata salivate. Ignoring the urge to bite her maid, Agata crossed the halls. *What if the Legatus is real? What if he attacked me? No. I don't believe in vampires.*

There was power in gold and silver, parsley and garlic, but not because they could ward off vampires. Infants met death at a midwife's hand because if they were born with a caul, it was thought they were cursed to become vampires. She had witnessed too many instances of infected, untended wounds that might have healed with a good scrubbing of potash soap instead blamed on vampires. Vampires were even blamed when a starving peasant elder failed to recover from a winter's chill when a hot meal might have saved them.

Agata bit the inside of her cheek; trying to pinch the craving away. She looked away from Elana's neck. The pulse within the luscious vein was too much a temptation.

The walls of the long corridor were painted green, but everything seemed black flickering in the candlelight. They passed several tapestries and the carved pillar showing Jakub's family heraldry with his emblem in the cadet position.

They slipped into the kitchen. The maid lit several candles. Light flickered around the room, casting the women in comforting softness.

The two hounds, which the manservant kept, looked up at them and wagged their tails in unison. The maid sliced off a hunk of yesterday's bread and set in on a plate.

Agata swallowed a bite. It tasted like ash in her mouth. As naturally as she could, she broke the rest of the piece in two and threw it to the dogs. They gobbled up the morsel as if their lives depended on it.

Meat was what her body craved. "Do we have sausage in the pantry?"

"Indeed." Elana sliced pieces of blood sausage and set it on the plate.

The hounds nuzzled her side, hoping for more. She listened to the creatures' heartbeats. Their backs trembled under her hand as she pet them. Her mind wrapped around their primitive dog minds.

Food. Lady. Pet. Food. Food. Lady. Pet. Food.

She threw them pieces of sausage.

"Perhaps some milk or beer would help you sleep?" Elana asked.

Beer sounded awful, but perhaps milk would sooth Agata's stomach. "Would you warm me some milk, please? And for yourself, if you wish it."

*

Chapter 5

Agata felt as if she had not slept at all. She could not allow the village to know of her weakness, so she rose to her feet. Agata grasped the bedframe to stop herself from falling. She could not remember ever feeling so dizzy. She considered her symptoms: exhaustion, unsteadiness, thirst, and strange cravings. She never felt this way when the winter chills ran through the town. She had not craved flesh when she was pregnant. She did not have any disease she knew.

What if the peasants are right and there is a Legatus? What if I was attacked by a vampire? Am I one of the damned? Has my hubris set me away from God's path?

Yet, Agata could easily hold her Crucifix as she ever could. Legends said Artemis had cursed the first vampires. Of course, if that were true, why should the Goddess of Wisdom and Craft care about symbols for God the Father, Son, and Holy Ghost?

Another part of the legend claimed vampires could not hold the purity of silver. Agata touched her most elegant shirt, with real silver and gold embroidery running down the sleeves. Her hand did not burn.

I'm being stupid.

Outside the window, the trees moved. She felt the wind,

not tempered by spring and the smoke in her fireplace whisper to her. The legends said as a vampire, she could become mist. No matter how hard she closed her eyes and dreamed, she did not become mist. She was simply Agata.

Now I'm being unquestionably stupid.

Elana entered her room. "How did you sleep, my lady?"

"Wonderfully after our trip to the kitchen," Agata lied. "Send word to my son. I visit Irina today after Mass."

Agata was not even dressed fully when Artur was at her door, his face set in a grimace. She had seen that expression on Mihai's countenance several times over the years. It was never good.

"Mother, I must insist you see Father Bogdan and take confession. He informed me about the ugliness in the church yesterday," he said.

"Your dear aunt stopped him from interrupting Irina and I while we prayed for your father," Agata said. "I sup with Irina after Mass. Tell Bogdan he may visit me at the evening meal."

"He says the sun must be up," Artur said.

"Fine. Bring him to me after midmeal then."

"A woman shouldn't dictate to a priest," Artur said.

"Perhaps not, but Bogdan is looking for scandal everywhere so he might find a better position. Your father's position," Agata said. "Do you want him to take this house?"

Artur pinched his lips together. "I know, Mother. He is a fool, but some whisper you lost your honor. Bogdan will use that if he can."

"I did lose my honor," Agata snapped.

He flinched as if she had slapped him. With a voice full of

shame, he asked, "What are you going to do?"

"I'm a fallen woman. I must ensure Daciana's future before that is known or find some way to regain my honor. If your father was here ... "

Artur's cheeks flushed. "Lucretia regained her honor by sacrifice and built a Republic."

Agata crossed her arms in front of her chest. "If I follow a heroine from our history, I might follow Chiomara's example, my son."

"That is madness. You're better off with Bogdan." With his uninjured hand, he slapped the door jam and slammed the door hard enough that it shook in its hinges. Once he was gone, she found a cup of spring water and gulped it down.

✳

Artur escorted Agata and the household servants to Mass. Except for his frown, there was no evidence of their argument. She kept her head down as if in prayer as she passed Irina, Lexi, Petru, and Daciana.

Daciana gave her a quick wave, but Irina kept her younger sister close.

In the second to front row, Agata genuflected. She easily looked at the Crucifix. She held her prayer book and hymnal, but all she could reflect upon was her unending thirst.

Trying to think of anything else, she thought about her argument with Artur. *Does my son expect me to commit suicide as Lucretia did?*

Since that was not going to happen, she pondered the legend of Chiomara. She might discover the man who attacked her. She might kill her rapist and regain her honor as the legendary queen did. Agata imagined herself climbing the Carpathians. *How could I go into the mountains? How could I take any man's head? I've never picked up a sword.*

Since her marriage, she had never left Râuflor. Before she had only been in her father's county. If she braved the mountains, whether the Legatus was an enterprise brigand, dishonored merchant, or vampire: how would she take his head?

Bogdan's eyes remained on the second row where she sat with her son. With a practiced face, he hid his emotions, but his body emanated with rage. Artur was right. He did not like being dictated to by women. Even the slightest analysis of the man showed Bogdan would make a terrible husband. However, in the depths of her mind, she wondered how he would taste if she bit him hard enough to make him bleed. *He probably tastes like sacrilege with a hint of slothful idleness.*

*

Accompanied by Elana and Florin, Agata took a basket of Cook's rose petal honey cakes to Irina's. The sunlight seemed even more violent today than the day before. In the market square, the two thieves still sat in the stocks. She wanted to offer them comfort but could not chance it when her own reputation had been blemished. Merchant Street was nearly empty as it often was on the Sabbath. Behind the row of shops, she could hear people inside the wooden houses and garden plots. Riotous noises carried through the alley and created a clamor with a mass of its own.

She turned the corner and spied Irina and Daciana

playing with a ball in front of Irina's house. Looking at her two daughters, warmth spread across her heart, and she felt as if she had smiled for the first time since the attack.

"Mama!" Daciana ran toward Agata.

Agata lifted her daughter up and kissed her. "Were you a good girl?"

"Yes," Daciana said. "Lexi and Petru played Little Rabbits with me, and Lexi let me ride on his back."

"He looks forward to the day he is a father," Irina said. "He will be a good father, I think."

"Yes, a tender spirit and generosity to children are the finest attributes of a man." Agata waved at Lexi, Lexi's father and Petru in the garden as they collected herbs for some potion or spice blend.

It is good, Agata thought, *Irina has a husband who is home.* As she had previously, she sensed the steady rhythm of her own sweet daughters' heartbeats. Below Irina's a softer third heartbeat. *What joy!*

"Are you with child?" Agata whispered.

"We don't know. Perhaps. I haven't bled this month," Irina whispered and made the Sign of the Cross to protect herself and the unborn child from any passing devils. The women and servants went inside her house.

Since Irina only kept a single charwoman, she poured watered wine. Agata opened her basket of rose petal cakes and a round of soft cheese.

After helping set the table, Daciana sat on Agata's lap, chattering nearly non-stop about the day's adventures until the men came inside. Agata wondered what Irina had told her husband and father-in-law.

"Mother of my new daughter," Alexander inclined his head to her took his chair, and lit his pipe.

"Father of my new son," Agata replied and inclined her head.

Petru's curly brown hair fell into his face as he bowed to his mother. His father's eyes stared at her in sadness. She ignored the smell of his skin; his hair. He stiffened as she embraced him, but that was the way of apprentice-aged men.

"Irina, I need you to keep Daciana longer. Artur insists Father Bogdan visit me tonight." Though it was a family lunch, she was careful to use Bogdan's title in front of Alexander and Lexi. The town's head priest and cousin of a count was a man to respect and fear.

"Don't worry, Mama," Irina said.

She could not think of a better way to tell her children, so she said it openly: "While I don't remember the entire attack, I drank a parsley potion."

Petru's face reddened, and he clenched his fists.

Alexander spoke: "The whole town knows the Legatus came down from the Mountains, Lady Agata. It doesn't change our goodwill towards you. Whether it was he or another man: we would kill the fiend if we could."

Agata lifted her head and met his eyes, hoping she appeared confident to her children and in-laws. "I will recover my honor before Jakub returns. I ask you to keep my little girl safe. Even from me, if I fail, and I become something I am not."

"Mama, you never believed in vampires," Irina said.

"I may have been wrong," Agata said. "I do still believe

people blame vampires when they should look to ill air, but that doesn't mean the Legatus doesn't exist as well. Or someone pretending to be the Legatus. I mean to discover who is in the mountain and take his head, if I can."

Irina wrapped her arm around Agata. "Mama, don't speak of such things."

"My lady, you don't have to prove your honor," Lexi said. "Vampires only leave their tombs at night. You walk in the day. You're not a vampire."

"I still must prove my honor. Swear to me that Daciana will be safe from all devils."

"We'll keep Cia safe," Petru said. His tone sounded more like a man's by the day.

"Irina's sister is my sister by law and by my heart," Lexi said.

"Your family is tied to mine," Alexander said. "Jakub Petruescu Christian is a great viteji. He will never fail you or

your children by setting you aside."

While she appreciated the kind words, Agata asked, "If I don't return, you will keep my daughters safe?"

Lexi glanced at Irina. He held his silver medallion. "I swear it, Lady Agata. We will find Cia a good husband when she is of age. And if whatever fate befell you, if it happened to Irina, I would not turn my back on her. I love her too much."

Lexi's speech did not alter her mind any more than Alexander's words had.

She embraced Petru. "I'm proud of the man you're becoming. Your aunt and brother will have your father's instructions on your future bride."

She embraced and kissed her daughters in turn. She hugged Lexi. "Be well, all of you."

Escorted by her servants, Agata walked away from the house.

Daciana cried for her. Agata's heart ached for her youngest, but she kept walking. She might not know what happened to her or even if she genuinely was a vampire, but when she embraced her children and smelled their sweet flesh, the thirst grew more intense.

✱

Chapter 6

With Artur and the servants watching, Bogdan held his Crucifix as if it was a shield against Agata in her own home.

"Back, wife of Jakub, if that's who you are." He thrust open the curtains and chalked the sign of the cross on the floorboards. "Or are you the wife of the devil?"

Agata stood in the fading sunlight. Her heart thudded in her chest. Her leg muscles tightened and her back spasmed, urging her to run. She wanted to turn away from Bogdan, but did not dare so much as flinch. He might have her hanged or burned as a witch if she turned from the cross. And above all else, she must protect her children. She tried not to squint, but the afternoon sun was so warm. She and Artur knelt in front of the priest. Though Agata trembled, she reminded herself silently, *I'm the wife of Jakub, not the wife of the devil. My children's mother. A midwife and dairywoman. Being a vampire doesn't change that.*

She smelled the rank scent of Bogdan's sweat as his greasy hand placed a wooden cross on Artur's brow. It made no sense; he usually bathed on Saturday nights to prepare himself for Mass.

"Confess Artur Jakubescu."

"When we were attacked, I was disarmed and failed my mother and our herdsman. Though my mother taught me well, I have a fuller sense, a man's sense, of duty before God." Artur's eyes brimmed with trembling tears, which did not fall. "I think the man thought he killed me before he attacked my mother."

Bogdan smiled, exposing his stained teeth.

Agata refused to quiver as he placed a wooden cross on her brow. He asked for her confession.

"I have nothing to confess, but I fear my body tempted an attacker. I fear I was dishonored, but I don't know. I want to tell my beloved husband first, but he is away at war."

Bogdan leered at her. "The Lord God will not allow an honorable woman to be dishonored."

That was a blatantly false statement.

There was coughing from the doorway. "There are several instances in the Bible where honorable women are raped through no fault of their own," Cook said.

Beside her, Artur's eyes pinched closed for a moment. Then he cleared his throat. "Indeed, Princess Tamara ... "

The priest narrowed his eyes at Artur and cut the words from the air with a wave of his hand. "You both lived. You both say you blacked out. This means you're not a witness, Artur. You do not know what happened. Perhaps your mother bargained to the devils who attacked you to let you live. She gave the only thing that was hers to give."

Artur gasped. "Mother, is that true?"

Her body felt hot. Sweat prickled her skin. Artur was young and might cling to anything to forgo shame.

"No. I did not give myself to anyone," Agata said.

Bogdan's lips creased into a deep sneer. "The question remains: are you an honorable woman or not? Think of your sons before you answer."

"I don't remember the attack. I fear ... I fear." Agata trembled. "But I don't know. I don't remember anything."

Cook lifted her hand toward Agata and then lowered it.

"Why do you hide the truth?" Bogdan smiled a wicked and terrible smile and looked around. "Artur is grown. He has an appointment with the count. You will have no protection."

"My husband will return to me," she said.

"Your husband is dead," Bogdan said. "Marry me and allow me to lead this household, I will protect you in peace. If you don't, then I suppose I could bring charges of adultery upon you to the town council."

"My mother is innocent!" Artur exclaimed.

"Innocence doesn't matter," Agata said softly to her son. "He is not threatening me with a lashing or even death. He is threatening us with scandal."

...And the Count would abide no scandal to his family name.

She met Bogdan's face and considered his words.

Hoping to buy time, she said in the most modest fashion, she knew, "I do not know my husband is dead. I have not heard word for seven months from him or anyone. If he had fallen in battle, his company priest would write to me. If I am to remarry, I must have confirmation my husband is dead."

"What if it was the Legatus who attacked her?" Artur said in a small voice. "She would be innocent!"

"All of you leave this room," Bogdan said.

Agata remained very still for a moment. She knew this might happen; she should have prepared for it. She should have hidden Florin behind a tapestry.

Bogdan stared at her, his teeth clenched. "This could have been avoided if you had just remarried. I would have left my marriage to the Church to protect our family. Then, woman, you would have had a protector."

"I will stand for the wife of Jakub," Florin hissed. "She has been a fair and kind mistress."

"And I will cut you down," Bogdan said, tapping the knife on his belt. "Does a mere servant believe he can stand before God's representative?"

Agata stood and moved between them. "Florin, do not let yourself be harmed. This house is just wood and stone, but you're a friend and excellent servant. Go with my son and help him in his studies."

Florin seethed but said through his teeth. "As it pleases, my lady."

"Son, take the servants into your uncle's home, take my surviving livestock. The count has a copy of Jakub's direction on your and your brother's future," Agata whispered. "Lexi and Irina will keep Cia close, but you must protect her."

Artur nodded. He dropped his eyes. His face was full of sorrow. "I will, Mother."

Agata raised her head and looked at her servants. "The good and kind Father means to bring charges of adultery on behalf of my beloved husband, Jakub. My only witness was my beloved son, who was also assaulted, so his witness is not to be trusted."

"What will you do, my lady?" Florin asked.

"I mean to regain my honor if I can, or I will find death if I cannot. I ask you to forgive me for leaving you all of whom I am so fond."

She could not show pain, only bravery. She grabbed her son tightly and embraced them. "I remember the day of your birth. I love you, and I am proud. Go to your honorable uncle, and live well, my son.

"Find situations for all who rely upon us."

"Enough!" Bogdan shouted. "It has been many years since the Legatus has harmed a soul in the county, due to our Good Count's sacrifice. However, there is one way to know if it was him." Bogdan pulled a small box from his robes. Inside was a golden-brown Prosphoron.

"The body of Christ will destroy your demons."

"Amen," Agata said.

He turned to the others. "Leave, all of you."

Agata's heart sunk into her stomach as she watched them scurry out in fear of the priest. Maybe she should have let Florin fight him.

Bogdan tied Agata's hands together as if she was praying. He walked around her spilling scented oil and holy water upon her shoulders.

"The Body of Christ. May God pardon and have mercy upon you."

Agata opened her mouth and expected him to lay a cube of the Prosphoron on her dry tongue. Instead, he pressed the entire loaf into her mouth. He smashed his meaty hand over her face, squeezing her mouth shut.

Choking, she tried to pull away. Her mouth tasted full of ash, just as it had with the regular bread.

Agata stared at the priest in loathing. *It is he, God's own messenger, who has desecrated the Divine Eucharist. If he had believed me unclean, how could he handle Jesus's flesh in such a way?*

Agata forced herself to let her saliva wet the bread and gently chew as it moved down her throat. She wanted to gag as the dry alter bread scratched her esophagus and crumbs burned her lungs, but she must not desecrate the Divine. She lowered her eyes to the floor and swallowed another piece. Then another.

"Now, you'll listen."

He put his hand to her breast.

She yanked her body away, her mouth filled with wet bread. She tried to swallow.

Bogdan kicked her squarely in the back. She choked on the paste and crumbs.

"If you won't give me this house, I'll just take it." He leaned close: "All I wanted was an industrious wife. A wife of Proverbs. Your husband is dead. Yet you still struggle. Take me as your husband, and I'll let you live."

She shook her head and tried to kick him. Her tongue and throat coated with bread paste, she ached to breathe.

He whispered: "You still defy me? I would've been a good husband. I would've let your children live. Now I will take Jakub's house and his wife's reputation just as I took the sheep from the sacrificial fields."

"Why?" She gasped, spitting crumbs onto her beautiful carpets.

"Because Jakub is nothing more than a fancy-dressed bully. Shining armor and a warhorse doesn't change the boy. He left this parish with everything; he will come home to nothing. That's what God promised me when I saw the sheep in the field."

"Jakub's alive ... "

Bogdan's hands wrapped around her throat. He squeezed. Her hands tied together, Agata could not find any leverage. She scratched his hands, and she pushed ineffectually against his grip.

He squeezed tighter. "If Jakub is alive, I would have preferred for him to come home and see his wife in my bed, but having a dead wife who was defiled is just as well."

Please, God, whatever happens to me, protect my children.

Her windpipe was crushed by meaty hands. She stopped struggling as God lifted her spirit from her earthly form. For a moment, the world went dim. She felt as if she was singing a donia; the lyrics were happy. If Jakub were dead, she would be reunited with him in heaven.

Bogdan dropped her corpse onto the floor. "Fool woman. All you had to do is marry me."

He kicked her.

Agata knew her body was dead, but she felt the foot hit her stomach. She could still hear, still see, even think. She knew it was imperative she did not move, not yet.

Let him think he won.

Bogdan opened the chamber door to the crowded hallway.

"Artur was right. His mother was attacked by the Legatus; she became a vampire. The Flesh of our Lord destroyed her."

Bogdan gestured to her body and the scattered crumbs of Prosphoron.

Listening to her son and the women of the household cry, Agata thought her heart would shatter, but she could not weep. She must not react at all.

His voice rising in triumph, Bogdan said, "I will return with a coffin, stake, and brick to ensure eternal rest. I will exorcise this house of any further demons. Florin, bar the doors.

"I suggest the rest of you leave as Lady Agata suggested earlier."

*

Chapter 7

Agata feared waiting. She did not know when Bogdan would return. Still, she listened to the pounding of boards on the front door and chains dropping the portcullis. It would be over soon. The servants were gone. Artur had gone to his uncles. The other children were safe. That's all that mattered.

She tried to look at her injured neck, but no longer had a reflection in her mirror. She found her silver and gold blouse and brushed her fingers against it. Surprised by the heat, she pressed her reddened fingers into a salve.

"Hmmm, why didn't it burn me yesterday?" Agata spoke aloud the most logical answer. "Yesterday, I wasn't dead."

She dressed in three layers, placing the blouse with real silver embroidery in the middle, she covered her hair with her plain maramă and packed her best. She put her gold Crucifix around her neck. It did not bother her in the slightest. With the knowledge that at least she was not damned, she packed her medicine bag.

Out of habit, Agata carefully locked the windows to the manor. Perhaps it did not matter. The poor or more likely Bogdan would raze the house soon enough, perhaps even the servants would make off with whatever treasures they found, but it felt good to lock the windows. Normal. She was the Mistress of the manor, and she would protect it as Proverbs said she should.

In the kitchen, Agata ate her fill of sausage and stuffed the rest in a bag. She found a bucket with a piece of torchwood and straw. She lit the straw, and when the fungus caught the smoldering ember, she loosely fit the lid so as not to kill the low flame. Listening to the men on the street-facing side of the house, she left through her garden door. Expecting an attack, she stayed near the wall and then sprinted to the apple tree. She ducked low to remain behind her garden and plucked several herbs that were supposed to protect people from the walking dead.

She crossed her old herdland. Her surviving cows grazed lazily at the spring flowers, which pushed through the grass. She had never felt as lonely as she had this moment.

If she was indeed a vampire, she had no people, no family anymore. Bogdan had seen to that. She was sure she had died an unnatural death. Death by priest probably made it more aberrant, but was the method of her death how she became a vampire?

There were many ways to become a vampire in legends, but none seemed to fit her circumstances. She had been baptized. She was not born with a caul, an extra nipple, a tail, or excess hair and was doomed to become a vampire, as the myths claimed. She was not the seventh child. Her mother ate salt during pregnancy.

Shaking these thoughts from her head, Agata silently prayed to the Blessed Virgin to protect her children, and she would regain her honor. She slipped noiselessly into the weir to remain out of sight of the shepherds tending their flocks. It was dangerous to move about the woods at night. If vampires were real than no doubt, other things roamed the forest. Perhaps the Ottoman's God and Djinn were also real. Maybe the Fair and Earth Spirits were real. If vampires were real, there must be truth in all legends.

Agata followed the meadow-covered foothills to the ancient Roman footpath, which led into the mountains. She carefully found her footing on the narrow trail twisting over the rocky hills. Sharp angular rocks stabbed her feet through her leather shoes. She wished she did not feel the chill. What was the point of being undead if she felt cold?

She smelled death on the air. As she moved across the path, she found torn pieces of a cow. Only scraps of flesh remained on the bones so she could not identify if it was one of hers.

She pushed a branch out of her face and moved on.

The forest was not as silent as one might think it would be. Noise filled the wood, just beyond Agata's sight. The gentle step of animals, the night birds who took wing and hunted.

The night grew late, and Agata's brain swam in a sleepy fog.

The rocky ground became covered in patchy snow. Snowdrop blossoms pushed out from under the frost. She thought of her children hanging Mărțișors in the apple tree. There were no Mărțișors in the mountains.

Dawn lightened the sky. Her eyes grew blurry and teared; light blinded her. She felt faint. She was so thirsty.

She needed blood and a safe place to sleep. *I must hide*

from the sun, but first I must eat.

She gathered a few sticks and lit a small fire from her smoldering torchwood. She melted some snow.

The water did nothing to quench her thirst. Agata ate the rest of her sausage. She groaned with a pang of voracious hunger.

Nearby, Agata observed a rabbit, nibbling on a dew-covered blade of grass. As if the spirit of a wolf had taken her soul, she dashed toward it, moving faster and faster. Before it could escape, she dove upon it and raised it to her lips. Her gums screamed as she felt her teeth expand.

The poor creature scratched her face as it struggled. Blood flowed into her mouth and echoed in her veins. Her humors sang in joyous rapture. She felt stronger than she had since the attack.

Once the rabbit weakened, she broke its neck and bit into its sweet flesh.

She found shelter in the hollow of an old tree. She picked up a heavy pine bough and covered the opening. She dreamed of her beloved Jakub and their children. She did not know if he was alive or dead, but she feared she would never see her family again. The rabbit proved she was damned. She hoped her children would forgive her for leaving, but no doubt they would be told to forget her. She was dead.

The sun crept higher in the sky.

She pushed herself deeper into the hollow, covered her face with her veil, closed her eyes, and tried to sleep.

She felt a strong instinct to bury herself in the soft loamy earth, but she did not want to dirty her clothes any more than the journey already had.

The wind pushed the clouds and branches. Panic caused her heart to flutter and legs to twitch as the sun moved over her hiding place. She clenched her eyes shut and reminded herself she was safer in the tree than she had been in her own house with Father Bogdan shoving the Divine Bread down her parched throat.

Agata drifted off, thirsting for more blood than a rabbit's body could hold. She awoke what felt like minutes later by a sunbeam moving across her cheek. She yelped as she felt the warmth. She tucked her face deeper into her woolens and tried to move the branches to provide better protection. The sun passed. Had she imagined that?

With a spark of inspiration, she slipped her left hand from her glove. She put it into the sun. Her skin itched, then smoked. She pulled her hand back and rubbed a cooling unguent upon her burn.

The sun had reddened her skin before, and she had many farmers whose skin had peeled after a long day in the fields. She had never been scorched. So the myth about the sun was true.

Speaking aloud eased her fear. "Our people have so many vampire myths. Perhaps, I shall find a less fatal remedy than Bogdan's?

"Or perhaps if all else fails, I will make remedies for vampires."

She chuckled at the thought.

*

Chapter 8

The sun descended behind the mountain. If the Legatus of the Mountains was a vampire, soon she would know it. If he was just a human using the myth, she would know it. She pushed away the pine boughs and clambered from the hollow. Her outer skirt was filthy and covered in blood, her blouse was bloody, but her inner clothes were unsoiled.

Agata climbed higher. With luck, she could make it to the old Roman fort before the sun rose again. Icy wind gusted and blew sticks and pine needles across her path, stinging her exposed skin. She crossed a slope of snow-capped boulders where the pines grew twisted and more desolate. The night air sparkled. The tips of the tree branches were lined with ice and frozen moss. The patches of snow became fields of snow. She picked up a large stick and pushed it into the snow. Agata traversed the barren earth with care as the snow hid that the ground was pockmarked with holes, some small enough to catch an ankle, others large enough to swallow her.

Through the trees, Agata caught sight of the gloomy four towers of the old Roman lookout. She wanted to run toward the apparition. She wanted to know if the stone was solid or a phantasm? She kept her pace, refusing to arrive any more tired, injured, or dirty than she already was. She did not know what she would find.

The north side of the fort was piled with snow, and the eastern wall had crumbled down the hillside. Needleless, skeletal branches twisted away from the fort. As she moved closer, she picked her way through broken siege engines, dented shields, swords, and pikes stained with ancient blood and rust. She observed Latin words carved into broken stone and found several carved phallic symbols that the Roman soldiers were known to keep as talismans.

She gazed at the darkened arched windows scattered across the walls and wondered if the occupants could see her approach. If so, she hoped they looked at her from the windows rather than the arrow slits. Squeezing between rotting wet wood and mossy stone, she passed through a broken portcullis. The ground of the keep was slippery with mud, gravel, and the ghostly feet of a thousand men, which had broken down the earth and left it unsuitable for crops.

The inner keep was protected by an ornately carved door emblazoned by a knocker in the shape of a lion. She knocked and waited. No one answered.

She knocked again and looked to the east. The sun would rise shortly, then it would crest the wall. She must hide from the sun. She pushed on the door. Unlocked! She went inside and closed it behind her.

"Good day?"

No one answered.

Inside the fort was as cold as it was outside. Agata's soft footsteps squeaked under the old cracked stone tiles.

She found a tarnished brass candelabra sitting on a dusty table covered in multi colors of ancient wax. She lit the remaining candles and used the flickering light to warm to her hands.

More Latin words were inscribed on the threshold.

The wall across from the front door was covered by a large mural of presumably the Legatus. He stood over a battlefield, his enemies, his enemies' dogs and horses, and city lay waste.

"Who are you?" A raspy voice said.

She jumped as a man with a bent back in a dirty, blacken tunic came from the shadows. Around his neck was his only sign of wealth: an amulet of silver. His hair was still thick but graying. His skin looked sallow. His hands were gnarled, his nails were yellowed. Yet he seemed too young to know the ravages of age. She felt his heartbeat in the air. She was sure he was human.

She introduced herself. "Agata Arturescu Vidraru, wife of Jakub Petruescu, a viteji of Christendom. I've come to meet the man who stole my honor."

"The other vampires are there, up the stairs, Honorable Lady. They rarely come down except when it suits them," the servant said, in a strange accent.

"Thank you."

So there are more vampires than just the Legatus. That may or may not be to her advantage. "How many vampires are there?"

"You will be the sixth," the man whispered. "Be wary."

"And what is your name, friend?"

"Titus Octavia Zelina, Honorable Lady."

She noted he used his mother and grandmother's names as his surname, rather than a father's. And he said it in the old Roman way rather than the contemporary manner.

"Thank you, Titus Octavia Zelina."

*

Chapter 9

Agata climbed the steps and moved through a heavy, wooden door with carved panels grayed due to a blanket of dust. She felt the warmth as she entered what once must have been a lavish great hall. Three fireplaces were lit and cast dim light around the room. The plaster was cracked and falling off the stone. Old Roman shields painted with mythical beasts lined the walls. The glass in the ancient leaded frame windows was cracked and broken and covered in rotting wool blankets.

Yet, life was everywhere. Spiders lived in every corner. Rats scurried along the walls. Pigeons and sparrows fluttered in the rafters.

Death aboded in the fort as well. Five vampires turned toward her. One man — *could it truly be the Legatus of the Mountains?* — sat in a marble chair surrounded by two carved stone wolves. Three women sat on cushions near his feet. They had different skin tones, but their complexions suggested death, or something unnatural.

Nearby on a wooden stool sat her rapist. Somehow, she instinctively knew her attacker the moment she laid eyes on him. Almost at once, as she had known her own mother, she felt connected to the man on a strange level. This attachment filled her with self-loathing. *Focus. This might be one of the vampire's tricks,* she thought. She remembered his rancid breath on her body during the attack and redirected her fury back to him.

His threadbare clothing rotted off his frame, and he looked like he had not taken a bath in over a decade. The edging on his shirt was yellowed. His red coat was frayed. He was tall and thin, handsome in an understated way. His skin was ashen, stark against his brassy blond hair. The blue in his veins seemed to complement his brilliant blue eyes. She knew his name without asking: Nicheloa Augustus Flavius, another Roman.

The Legatus's booming laughter rang to the rafters and startled the living creatures in the hall.

She did not see Nicheloa move but smelled his putrid breath. He whispered beside her. "So you have come to us?"

"You took my honor; I have come to claim it."

"We've no honor here — at least in the limited way you define it. On your knees before the Legatus of Carpathia, woman," Nichcloa hissed. "The Legatus claimed he felt the creation of another vampire."

"How dare you, I am Agata, wife … "

"You're the least of us; take your place at your master's feet." With his hand on the back of her neck, he dragged her across the hall toward a throne. With his greater strength and weight, he forced her to her belly.

"This woman comes to you, my Legatus."

Agata elbowed Nicheloa until he released her. She scrambled to her feet and raised her chin to meet the vampire's gaze. "I am Agata, Daughter of Count Artur Vidraru, the wife of Jakub Petruescu Christian. Whom do I have the honor of addressing?"

The Legatus of the Mountains appeared to be a man in his prime, but there was something ancient in his face. A twisted lump spoiled his otherwise aquiline nose. His tanned complexion had an undertone of blue, a symptom of death. His piercing brown eyes were nearly hidden under bushy eyebrows and his unbrushed thick mane of black curls. A short beard and mustache overtook his stern and terrifying face. He was not tall for a man, but his broad shoulders and muscular arms were exposed by the Roman style tunics rotting off his body. His undertunic was torn thin gray linen —perhaps it was once white— its frayed hem was dirty and blackened. His brown outer tunic looked like it once might have been red. It seemed too cold for such thin garments.

"I am Gaius Lepidus Severus, Legatus of the Carpathian Mountains. Do you throw yourself upon my mercy as did my other concubines?"

He gestured at the three vampire women, but his piercing eyes did not leave her face.

The women's uncanny expressions showed nothing but disapproval and sadness. They watched, not speaking. Two were darker skinned, luminous brown eyes and long free black hair that hung freely down their backs. They appeared to be in their twenties. The other was pale with blond hair and blue eyes. She seemed to be the same age as Irina and bore bruises around her neck from someone's cruelty. With three beauties, she doubted Gaius would be interested in a thirty-two-year-old mother of five.

"I need no mercy. I am a lady of honor. I have no master

save the Lord Above and my husband whom I promised to love, honor, obey with a kind heart on the day of our marriage," Agata said.

"You're brave but foolish. Crawl to me," Gaius said.

She refused to even lower her gaze. "Even my husband would not dare order me to crawl, or he would find his next meal poisoned."

Gaius stroked his chin. "You're no noble here. Just a lesser vampire, made by a lesser vampire. If you want my protection, show me your hair."

Agata did not comply; Nicheloa ripped off her maramă. The linen fell to the stone floor. She refused to cry as he unraveled her coils and plaits.

"Another raven beauty and not a touch of gray," Gaius said. "Though you're rather old, you're still pretty enough. You may be my fourth concubine."

"I've entered in no such arrangement with you; I stand before you as the wife of Jakub," Agata said.

"You bore me, woman. Kneel."

Agata felt her knees buckle, she locked them in place. *Gaius and Nicheloa are spoiled children,* she told herself. *I will not kneel.* His mind slithered over hers. It felt as if a thousand insects crawled up her feet, legs, back and over her hair. She would not be cowed.

Seconds later, she was on her knees.

The women did not move or even blink.

From her prostrate position, Agata said, "My people call you the Legatus of the Mountains. Is that a self-appointed rank?"

Gaius rose to his feet.

"Are you the warrior in the mural below or are you simply a leader of frightened women?"

His fangs expanded as his face twisted with rage. His mind slipped away from hers. The sensation of insects on her flesh disappeared. Domination was forgotten for the time being. He raised his hand as if he would strike her. "Was it your husband who wrung your neck? Look upon my women, and you can see I am not above such things."

She hid her trembling hands under her long sleeve. *Gaius exists in the ignorant darkness which brought forth the collapse of the old Empire.*

Gaius walked around her, studying her. "I didn't create you, but I will keep you. If you exist in pain, it is because people make their own misfortunes."

"If you truly are a Legatus, is Nicheloa your Lictor?" Agata asked.

"Yes."

"Then, I challenge you for my honor and freedom."

The women's eyes moved quickly. They glanced at each other, then to Gaius, Nicheloa, Agata, back to Gaius.

"With swords, axes? Have you ever held a weapon in your delicate hands? I might crush you," Gaius said.

"With the weapon of my choice, and when I win, you will do what I ask of you," Agata said.

"A woman's weapon is always poison," Gaius said. "And nothing can poison me."

"I'm a learned midwife."

"Even a midwife cannot poison a vampire," Nicheloa said.

"I bring forth life while you live in a tomb with the rats

and spiders," Agata said. "You have no idea what I know."

"So be it. When I win, I'll torture you until I bore of it," Gaius said.

With those words, his women drew closer to one another. The pale one covered her throat. They feared Gaius. Nicheloa's eyes dropped. He also feared him though his experience as a soldier made him better at hiding it.

"It might be centuries until I tire of you." Gaius smiled.

Agata has seen terrible wickedness before in men. Gaius thought she was a plaything and assumed she would lose. To him: the challenge was a diversion to break up the centuries. *These fiends are beyond worthless.*

"As for weapons, I choose the quality of my own mind," Agata said.

"A woman's mind, what good is that?"

Though she ached to school him, she did not speak of ancient texts or legends. "When I win, I want my freedom and honor returned to me."

Gaius waved his hand in a listless gesture. "Yes, yes. So this battle of wits commences. What shall we do, tell riddles?"

"No. I will heal your servant and remake this dungeon into a home in a week."

Gaius's eyes opened wide. "How is this a battle of wits? What woman's trickery is this?"

Agata did not answer him. "My first question: What is the remedy for your servant, Titus Octavia Zelina's, ailment?"

"Why would I care? He's just a servant." Gaius said. "He's a human; humans die."

"Is that your answer?" Agata hid her elation at his

confusion.

"I suppose you have such knowledge," he said with scorn.

Below him, one of the women with raven hair pulled the younger pale woman close to her breast. The other shifted between them and Gaius as if they expected him to harm the girl.

"As I warned you, I'm a midwife," Agata said calmly.

"Perhaps, you should have insisted upon the riddles, my legatus." Nicheloa smiled with his blue eyes. He, too, found Agata's challenge diverting, but he was a different type of man than the Legatus. "Besides, even if you lose this woman's challenge, don't forget you won our bet that I created a vampire."

Agata felt a connection with Nicheloa again. She ignored it.

Gaius calmed and chuckled. "You are correct, my friend."

Nicheloa said, "I'm poorer since you lived. I have no way to keep a woman without my lord's blessing."

Agata considered it was wrong to overlook Nicheloa, especially since she was planning to kill him. To him, she said, "I was made poorer since you stole my cows." Then to Gaius, "Titus Octavia Zelina has the sailor's disease."

"Prove it," Nicheloa said.

"Goodman, pray to tell me do your joints ache?"

Titus looked at Gaius in terror.

"Answer the woman's questions," Gaius said.

"Joint pain, Lady," Titus said.

"And pray, how old are you?" Agata asked.

"One and thirty."

"Open your mouth. I'm wagering my freedom your tongue

is spotted," Agata said.

Titus obeyed. His gums were bleeding, and several teeth had been lost. And of course, his tongue was covered in spots.

Gaius's sneer disappeared.

"I must make him and all your human servants a needle broth. Though it is sharp in taste, they must drink it for one week, but we shall see an improvement within days," Agata said. "Titus, please collect stems of new-growth pine. New growth is a lighter, brighter green."

"My Legatus?" Titus asked.

"Do as the woman asks. I want to observe the miracle of a human who grows strong again," Gaius said.

✳

Chapter 10

Other than the bit of shouting of a woman's trickery, which sprinkled dust from the rafters onto the stone floor, Agata was happy. There had been no violence. The sun rose higher in the sky. Eventually, the Legatus and Lictor went down the stairs to the old barracks.

"Gaius doesn't come into the harem. You will be safe there. Come," the woman with long straight black hair said. "He calls it a place for the weak. Still, take care with your words, Titus is not our ally and his daughter, Ulpia, is dawdling and slow."

Agata was not sure if she could trust the concubines or servants, but she had no other choice. "I am called Agata."

"So we heard. I am Sylvia, that is Phillipa, and the golden one is Julia."

Sylvia opened the carved door. The harem's stone walls reflected filtered light. Mold hid in the corners and between the stones. Carpet beetles scurried before Agata's steps.

Phillipa closed the first set of shutters, casting the room in greater darkness. Over the screens, the sheer linen moved across its rail. Velvet curtains drifted slower. It did not take long for the room to fill with stale, musty air.

The women ignored the furniture and lay on the floor. Agata could see why. The rotting leather did not look like it would hold their weight anymore. She did not want to place her face on the musty rug or a moldy cushion but saw no other choice. She reclined on the floor with the other women. On the east wall sat a shrine covered in figures of the old pagan Goddesses from the Empire. Pots filled with cosmetics, ribbons, combs and womanly apparel sat on shelves. Discarded ripped fabrics and crockery lay in the corners.

This close, even in the darkness, she could see the bruises on the pale girl's neck were deep and purple. Agata's heart went out to her. She touched her own neck. "May I help you, Julia? I have a salve."

The younger woman did not meet her eyes.

"Your remedies will only help so much. What she needs is blood," Phillipa said. "We have been forbidden to give it to her. Gaius keeps Julia in penance."

"Still, I might help the pain. I have my own bruises."

Agata opened her case and rubbed a salve upon her neck.

"You were strangled too?" Phillipa said. "Not by Nicheloa, that's not how he takes women."

"Was Gaius, correct? Was it your husband?" Sylvia asked.

"No. My husband is at war. I was alive after Nicheloa raped me, but our parish priest killed me, claiming I was a vampire."

Phillipa chuckled. "And he was right. You are a vampire."

"It was an excuse," Agata said softly. "The priest actually just wanted my house."

"Men always want something," Sylvia said.

Julia glanced over at Phillipa.

"If you think it will help even with the pain, Julia wants to try the salve," Phillipa said.

Agata gestured for Julia to sit in front of her. "The home I built with my husband is in the western shadow of the highest peak. Where are you all from?"

"My mother is Breton-born, she came with her lady as a maid, I was born somewhere close." Julia lifted her pale hair off her shoulders so Agata could dab the unguent on the back of her neck where Gaius's fingertips had drilled into her flesh.

"I am from Spain," Sylvia said. "I was stolen from my

people and taken to the Capital. And Phillipa is from Rome. She is the eldest of us. Nearly as old as Gaius."

"You're his wife?" Agata asked.

"A freedwoman. He changed me for his pleasure." The disgust in her voice was apparent. "Then he claimed me as his concubine."

Finishing her ministrations, Agata wondered if she should tell the women there was no more Empire. Did they know of the spread of Christianity throughout Europe or the centuries of invasions the Goths, Mongols, and Ottomans?

Sylvia said, "I don't think any man or woman has rejected him since. He doesn't like it. It's better to just accept Gaius; he isn't a terrible lover."

"I'm the wife of Jakub." Agata moved a cushion and yelped as a rat raced toward the wall.

"Now you're the concubine of Gaius," Phillipa said softly. "Fight as you will, but Gaius will have you."

"Gaius does not follow the Roman order of things. He does not care if your Jakub has had you or Nicheloa or that you bore children. All that matters is now you're a vampire of his bloodline. He claimed you as his. It brings him a twisted joy to take something from Nicheloa," Sylvia said.

"But if I win the challenge?" Agata whispered.

Phillipa sighed and picked up a comb to plait Julia's golden hair.

Sylvia shook her head. "He won't let you win."

"But I must win," Agata said.

Searching through the discarded and broken items in the corner, she found a pot which used to hold some sweet-smelling cosmetic. Not knowing what used to be in it, she set it aside; she needed clean crockery if her remedy was to work.

"Don't worry about his threats of torture," Sylvia said. "Torture doesn't interest him. He will have you a few times and grow bored. However, he won't let you go. He feeds us, clothes us in silk when Nicheloa can find it, protects us from the changing world.

"All he asks in return is to make love on occasion and Phillipa to dance for him. When she is well, Julia will sing. I will play my flute. Perhaps, there is something you can do to entertain him. Otherwise, he leaves us to our pleasures."

Agata was careful to hide her thoughts, but she wondered what pleasure was found in a rotting old fort.

Sylvia apparently did not like her silence. "Let us muse for a moment. If Gaius lets you win, what prize will you ask for? Will you ask to be his wife so you might rule over us?"

"No. I will ask to go home with proof of my honor."

Phillipa's mind wrapped around Agata's. It was soft and cold as if fresh snow was falling upon her cheeks, yet it was terrifying to have one's own spirit eclipsed by another stronger will. Thankfully it was over quickly.

"She tells the truth," Phillipa said to the other women. "She thinks if she finds her honor, her husband's family won't forsake her."

"How sad." Sylvia shook her head.

Phillipa looked over Julia's shoulder. "Agata, you must realize if your husband doesn't forsake you, he must forsake your children. Let him go. Stay here and be the Legatus's concubine. One man is rather like another after a few centuries."

"I thought a Legatus leads men?" Agata asked. "On horses."

"He used to have men with horses, but they died long ago. Now there is only Nicheloa," Phillipa said.

"Well, there's one other thing," Julia whispered.

"Hush, Julia," Phillipa tapped the top of her head with the comb. "Speak no word that might be used to harm you." She finished the braid and tied it into a bun. Then wrapped it in a long cloth.

"Is that why you're being punished? Did you try to kill Gaius?" Agata asked.

Julia shook her head. "I'm not brave enough. I ran away."

Phillipa drew the younger woman closer to her. "But she won't again."

There was a knock on the door. A skinny young girl probably no older than nine popped her head in. Her tangled hair hung about her shoulders. Her Roman style toga praetexta was threadbare as was the faded purple band around her waist. Around her neck was a silver amulet to ward off malevolence.

"Lady, my father asked me to bring you this basket." She bowed and left.

Agata looked inside and found pine needles of good quality. "Where do I get water?"

Sylvia gently touched Agata's wrist and drew her close. "We will not help you destroy our coven. Besides, the old well is dry."

"We've no need for water," Phillipa said. "We drink blood."

Agata adjusted her layers of clothing. She would have

liked to strangle the vampire women for their acceptance of their fate, but she needed allies.

"I don't want to destroy your coven. All I want is my honor. You've human servants—even if we don't need water—they do," Agata said. "There must be a source."

Julia motioned to a rope hanging from the ceiling in the corner.

Silently cursing herself for her stupidity, Agata rang the servants' bell. The young girl reentered, trembling, and holding her elbows close to her body.

"I need water, girl," Agata said in a tone that meant she was to be obeyed. "Finish the task and report back directly."

"Yes, Lady." The girl scurried in haste as if a devil was behind her.

"Agata, the girl and her father are slow in the mind," Phillipa said languidly. "Don't be cross with them. Come sleep. The sun is out, but there's always a new moonrise."

Agata declined.

The other women made themselves comfortable and warm in the shadows.

Once Agata was sure the other women slept, she removed her lower layers of clothing and hid them in a broken wardrobe. If the other women wanted her things, she might lose all that was hers, but they seemed uninterested.

The concubines must want something. Julia ran away for some reason. Sylvia and Phillipa were compelling in the way, intelligent women always were. They knew something or wanted something more than this quiet harem filled with rats and bugs, but what?

Ulpia returned, carrying two full buckets in her small strong hands. "Do you need more, Lady?"

"I need a clean pot. I'm trying to make a tonic to heal your father."

The girl followed her directions to the letter.

Ulpia was not slow as the concubines warned her. She poured the bucket of water into the pot and set the pot to boil with instruction.

Agata removed the brown papery sheaths from the base of the needle. Not wanting to let the other women know of her knife, she tore the needles into smaller pieces and crushed them between her hands. She put the needles in the pot of boiling water and let them steep for five minutes.

Agata took a sip to ensure the potency. "Now, Ulpia, bring me to your father, so I might help him."

✳

Chapter 11

Holding the still-hot pot of pine-needle tonic, Agata followed the scrawny girl down the long dirty corridors to the fort's old scullery. A tallow lamp hung from the ceiling, casting light around the room.

Large jars marked lanolin or oil lined the wall. Blocks of ice and snow melted in large troughs, which drained into old barrels.

She noted how Titus or some other servant had stacked a smaller brick to create a small firepit inside the large ancient fireplace. Sheepskin pallets lay inside the structure. From the ceiling hung silver amulets and old clothing.

Agata wiped a dusty pewter cup and poured Titus a dose of tonic. Titus grimaced as he sniffed it.

"Drink for your daughter, if not for yourself. And the child must drink as well. It will stop any of your bad air harming her lungs."

"But I don't want it," Ulpia whined.

Titus threw his head back and drank the tea. He handed Agata back the cup. She poured another dose for the girl.

"Drink, Ulpia; the lady commands it," Titus said.

"But, Papa, we put pine on the dead."

He patted her shoulder.
"Drink."

"It smells gross."

"No. It's not the best-tasting thing," Titus admitted, "But it will make you strong, Ocella."

"But ... "

Titus's voice changed as he scolded, "Ulpia Titus Octavia, if I have to tell you again..."

Ulpia did not wait to hear her father's threat. She tilted her head back and gulped it as fast as she could. "Yuck!" she cried.

"You can drink milk or water as you wish now," Agata said. "Are there any other servants in the fort?"

"Not any longer." Titus poured the girl a cup of water. She drank it just as fast.

"Any longer?" Agata asked.

"Ulpia, ask the lady what your next job is," Titus said with a look at the girl's head. He would not speak in front of her. Her life might be hard; he would not make her harder.

"What should I do next, Lady?" Ulpia asked.

"Have you any vinegar?" Agata asked.

"No," Titus said.

"Gather more needles. This time the color doesn't matter.

We will boil them and wash the walls and floors with the solution. I also need a bucket of ash and fat from a slaughtered animal. We will be making soap. It's fun."

Ulpia scurried to do her bidding.

"Tell me of the others," Agata ordered.

"The Lictor finds infants left out by farmers." Titus went on to explain how in a lean famine year; the vampires ate the infants.

"How cruel."

"They are killed quickly, and with mercy, more mercy than their fathers gave them when they're set out to freeze," Titus said. "However, at times, the Legatus decides not to kill them. He brings me a child to serve the vampires. How or why he makes the decision, I do not know."

"So she is not yours?"

"I've never known a woman. You don't have to fear me, Honorable One. I'm a eunuch. All the boys are eunuchs. Other than the Lictor, the Legatus doesn't keep intact men around his women."

"You've had other children?"

"They died just as the other children died when I was a child. There's little food and vampires can be cruel. I keep a strict watch over Ulpia. She's past the most vulnerable age. She has gone hungry too many times to ever become a true beauty which should protect her from the Lictor's vileness when she is older."

"And the Legatus?" Agata asked.

Titus sighed. "The Legatus keeps women out of habit. He will keep you safe; he will make love to you on occasion. He will feed you and the other women the blood of the cows and sheep which he receives in tribute. Do as he says and you've nothing to fear from him."

"What do you eat?" Agata asked.

He explained how some meat is thrown to the servants, but he set snares for rats and rabbits. Ulpia collected berries and mushrooms when she could find them, but very little grew on the mountains.

"I will write this recipe for a tea down for you and your generations of children. It will keep them strong when they can't find berries," Agata said.

"Thank you, Honorable One," Titus said.

✳

The sun was high. Agata lay in the harem and listened to the sleeping women. She ached with her need for blood, but nothing compared to the pain of leaving her children. Dwelling in impotent rage took time that Agata did not have. Gaius's threats of torture was nothing compared to that pain. She must win. Unable to sleep and wanting to know more about this strange place, Agata followed Ulpia, who held a wreath of pine down a long dark hallway.

The skinny girl knelt before an open hole with generations of human and animal bones. She invoked Artemis and several other childhood Gods and dropped the wreath upon the bones.

"I feared I would have to throw Papa in there. I'm glad you're making him better, Lady."

"You heard me behind you?" Agata said.

Ulpia turned. "Papa taught me. Vampires become more silent with age, yet I must know where their feet fall."

"You're a clever, industrious girl, but you don't fear us?"

"Why would fear one of you wretched things?" Ulpia said. "I'm Ulpia, daughter of Titus, son of Octavia, daughter of Zelina, daughter of Crassus, onward for millennia. All I must do is keep to the light."

"I see the wisdom in your words."

"The sun is up. If you don't sleep, eventually, you will go mad and run into the sun like the other vampires. The harem is safe from the Lictor. The Legatus never visits it; when he wants you, he calls you to his room in the barracks." She spoke in a jaded, wearied voice which sounded too old for a young girl's lips.

"I still have work to do," Agata said.

"Even a vampire needs sleep to work," Ulpia said. "I'll take you back to the harem until nightfall."

Agata lay beside Julia, who lay beside Phillipa. Half-asleep, Julia cuddled toward her and wrapped her arms around her and rested her cheek on Agata's shoulder.

Staring at the darkened ceiling, Agata tried closing her eyes. It did not matter. Eventually, she rolled to her side and pulled Julia closer. She wept for the wounded young woman she barely knew, her own children, her destroyed cattle and everything else she had lost. Eventually, an uneasy sleep took her.

Agata dreamed of millions of insects, spiders, and rats biting her, crawling inside her and eating her innards: deget by deget, palmă by palmă. The vermin took over her body.

She awoke with Phillipa shaking her shoulder. Her perfect ringed curls draped over her, like snakes. Agata shuddered and pushed the image from her mind.

Agata sat up. Beside her, Julia still slept. Phillipa gestured for her to follow. "Walk with me. The sun is setting."

Phillipa led her to a shuttered balcony. Agata held back for a moment, but the other woman walked out first. "You need not fear. The sun is down. You will sense such things in time."

The sky was streaked with lavender. Below the mountain, the valley was dark, but single points of warm light broke up the darkness. Agata wished she knew which town was hers, but she did not. From this position, she did not even know if she was facing west or east.

"I witnessed your plot when I looked into your mind. You mourn your lost life and put yourself on a fool's errand," Phillipa said.

Agata tried to turn away, but Phillipa gripped her wrist with a surprising amount of strength.

"You will stop me?"

"Only if you harm my sisters," Phillipa released her. "I speak to you as another mother. Julia fills the place which has been empty since my daughters' deaths. I protected her from Gaius's anger when she ran away. She has not been forgiven. I will kill you if you endanger her place in the coven."

"I have no intention..."

"I don't care about your intentions. Your passions play a

dangerous game. More dangerous than you realize. There have been other concubines and soldiers. When they betrayed him, Gaius tossed them into the sun or worse."

Agata opened her mouth. "I ... " she stopped and asked an intelligent question: "How many others were there?"

"In a thousand years? I've lost count. At least, hundreds. Gaius drinks the blood and has them burnt to ash."

"Then, what is your counsel?"

"Forget your errand," Phillipa said. "Heal Titus if it pleases you to do so, but forget your task."

"You had children?" Agata asked her. "You must understand I want to go home."

"You can't," Phillipa said. "If you love your husband and children: you must not go home. Never. Even if you regain your honor, you still cannot have the life you had."

"Jakub will not forsake me if I have my honor. His family ... " Agata took a deep breath.

Phillipa squeezed her arm gently. "You will harm them. Your need for blood will grow. You are fighting it now. To come into eternity with you, Jakub will have to also leave your children. Let him remarry, grow old. Let him die with the children as my husband died."

"But I cannot fail. Gaius will torture me if he wins."

"He won't if you throw yourself on his mercy," Phillipa said. "You're surprisingly naive for a mother over thirty."

Since she did not have a handkerchief, Agata wiped her nose with her hand. She sensed there was more to Phillipa's counsel, but she did not have her gifts. She wished she did.

Phillipa sighed. "No, you don't. It's confusing to hear

others' emotions, thoughts, and spoken words. People often feel several ways about any given subject. Their thoughts pound upon my mind." After a pause, she continued, "It's quiet here in this fort. A learned woman such as yourself must see the value in that for someone like me. Perhaps I don't love Gaius anymore; perhaps I still do. Perhaps I only love the man he was once."

"You said he claimed you."

"Gaius was a senator's son. I was his oracle... and I took him as my lover... He could have never married me, but he claimed me as his. Once I wanted to be his. Still he listened some of the time. He has been warned."

She sighed. "Sylvia is right, there are worse men in the world."

✳

Chapter 12

Agata's ears rang with Phillipa's counsel. She did not know what to do, so she set to cleaning the harem. Lounging amongst the cushions, Phillipa, Sylvia, and Julia watched Agata and Ulpia chase rats from the harem with a broom.

"Why are you doing this?" Julia asked.

"Are any of them pets?" Agata asked.

"No."

"Then I'm getting them out of here."

"Gaius probably won't even see this room," Phillipa said. "Gaius likes things the way they are."

"She tries to curry our favor," Sylvia said. "Daughter of a Count indeed. Perhaps you're the servant of a Count."

Panting from the excursion, Agata stopped. "I am who I claimed to be. That fiend isn't the only reason I'm doing this. I don't want to live with rat feces, spiders, and fleas."

"No disease can harm vampires. The fleas don't even bite us. They want warmer blood," Phillipa said.

"But Titus and Ulpia might be harmed by illness." Seeing their uncaring expressions, she added quickly, "Please tell me you do not enjoy sleeping with the rats and spiders."

"Of course not, but eventually you'll also tire of human

work."

Phillipa stood. Sylvia followed her out of the harem arm in arm. "Julia?"

"I think I'll help Agata," Julia said softly.

"Remember what I told you," Phillipa warned. Agata was not sure if that was directed at her or Julia.

The younger woman nodded and picked up a pile of old broken crockery from the corner and set it in the basket which Agata had designated for ripped and broken things. After she finished, Julia took the spiders from their webs and set them outside the window.

Her gentle hands surprised Agata, yet twice the hands made the work lighter.

"How did you come here?"

Julia glanced out the door first. No one was there. Then out the window. "I was laundress, and Gaius saw my golden hair and became enamored. He had Nicheloa steal me from my home."

"Do you want to go home?" Agata asked.

"My mother is dead," Julia said. "Titus's mother Octavia was younger than Ulpia when Nicheloa brought me here."

"Then why did you run away?"

She pinched her lips together. "Boredom, I guess. I thought I'd have a better life, but a week on the mountain, eating rabbits, being cold and afraid of the sun, of the villagers, even running into Nicheloa, I returned.

"Gaius was angry at me. He yelled so loud I feared the fort might come down on our heads. I accepted being chastised — Phillipa did not let him really injure me — and we all go on with our existence."

"Are you happy?"

"I exist," Julia said. "I'm not sure vampires can be happy, but I love my sisters."

Agata separated the torn linen from the rest to re-stuff the harem cushions. "Do you remember how he turned you?"

Julia looked out the door again.

"Nicheloa raped me," Agata said. "But I don't comprehend how I was turned. I've thought about it many times as I climbed the mountain. My people have many myths about the vampire.

"Some claim vampires are born with a caul, must be the seventh child of the same sex in a family and lead a life of sin, die without being married, die by execution for perjury or suicide or from a witch's curse."

Julia's laugh was musical. "I wasn't married, but I don't even know any witches. Do you?"

"No."

Julia peeked out the door one more time. "Gaius took my blood from my wrist, then he told me not to be afraid and bit me over my heart. He held me close as I bled into him. My heart stopped. He then gave me more of his blood. I was dead, but not. Then he gave me the blood of a boy because I was so ravenous that I ached."

So the myth about biting over the heart is true, Agata thought.

"How strange. That isn't what happened to me at all. Except I knew I was dead, but not, and very thirsty."

"I don't know much about it. Gaius made it clear I was not allowed to transform anyone. He says I'm too young. He is less restrictive with Phillipa ... but ... ”

"He's the head of this House," Agata finished.

"And expects to be obeyed," Julia nodded. "Phillipa can trick him into doing what she wants most of the time."

"She seems very wise."

"She is," Julia said. "And she's always been kind to me."

Titus entered the harem. "Honorable Ladies, the Legatus of Carpathia orders you to the hall."

Agata hated leaving work half-done, but she knew it was essential to conform and observe. As they entered, Phillipa and Sylvia sat quietly on their cushions. Phillipa had a slight look of triumph on her face. Agata hoped she had not made a fatal mistake by speaking to the youngest and least educated vampire.

"Julia, come here," Gaius ordered.

Julia glanced at Phillipa but hurried to him. She gasped as he pulled her onto his lap. He combed Julia's long blonde hair with his fingers.

"I was told you are helping Agata with her task," Gaius said.

She sat perfectly still. "Yes."

"Why?"

Her eyes were wide and panicked. "It's something to do. Different, Legatus."

His finger traced her pink ear, but his eyes were on Agata. "You oppose with my methods, Agata."

"I don't know your methods."

"It causes you distress to see marks on Julia's neck. Phillipa said you tried a salve on her last day."

"Cato the Elder said, 'the man who struck his wife or

child, laid violent hands on the holiest of holy things. Also that he thought it more praiseworthy to be a good husband than a good senator.' "

"Cato the Elder did not have to teach a rebellious vampire," Gaius said. "What would you have done? Let this vampire roam, hungry? Eventually, she would have attacked a village, perhaps the one with your beloved husband and children in it."

Agata did not answer him.

"Phillipa and Sylvia cause no problems because they experienced life before they were transformed. Nicheloa and I are the same. Even you, in your state of rebellion, are working to make our world more inhabitable, not less. But Julia was made from a woman who was still half a girl."

"You made her."

"And you have had children. Did you not teach them to obey?"

"Yes, but there are better ways than with bruises," Agata said.

"If the marks displease you so, I will remove them." He opened his wrist and told Julia to drink. She pressed her lips to his wrist. She swallowed his blood and cried out. As if it was magic, the bruises around her neck vanished. The flesh of her neck became immaculate.

"You see, I'm not an ogre."

"Thank you."

Gaius stood and told Julia to return to her sisters, which she did. "What else can I do for you? Should I remove the bruises from your neck? Is this why you couldn't bear to see the young one chastised because your husband did the same to you?"

"My husband is a great cavalry officer on the front lines of battle. He does not know my fate." Agata said. A single bloody tear rolled down her cheek. She wiped it away.

He stepped closer to Agata.

"Don't touch me."

Gaius's voice was soft. "Your love for your husband is heart-wrenching to watch, but he will forsake you. He must. If he remained with you, your hunger would eventually kill him."

Her voice trembled as sorrow overtook her entire body. "Let me return to my work. I will be washing the linens and cushions in the harem so they might dry in the day's sun."

"I won't see the harem."

Agata put her hands on her hips. "You may be the ruler of this house, but you're not the only one who lives here. As long as I live here, I won't sleep with rats."

There was a moment in which the concubines stopped breathing.

Gaius laughed. "I dismiss you to return to your efforts. Julia, remain with your sisters."

Phillipa left her cushion and wrapped her arms around his. "Gaius, you always say a person makes their own misery. If Julia's punishment is over, please, may she have a little freedom? Agata is her sister too, and will no doubt keep an eye on her...

"Let Julia know the old pleasure of a job well done. You know how her young heart craves more affection than we can provide," Phillipa said. "Did you know Agata has a daughter no older than Julia was? The girl is newly married and pregnant with a grandchild."

"Is it any wonder Agata acts so irrationally?" Sylvia took

his other arm. "And you never blame a newly-formed vampire for senselessness human passions."

"Ah, very well. Whatever gratifies my concubines satisfies me," he said.

In her mind, Phillipa's voice rang out as if she had spoken. *However, be clear, Agata, you're not above Julia. Julia works as she wishes.*

Dismissed, Agata left the hall. Julia silently followed.

Agata was pleased the young vampire's wounds were healed but felt used. In truth, she was even more confused about Phillipa and Sylvia's intentions.

*

Chapter 13

Going room by room, Agata, Titus, and Ulpia washed the ceilings, walls, and floors with pine-needle solvent. The bricks bled with rust. Most of the rooms were abandoned and neglected, tiles littered with leaves and old bones of victims. She knew she ought to be afraid. There was too much work to do in the time allotted. Yet, she was too busy to think of the consequences of failure. When she was not moving, her silent days in the harem were worse than her toils. The rhythm of life in scrubbing floors, lowering herself to witness the time-worn dirt and damage, kept her calm.

Bugs and dust flew off the ancient carpets as they were beaten. The leather and wooden furniture were rubbed with lanolin until they gleamed. Anything so damaged it would not hold her weight was dissembled for parts or burned as fuel.

Old threadbare cushions, rags, and tattered fabrics were soaked in water and pine oil and left on the roof to dry, collected again after nightfall. Once dry, Agata started to re-stuff and wrapped cushions, but Sylvia surprised her.

"I know how to sew. I will help with this task, but only this task," she said.

Julia assisted as she liked. Agata noticed when Nicheloa

was around the fort, she stayed near Phillipa. When he was out collecting the sacrifices, she happily chased bugs and rats. Her most effective action was to collect all the broken crockery and till the soil next to the old kitchen. She lined the patch of tilled earth with the broken pottery to make a garden for Titus, Ulpia, and any future human children.

As Agata moved through the fort, she found an old trove of weapons and dead husks of men, long mummified in banded iron armor stacked on their rectangular shields. Their swords and pikes at their sides were covered in a thousand years of rust, dust, and spiderwebs.

"Thinking of using those?" Nicheloa asked behind her.

Ulpia dropped her rag and scurried behind Agata. "Leave me be; you are frightening my helper." Agata did not stop scrubbing rat droppings off the floor.

"I will not harm you; you're my legatus's woman."

"If I am a woman of Gaius, you have already harmed me." She dreamed of reaching for a pike and decapitating Nicheloa where he stood. Between her lack of instruction and his training, Nicheloa would crush her within seconds. *Keep your own head.* "Who are these men?"

"Former legionnaires," he said.

She looked up from her cleaning. "Why are they here? Were they vampires too?"

"A woman knows nothing of esprit de corps. They gave themselves to Gaius after he was turned." His voice was devoid of the emotion of brotherhood of which he spoke.

"So, though you carry the title of lictor, you're an errand boy. You deliver the sacrifice, steal the women he wants."

"A man needs a job, and Gaius hasn't needed a bodyguard for centuries."

Agata stood up and stretched her back. She wished she did not feel connected to Nicheloa. "Ulpia, go help your father."

Ulpia gladly escaped the room.

Nicheloa was taller than she, but she looked him in the face. "Why did you make me a vampire?"

He looked away. "I didn't mean to create you."

She moved, so she was in front of him again. "Tell me."

Nicheloa ran his fingers through his short beard and grimaced. "It will pain you to relive it. Forget it happened and go on with your existence or walk into the sun. If it pleases you, know Gaius upbraided me for my carelessness."

"Tell me."

"The sacrifice wasn't in its field, so I went to find another. A vampire can't be soft on such things. I saw your cows. Then your man ran out of the small barn like a rabbit."

"Robert wasn't my man. He was my herdsman," Agata said.

"Regardless, the stank of his fear was delicious. Do you know how much blood and flesh are in a grown man? I was so excited to have it all for myself, and Fideles, my horse. I felt as if I were an Emperor!

"Then your boy shouted. If I hadn't drunk from the herdsman first, neither of you would have lived. I left your herdsman for Fideles." His eye grew dreamy. He touched the scabbarded dagger on his belt, his fingers lingering on the leather. "Besting the boy was nothing. However, I prefer a soft woman over boys. I dominated him so he would sleep until morning and took you."

"Since I killed the herdsman, I assumed you were a widow. Who cares about the rape and murder of a herdsman's widow? So, yes, I took you, but let your son live, relatively unscathed. You should be happy." She wondered why he was defending his actions. He obviously believed raping her wasn't a crime — especially after destroying the man he assumed was her husband.

Agata said, "The herdsman died, but the boy lived. Will they become vampires?"

"I didn't spill my blood or seed on them, so no," Nicheloa said. "I obviously spilled something in you. You ought to thank me."

"I thank you for my son's life." Her voice cracked.

His tone grew soft. "You're my creation. I caused you pain once; I won't do it again."

"Don't mock me. You took me from my family and now claim I belong to another man." Fighting her urge to weep, she threw her rag at Nicheloa. He stepped out of the way before it hit him and landed on the floor with a splat.

"I do not mock you." Nicheloa picked up her rag and returned it to her. "I only mean I didn't want to change you. I dominated your mind. You were supposed to die. You weren't supposed to wake as a living vampire, to be killed by a priest, and walk in death for eternity."

"My husband, Jakub, is a cavalry officer; protecting our land from the Ottomans. I am not a widow. You raped a married woman," she accused him. "You claim to know esprit de corps. That means you should call Jakub your brother too. You raped your brother's wife."

Agata's sniffed, fighting tears.

"Yet, your Jakub isn't here, is he? He left you alone." He stepped closer. "How long had it been since your husband found peace in your arms? A year? Longer?"

God I hate you, she thought. In her heart, Agata did not hate Nicheloa.

"I took you, so don't bother lying. How long had it been since he even looked upon you?" He pressed the line which had taken residence above her eyebrow. "Has he seen that?"

Agata pushed away the lump in her throat.

"You're a vampire now. Among vampires, you simply are Agata. You will live forever as young as you are today. Why you wish to be a charwoman is beyond me.

"If you want Jakub, seek him out. You already know he will forsake you. Isn't that why you came here? The count's daughter; the soldier's wife, you know you would be cast aside. You are adrift."

She pushed him away from her. "I came to claim my honor as Chiomara did!"

Nicheloa laughed. "And you believe you will have my head by scrubbing floors?"

Agata went back to her work. "I don't have a plan yet. But I shall never allow Gaius to have me."

"You should," Nicheloa said. "Join your sisters in the harem. Gaius will lavish you in gold and fine fabrics when I can find them. The beasts he collects are for you and the other women. He eats the heart; I eat the kidneys. The rest is yours, the horses, and servants."

"Never!"

"If you belittle his generosity, if you continually disobey Gaius, as others did before you, he will have me kill you in some terrible way. Our horses will feast on your flesh and blood so as not to waste such a treasure."

It was not an empty threat.

"Phillipa told me there were other concubines," Agata said.

"There have been several mistakes in the past thousand years. I am not a fool, Agata, or I would be dead. You may spin remedies rather than turn a song, but that means you are useful to this coven. Your presence might mean our servants live into old age. However, this work is beneath you," Nicheloa said.

"Perhaps, this work is beneath me, but if I don't do it, who will? There aren't enough servants to keep the fort."

"Then I'll find you servants." He bowed and turned away.

At the door, he said, "I am sorry for the pain I caused you."

"I don't care if you're sorry!"

The tears came then, too powerful to stop. Blood spilled upon her cheeks, her blouse, her freshly washed floor.

From the hallway, she heard Titus speak: "Lictor, the Legatus of Carpathia orders dinner."

From the door, Titus bowed. "Honorable One, you've been summoned to the hall. Please don't cry. Everything is well." He wiped away her tears with a clean rag.

Agata followed Titus to the Great Hall. Gaius sat in his throne. His eyes did not alight upon her any more than he watched Phillipa dance. Agata did not doubt he ordered it. Phillipa's crumpling veils spun around her. Her long brown legs kicked upward and then she jumped, so high she seemed to soar. At least, Julia and Sylvia watched her with appreciation.

There was a fourth cushion set beside the other women. Agata sat on it. Wooden goblets stood on a tray beside the throne.

Nicheloa brought in the warhorses first. Their fanged mouths clattered in anticipation. Eerie neighs and snorts echoed over the stone.

"Nix and Fideles," Sylvia whispered to Agata.

Nix was black with white socks and a white blaze. Fideles was a gray. Used to carrying armored men, both horses bodies were heavily muscled. Their manes glimmered in the candlelight.

"May I, Gaius?" Julia asked.

He waved at her in a bored manner. "As it pleases you."

Julia crept to the horses with her hands out toward them. The animals were obviously used to the girl, but Agata felt uneasy as their fangs nipped at her fingers.

Nicheloa brought in one of Agata's cows.

Did no one care that I love the creature? That I brought her into the world so my sons and daughters might inherit wealth since they were provided nothing else as a birthright. She did not bother speaking the question aloud since she knew the answer.

Gaius clapped. "Enough dancing. Now, my women, the Lictor has brought us a cow. Enjoy my generosity."

Julia returned to her cushion as did Phillipa.

Nicheloa set two long wooden troughs in front of the tethered cow. He pulled a knife from his belt. He slit the cow's throat. The beast took a step and fell, bleeding into a trough. Agata could not stop her pounding heart as she watched the scarlet drain into the gutters. One for the human vampires and one for the horse vampires. Her mouth watered, but she did not move, she was so mesmerized by the blood.

Sylvia groaned in hunger beside her. She glanced at her companions. The women's eyes grew wide, but Gaius's face did not change. There was no emotion behind generosity. He did not seem to even take pleasure in it. Just as Titus and the women informed her, Gaius performed perfunctory services to his underling, because it was expected of him and kept the peace.

Nicheloa sliced into the cow's belly; her entrails fell onto the floor.

The concubines left their cushions and jumped upon it and tore its dead flesh.

"Will you not eat, Agata?" Gaius whispered. "You must be hungry with your exertions."

His will overcame her resistance.

Agata found herself kneeling beside the other women and eating pieces of fresh intestine, sucking the blood from the muscle.

They took their cups and dipped it into their trough. The drinking of blood brought laughter. She drank the crimson liquid and found it more pleasurable than the most exceptional wine. With every gulp, injuries she had suffered disappeared. Her body knitted itself back together. However, Agata refused to lose her mind to the bloodlust. She watched how, blade in hand, Nicheloa cut out the cow's heart.

He carried the bloody heart to Gaius.

The Legatus's pupils dilated and his fangs expanded. He took a bite. Blood streamed down his face, and for the first time, Agata saw exquisite joy in his eyes.

His task done, Nicheloa knelt beside Agata. He bit into the cow's kidneys. All this was done without words or instruction. All ingrained habits.

*

After devouring the heart, Gaius rose from his throne.

Agata followed him. "Thank you for insisting I drink from the river of living waters."

His eyes studied her. "Those are strange words."

So Gaius did not know scripture, interesting. "Do you not know the story of Jesus?" Agata asked.

"I was already a vampire and striking bargains with your ancestors when the prophet of Judea and his cult spread throughout Rome. Your faith is a strange one, but I do not tell my concubines who to worship. A Christian woman ought to be obedient as a Roman woman."

Agata said cautiously, "I wanted the blood, but didn't. I felt your encouragement. I don't know why, but after I drank, it felt as if the bruises on my neck are gone."

He brushed her hair off her shoulders. He did not balk at her crucifix anymore than she had. "They have yellowed and are healing. That was just a cow, but the more blood you drink, the quicker you'll heal. My blood is the living waters as you put it. I can heal you if you'll be mine."

"But I love Jakub."

"More's the pity. But you will forget him in time," Gaius said. "However, remember I won't wait forever for your broken heart to heal. You will be mine when I call you."

Agata figured saying nothing was better than arguing. He placed his hands upon her shoulders. When she did not respond to his touch, Gaius pushed her away and returned to his quarters without requesting any of the women's company.

Agata resumed to her errands and kept mental notes. The vampires and servants could consume most of the cow's organs in one day. The rest of the blood was drained for tomorrow, and the muscles were hung for several weeks later. As requested, Titus carved the fat for making soap and candles. The skin was soaked and hung outside to tan.

*

Chapter 14

The sun had risen when Agata had returned to the harem. Though she was satiated by the cow's blood, her hands and back ached.

Julia lay sleeping, her head on Phillipa's lap who held her and stroked her hair. Sylvia met Phillipa's eyes. She rose and slunk across the carpeted floor. She wrapped her arms around Agata and pulled her to the floor. Agata did not fight as Sylvia covered them both in a rug.

"It was idiotic to reject Gaius," the other woman whispered.

"I love Jakub and I want my family back."

"Then kill the Lictor and return to humanity. Return to your children if you can," she said. "Gaius might not know what village you are from, but remember, Nicheloa does."

"I can't kill him."

"Your heart is going soft?"

"No. I'm not physically strong enough, but I still plan to have my vengeance. I must use my mind," Agata whispered.

"Good." Sylvia smiled. "If you mean what you say ..." she paused. "I could live in eternity without men to tell us what to do. I would be Phillipa's lictor."

It sounded like the truth. Agata wondered if it were a trap or a hint they would help her. She wanted to believe the women thought of her as one of their own. By her conversations, she already understood vampires did not have human principles.

Sylvia pressed her lips against Agata's. "If Phillipa ruled, we would live justly. You might stay here safe with us." Her soft black hair fell upon Agata's flesh and tickled her.

Agata whispered, "I've only kissed Jakub like that. Gaius ..."

"Doesn't share us with men, but what we do with each other in the walls of the harem is not his concern. No vampire remains innocent. Not even that one."

Her eyes flickered over Agata's shoulder to where Phillipa sat with Julia. "Gaius bores of them quickly when they are created that young. They never last long. If Phillipa didn't love her so, Julia would have met her final death decades ago."

Sylvia sighed. "There isn't enough food in this place to support an army of vampires, but we are safe enough."

"I feel your desire," Agata whispered. "But I can't fulfill it; my heart belongs to another."

"Then rest well." Sylvia slipped out of the rug.

Agata watched as Sylvia returned Phillipa. As kind as any mother, Phillipa lifted Julia off of her lap and tucked her under a rug. She kissed the girl's brow.

"You could still join us?" Phillipa said.

"No, thank you."

Arm in arm, the older women went to the other side of the harem for their pleasure, and no doubt, whispers.

Once the harem was quiet except snores and rhythmic

breathing, Agata counted to one hundred. Still no noise. She rose.

She crept across the room and checked the wardrobe. Her clothing and medicine kit were not touched. She removed her silver embroidered blouse. Wearing gloves, she carefully ripped the first seam holding the left sleeve onto the bodice. She loosened the threads on the second seam. It would rip easily.

*

Chapter 15

Most of the books in the old library were nothing but torn vellum and rotten leather. Many wax tablets were cracked with age. However, Agata found a wooden box filled with letters on parchment. She peeked through them. She could read Latin quickly enough, even if some of the sentence structure of the old Empire were strange to her.

The letters told the story of the newly transformed Gaius requesting military help from his father, a senator.

Gaius admitted he had hired the wrong prostitute. At first, he believed he was cursed by Venus in the medical way, but the blood lust grew until he killed his private physician and later his steward. He drank from captives, but when they ran out, his soldiers sacrificed themselves to feed him.

In the next letter, Gaius explained how he turned his officers and "a modest Roman woman whom the Gods gifted with unnatural intuition."

Another letter informed Gaius his father was dead. By the dates, Gaius still wrote to his father's ghost. Over the centuries, he turned women for his men, and he experimented on the vampires who didn't obey his will.

Agata paused. There was noise in the hallway. She left the

letters and went back to scrubbing.

"What are you doing in here?" Gaius roared. As he entered, he pushed Ulpia out of his way, knocking her into the wall.

Titus glared at his master. There was palatable hate in his eyes, but the eunuch said nothing.

Agata dropped her rag into the bucket. She hurriedly crossed the room and picked the whimpering girl up. She checked the bump on her head and then kissed her forehead. "You're all right."

The girl cringed under her touch, so Agata gently passed her to her father. Titus wrapped his arms around his daughter and drew her close to his chest.

She stared at Gaius and hoped her rage forced insects to crawl in his brain. "Though many of these books are already dust and droppings, I shall stop the rats from eating these volumes. If you do not wish us to clean this space, we will leave."

"It's fine," Gaius said. "I generally don't find women near the barracks when I don't call them."

"It's not fine," Agata said. "You are not to speak to me in such a way, nor should you knock down little children. You might have killed her."

Gaius growled: "Then we would drink her blood. She's nothing to me. And you're losing importance by the night."

Titus's face grew purple with rage, but Gaius did not turn toward the man.

"I am not afraid of you, Gaius," Agata said.

He grabbed her shoulder. "You should be."

Expecting a slap, she ducked and covered her face. He pushed her away from him.

"Clean this room as you will. Run your errands as if you were still a human woman, I do not care, but do not disturb me again."

He stormed away.

Agata knelt and looked Ulpia in the eyes. Her pupils were similarly sized. "Are you all right, sweet girl?"

Ulpia nodded.

To Titus, she said, "Do you want to take her to her pallet?"

"No, Honorable One, she seems to be fine and better she remain beside me."

Ulpia and Titus returned to their chore.

Agata returned to the letters which became a journal of sorts. She must learn what it was to be a vampire. She discovered Gaius once had a male concubine who ran away. He cut off the lad's hands and feet. Though Gaius did not cauterize the wounds, the man did not bleed out, but crawled around until Gaius reattached his feet and hands. *Interesting*.

Agata wondered what else she might cut off and a vampire would still live. Perhaps Gaius would let her have Nicheloa's head if she did not kill him.

*

Chapter 16

The rest of the week flew by. The vampires feasted on the cow's remnants each twilight. Each night, Agata wondered if she had bitten off more of a job than humanly possible. When doubt pressed against her heart, she looked to Titus, who had grown strong again.

The old fort became livable: even for the undead. As she faced her seventh dawn in the harem, Agata carefully dressed in her delicate silver threaded blouse.

She stood in front of Gaius. "In seven nights, I created a habitable home for you and healed your servant, Legatus. Now I expect you to keep your bargain."

"You wish to be my wife?" Gaius asked. "Is that why you are dressed so fine?"

"Hardly. I am the wife of Jakub," Agata said, not hiding her disgust.

"What does the younger son of a count rate to a legatus? Your own count sends me vassalage each full moon as did your father."

"But I love my husband; I don't love you," Agata said.

"I do not require your love. I require your obedience," Gaius said. "You must learn that if you are to survive eternity.

Just as you must learn, though you love him, your husband will forsake you as required by your strange faith."

"Which is why I will take Nicheloa's head to show my husband that my honor was restored. I don't want to harm another soul, but I must have my honor following the example of Chiomara."

"What?" Gaius's fangs expanded.

Nicheloa's eyes opened wide. He began to laugh. "I told you, Gaius, women do not understand our kind. She truly thinks you would give me up."

"By Gaius's own words, removing your head won't kill you," Agata said. "And I'll return it when I am done."

"You expect me to walk around without a head?" Nicheloa asked.

"I might take that one instead." She pointed below the waist. "You can live without that for a while."

The concubines sat straighter. They looked to the sky. Phillipa's face was neutral, but it felt as if she was smiling.

"You can't have my lictor's head," Gaius said. "Or his manhood."

"Then you're not worthy of the office you bear. I healed your servant and have turned this into a home with the power of my mind. You promised you would do as I asked ... "

Gaius rose. He slapped her. "Take your place among the women, fourth concubine, before I throw you into the sun."

Her ears rang and her cheekbone throbbed. "My name is Agata, and I am the wife of Jakub!"

He slapped her again.

"Take your place or go into the sun." He grabbed her

shoulder. He cried out as the silver thread burned the pattern onto his right hand. Agata ignored the sharp pain which rippled through her. Nicheloa and all the concubines gasped from it. Gaius threw her to the ground.

Agata felt the wind knocked out of her lungs and a low burning in her right hand, but she smiled.

"I have no need for presumptuous women, and you already said you don't want to be my concubine. Nicheloa, take her or destroy her as you please."

Agata ripped off the loosened sleeve of her silver threaded blouse. "I must regain my honor."

She jumped on Nicheloa's back and drew the sleeve against his throat as a garrote. She twisted the linen to ensure the thread was against his flesh, but it was the flesh of her throat which was burned by the silver. She screamed in agony as did Gaius who clutched his own throat. She dropped the garrote.

In her mind, Agata heard: *We won't help you take Nicheloa's head, but we would take this place from Gaius if we have an opening.*

Nicheloa pushed her to the floor. He drew a knife.

She looked up at his throat. Though Nicheloa's flesh bubbled and was scorched and blackened, Gaius was still smooth. She touched her own throat. She did not feel blisters under her fingers.

"Wait," Gaius said.

"You said she was mine."

Pushing Nicheloa aside, Gaius grabbed her and lifted her to her feet. He punched her in the face.

"Lady Agata! Noooo ... " Ulpia's voice pleaded. "Don't

hurt her!"

She felt blood squirt from her nose as she fell onto the floor. He kicked her in the stomach several times.

Through her bloody tears, there was a blur of movement as Ulpia jumped on Gaius's back. He grabbed the girl by the throat and threw her across the room. She screamed as she crumpled against the wall. Titus raced to his daughter. His expression exposed the sorrow in his heart. She knew what it was to lose a child. Gathering Ulpia in his arms, he ran from the room.

"You said she was mine," Nicheloa said.

"And you were going to kill her so I changed my mind. She is mine. Rape her with the knife before you kill her."

Gaius handed him a leaf-shaped blade.

Nicheloa pressed his lips together and came toward Agata, knife in hand. His eyes showed he did not like his task, but he learned long ago. *Obey Gaius or die.* "You brought this torture upon yourself and me, harpie."

Agata forced herself not to retreat. *Of course, the pain will ricochet as before... Gaius punishes us both... Beyond cruel.*

Titus raced into the hall with an ax. Putting all his weight behind the blow, Titus struck Gaius in the back of the neck.

Holding the gash in his neck, Gaius arched his back and screamed. All the vampires shrieked with him. The concubines writhed on the floor. Nicheloa fell to his knees. The sound echoed off the stone walls until it sounded like a thousand vampires cried. She shoved her hands over her ears, wounded by the noise. No, it was her own pain. Agata could not breathe.

Titus lifted Agata to her feet. Agata's heart froze, then beat faster. She tried to protect her face from the coming strike.

He pressed Nicheloa's dagger into her hand.

Confused by the action and pain, but knowing she must act, she stabbed Nicheloa in the side of the neck. The pain echoed in her own body. She tried to remove the blade to cut his throat, but it stuck. She drew upward. It stuck again. The ballads never told her how hard it was to make

a

killing blow.

Titus handed her his ax.

The weapon was heavy in her hands. She squeezed the rough handle tightly and raised it above her head. Using all her strength, she brought it down.

With Nicheloa still on his knees, Agata sliced his head from his shoulders. Blood spurted across her face, across her skirts.

The shrieks from her own mouth deafened her capacity to reason. Looking at the bloody dagger left in Nicheloa's neck and his severed head, Agata thought she might vomit. Gaius's furious scream pealed between his lips. It reverberated through every vampire. He held his own head as if he expected it to roll off his shoulders.

Blood pooled across the stone tiles.

Nicheloa's eyes were still open, moving. "Damn you, woman. I knew I should have just killed you!"

"We will have no more of your cruelty, Legatus," Phillipa cried.

"You will take what I give you," Gaius screamed. "And ... "

The concubines jumped on Gaius. The other two women's voices were screams of wild terror and fury. Only Phillipa's voice was more than a feral din: "For Jason!" She ripped Gaius's tunic. "For Claudia, For Laurel."

The women sweated blood as their hands ripped at his clothing and hair. Their nails ripped his skin. Phillipa kept screaming names. "For Paula. For Liliana ... "

Gaius punched Sylvia. Her head fell to the floor with a crack. Phillipa kept screaming names of former concubines.

Julia screamed as Gaius took her by the throat and threw her across the room. She jumped on the puddle and began to lick Nicheloa's spilled blood. Her wounds disappeared, and she grabbed on Gaius's head and exposed his throat.

"They were nothing; you're everything, Phillipa," Gaius screamed.

Phillipa ripped the dagger out of Nicheloa's neck. She stabbed Gaius in the throat. Agata could not move. Julia and Sylvia screeched, but Phillipa kept stabbing.

Gaius's words were drowned by Phillipa's yell. "Come, Sisters!"

Agata followed the women as they chased him from the hall, down the stairs, and the fort. His screams evaporated, pursued by laughter. They gathered loose stones and threw them at Gaius.

Titus came up behind her. "Escape now, Honorable One. The vampire women did not win their freedom only to give it to you."

The three women turned toward Agata. Titus stepped back as if he had not spoken.

"Do you think to rule us?" Phillipa asked.

"We had discussed it in depth long before you arrived. Phillipa will lead in Gaius's stead," Sylvia said, her fangs still exposed.

"As you will," Agata said.

"We can kill you without pain to ourselves," Sylvia whispered, taking a step toward her. "Do not think we were so foolish to underestimate you the way Gaius and Nicheloa did."

"Will you remain in fealty? Or go find your brave one?"

Phillipa asked.

"I must find Jakub."

"Then may your foolish love protect you." She kissed Agata's cheeks.

"May I take Nicheloa's head for Jakub, Lady Phillipa?"

"No. We must burn it along with his body," Julia said.

"If he reattaches his head, Nicheloa may yet take vengeance upon us. We cannot take the chance, Phillipa," Sylvia said. "Gaius must be kept at bay. His strength was his Lictor."

Agata could see the answer on Phillipa's face before she said, "Forgive us, Agata, but we must burn the body as the sun rises. You have fought beside us as a sister, so we will care for you during the execution and let you go in peace, but you have no claim upon anything within these walls."

The women were unnaturally quiet for victors in battle. Yet, Agata also did not feel like celebrating. There was nothing to celebrate. Men spoke of honor in battles, but all she saw was bloody butchery.

Titus smiled as he dumped straw and sticks in a pile into the fireplace furthest from the throne.

"Why are you helping us?" Agata said softly.

"Gaius said the words, but Nicheloa took what is mine. And Ulpia will be safe from his lechery. He killed my other daughters."

Sylvia and Phillipa dragged Nicheloa's body to the fireplace. Agata set down the head.

Julia handed Agata a torch.

Phillipa asked, "Do you want us to pray for you, brother?"

"Get it over with, you harpies," Nicheloa said. "I die happy knowing you'll suffer for your treason, you hag."

"I suffer happily knowing you'll die." Agata threw the torch onto his head. The hay caught quickly. Then his hair. The odor of burning flesh and greasy smoke filled the hall.

The other women set fire to his arms, torso, and feet.

Agata clenched her fists as his flesh smoked and blackened.

His skin blistered by the heat; she screamed and patted her own face. Over her cries of agony, Nicheloa shouted: "I knew you'd scream first."

Tears running down her face, she collapsed to the floor and clutched her knees to the chest.

Julia came beside Agata and embraced her.

Ulpia poured boiling tallow over Nicheloa's head and into his open mouth. He shrieked and sputtered then.

Agata curled into a ball, trying to drown the pain of being burned alive.

Sylvia set up the troughs, but Agata barely registered the mooing of another cow. She did not hear its panicked bleats as it was slaughtered. She only knew it was dead when she tasted the precious irony blood that filled the cup, which Julia pressed against her lips.

*

Chapter 17

At the next nightfall, Titus and Ulpia escorted Agata down the stairs of the fort. The walls of the Roman fort were still warm from the day's sun, which grew stronger as the day's lengthened. Julia's garden plot held tiny seedlings which quivered in the mountain breeze. Further afield snowdrop blossoms had pushed through the frozen ground. It must be an omen of good tidings for the coven.

"What about you? Come with me," Agata asked.

"I'm bound to this place, Honorable One. Whether Gaius or Phillipa rule, they will eventually bring more children that someone must protect, but you're not bound to the fort. Your heart is bound to your *viteji*. Find your home, and the Earth will protect you. Wrap it around you, so you might sleep."

"Thank you."

Though the night was beautiful, Agata feared the coming dawn. She perceived she might not make it in time. She must find shelter. She sought the tree she took protection in, but all the trees looked the same. None had a large opening.

A howl echoed through the cold night. Gaius was not dead. He was weakened, but he was not dead. He might follow her. She saw a wolf's shape in the darkness. *Could it be him?*

Agata ran as fast as she could. She found herself skipping over rocks, skidding down steep hills of gravel, bounding over boulders. Branches grasped upon her arms, ripped at her skirts. She ran faster; her sides felt they might split.

Her heart and lungs wanted to burst. Weakness overtook her muscles.

The sky lightened in the east. She sought a place to hide.

An eerie neigh rolled over the valley. *Oh my God, did Gaius have his horse? Weapons?*

She ducked behind a tree. She held her breath as hooves crunched through the icy snow. Trying not to make a sound, she peered around the trunk. Fideles and his rider, covered in old livery and armor, approached.

"Hello, Sister," Sylvia said. She reached out her hand to Agata. "Come, Gaius has Nix. Phillipa worried you might not make it home."

She pulled up Agata behind her.

"But the dawn?" Agata whispered.

"Fidelles knows where Nicheloa hid from the dawn."

"Hid?"

Sylvia laughed. "A learned woman such as yourself must realize he had his hiding places. Some of the county seats are over a night's ride from our fort and he was leading livestock."

Seeing the obviousness of it, Agata laughed with her. The concubines were free. Agata was free, she had her vengeance, if not proof of it. What else was there to do except go home?

✳

Chapter 18

The vampires emerged from their hiding place. Fideles knew the way to Râuflor without guidance from Sylvia or Agata. He had made the journey thousands of times over the long centuries.

Within hours, Agata saw the thick town walls, towers and familiar roof-line of her house against the herdlands. Her heart nearly burst from joy, but an icy feeling crept in her chest.

She had led Sylvia to the town where her children lived. A vampire anticipating freedom for as long as Phillipa would look for assurances that Agata would do nothing to harm them.

At the sacrificial herdland, Sylvia lowered Agata from Fideles back. A single white ewe chewed grass. *Was that the missing sacrificial sheep? Why was it here now?*

"The treaty still stands between Phillipa and the counts?" Agata asked.

"The legend of the Legatus protects us all. I will return on the seventh day of the full moon as Nicheloa did before me," Sylvia said as she dismounted.

The ewe bleated in fear and bucked as Sylvia bit into its throat. Watching the other vampire watch her, Agata bit into the sheep's shoulder. She drank until its heart slowed. Sylvia and

Agata left the rest for Fideles.

While the horse fed, Sylvia embraced her. "Let the Gods blessings fall upon you, Sister," she said. You have several hours till the dawn. Use it well."

Agata crossed outside the city walls to the meadow near her home. In the darkness, she climbed the wall and slipped into the garden. Up close, the boards were gone. After only a week and a day, someone already lived there.

Anger bubbled in her stomach, then self-terror. Agata was capable of killing. What if it was simply a servant or one of the children? Exhausted from her journey and satiated with sheep's blood, she needed rest. She would not enter the home, an unthinking beast.

She did not fight the instinct to dig into a planted mound of soft, sweet Earth. Her nails and fingers moved the tilled soil easily. The spicy, savory smell of her herbs surrounded her. She fell asleep, deep in the Earth, and knew sleep like she had not known since she had become a vampire.

*

Agata unlocked the door to the kitchen. She quietly moved through the house and ensured the other doors and windows were locked. Someone had been there. Hopefully, it was just Artur or perhaps Florin moving furniture or cleaning the pantry, but she was not sure. She was not even sure of the date. Only that the sun had set and night had come.

She moved through the hallways. There were no signs of servants. Dust had settled in the corners. Items had been rearranged. She needed a priest to quarantine her in her house, but could not trust Bogdan, one of the church's other priest, or even the count's priest, Father Alexander.

Considering Titus's words, Agata returned to the garden. She filled an oil sack with Earth.

Through her bed chamber's window, she saw movement on the upper floor. *Could it be Gaius? Could he have followed her home?* She did not sense him or any vampire nearby. She studied the form: *Bogdan.*

Fighting rage, she went inside. She placed the oilsack of Earth beside the bread oven and climbed the steps. She would see if human blood was as potent of medicine as the other vampires claimed.

At her chamber door, she said, "Have you made yourself comfortable, cousin?"

Bogdan screamed and held his cross in front of him. "This house belongs to me now, whore of a vampire. Bow before the power of God's glory."

"I do bow before God, but I don't believe you're his representative any longer, Ox. Plenty of men were forsaken in the Bible after they did not follow God's law."

Agata ripped the cross out of Bogdan's hands. She kissed the cross then gently set it upon her dressing table.

She pushed him onto the bed.

"I followed every rule the Good Book claimed a woman must follow. Yet a feeble, cruel priest stole my house and my honor. You wanted Jakub's wife," Agata said smoothly. "Now I am what is left. With your last breaths, you will know me."

Bogdan's eyes brightened as she climbed on top of him.

Even though I threatened his death, he is aroused. He's

an idiot as well as an ox. Still, he is proof of the endurance of childhood pain. After I kill him, I must protect my children's inheritance as well as I can so they are never Bogdan.

Whether lust or shock or fear stopped him, the man lay waiting. Agata bit him in the femoral artery. A flood of human blood flew into her mouth.

Bogdan kicked when he realized she bit his leg. He tried to push her off; she bit down harder. Fangs expanded through her gums and latched onto his muscle. She drank in the salty lusciousness.

The rush of blood heightened her senses. Nothing she had ever experienced compared to drinking the blood of one's enemy; she wanted to suck Bogdan dry.

He screamed. She wanted to make him scream again.

Agata craved for more than his death. She desired to eat his covetous eyes while he was still alive, then perhaps rip off each of his toes and fingers. She might listen to him beg for his life as she slowly took it.

No. She would have her vengeance, but she would not torture him. He was still Jakub's cousin.

His voice grew weak.

The flow of blood diminished. She searched his pale, sickly face for death.

"I ... " Bogdan gasped and tried to push her away. She was stronger.

"I won't turn you, but I have to kill you. Your hate of my husband might hurt my children someday." She kissed his lips and bit down, tearing at the flesh inside his mouth.

He gasped his last breath, sputtering saliva across her

face. Agata continued to drink until his blood thickened, and his heart slowed. She felt the moment his heart stopped.

She had to plan. Someone knew where Bogdan was, and they would look for him eventually.

Let them believe he was a vampire too, perhaps not like Gaius, but a wretched thing.

Feeling stronger than she had since she changed, Agata carried Bogdan's body to the Kirchenburgen. It was silent this time of night.

She decided to place his corpse in the traditional method to kill a vampire. Count Mihai would be forced to claim Bogdan died a vampire. The populace would burn the body and drink the ashes.

She crossed herself. "God, forgive me. Judgment and vengeance are yours, but this man wronged me. I must protect my family."

Agata set the body in the pulpit. She pounded a nail into his forehead, put a stone in his open mouth, and hammered a wooden stake through his heart. She set a crucifix in his pants and left the hammer in his hand. Then she scrawled a note: I AM VAMPIRE.

She scribbled letters to her children and raced across town to Irina's home with an appeal to bring her fresh meat and blood once a week. She pressed the notes under the door and went home, satisfied in her night's work.

On her way, Agata tore the Mărțișors with silver tokens off the trees. Careful not to burn herself, she encircled the house and herb garden with the silver charms so she could not escape, but could still access her medicinal plants.

She wrote QUARANTINE DUE TO THE PLAGUE on a board and attached it to the front portcullis of her house. She took the silver thread from her best garments and blocked the portcullis and shuttered windows.

Agata would wall herself into her home. Even she ate nothing, but the flesh of rats, she would never hurt her family and neighbors. She was a lady of honor.

*

Chapter 19

Weak from the lack of food, Jakub's stomach had not stopped rumbling for a day, but he needed his family more than sustenance. He should have rested Castor, but he wished to see Agata and his children: Artur and Daciana ought to be home, at least. Perhaps, they could send word to Petru and Irina to come.

During his years away, Agata had written to him nearly every week. Then her letters stopped. He had not worried. Several times during the last offensive, he was delivered several messages at once. The battlefield, even his enemy, had shifted relentlessly. One day the letters would catch up to him—even if he was home first.

Once home, Castor could graze on fresh grass and herbs to his heart's content. After Jakub slept in his wife's embrace, he could visit with Irina and her new husband. It might be he was a grandfather. Agata would most likely be thrilled to be a grandmother; he was not sure if he was happy about being a grandfather. Even if his body ached with every morning, thirty-eight summers seemed too young.

From a distance, the house looked the same, but different. The herd and herdsman were not in the pasture. The stone road had grown mossy as if horses and carriages did not come this way anymore. Agata's herb garden, which she had tended with such care, withered in places, and overgrew in others. No lights were cast from the windows. Spiders had woven silver threads over the outer door. He saw the sign: QUARANTINE DUE TO PLAGUE.

His insides twisted. His training forced him to unburden Castor and let him graze.

After seeing so much death, if his wife and children had died from the plague, Jakub no longer cared about his fate. With the side of his fist, he pounded on the door. "Hello!" he cried. "Someone! Anyone! Hello!"

He heard someone shuffle inside.

"Agata? My lady? If you're there, you must let me in." He pounded on the door again. "I can hear you. Agata, is that you?"

"Jakub," his wife's sweet voice whispered. "Is that you?"

"Yes, let me in!"

Agata's gloved hand opened a window. Then she backed away from him.

Her apparition looked too pale for health, but she was not pockmarked, nor did he see any blackened gavocciolos or rotting flesh.

"I see no black death," Jakub said.

"I sent Daciana to be with Irina. Petru is doing well in his apprenticeship with Lexi, so he is there too. Artur is with Gavrilla. I will die here but go see the children. Let them know I love them."

He pushed the wooden door with his shoulder. "Let me in! I have no life without you."

"Jakub, my love, if I will let you inside, you must cast me

out and I will die."

"So you might die in the wilds? Never!" he said. "Let me in! I'm your husband. You must let me in."

The door creaked open.

Inside, the smell of furniture oil met him. Though no light shined through the closed windows, the furniture gleamed as if it had just been polished, and the rooms were clean. As he stepped into the darkness, lingering disappointment that he had come home to this, pressed in on him. *Why had I been on the battlefield if not to protect my family?* He could claim honor, and he served his Voivode well, but he had failed as a husband.

His wife's eyes wafted with bloody tears. "I have sent the servants away and moved into the kitchen, my love, but how I prayed I would look upon you again."

"I will not leave you until you make sense and tell me of your illness. Why do you cry blood?"

"I'm not contagious due to foul air. Only blood. I can prepare you a bath. See to Castor and I'll prepare it."

"I already have seen to my horse."

Agata boiled water in a pot. She took the rest of the water from her collection of rain barrels. Her hands trembled under the weight of the buckets, but she poured each one into the bath. Agata had always been industrious, but the work she did was beneath the lady's hands. It was work for a steward.

"Where are the servants?"

She threw rose petals, orange peels, and rosemary into the boiling water.

I always loved that perfume. Even in her sickness, Agata looks to my needs.

"I sent them away after I was attacked," Agata said. "I caught this infernal disease. I thought I was with child and now I'm this. Artur tried to protect me, but he was overcome by a stronger foe. Don't blame him. You mustn't blame him. How could any fourteen-year-old apprentice match a grown man with centuries of experience?"

Jacob had seen many raped. Common women, boys and girls who did not have even a foot soldier to protect them.

I should've been here. Jakub did not blame his son, he blamed himself. It was Jakub who had vowed to protect his wife.

"I no longer sleep well. I'm going mad. Did I tell you Petru and Daciana are with Irina? They are safer there. Artur learns from his uncle's men."

"And the one who raped you?"

"I killed him. I think." She took the boiling pot and poured it into the tub of cooler water.

"What do you mean, you think?"

"I hoped I could show you his head like Chiomara, but I stabbed him in the neck and couldn't get the knife out. I took an ax to him. The other... v-vampires threw him onto a pyre."

Other vampires?

"You're a brave lady, Agata," Jakub said softly. "But vampires are legend. We used to laugh at peasants who believed in such things."

"We used to laugh at many things, but that doesn't make my fate any less true."

She stopped by the window and put her hand in the sun. Smoke wafted. He pulled her back inside.

"I don't think I have been forsaken by God. I can still

do nearly everything I could before. But silver seems to cause a reaction and so does the sun. I'm writing a book about such things for Irina. No superstition, just medical fact."

Agata took a deep breath. "Now, when you take another bride, see that she is kind to the children and industrious. That's how you'll know she'll make a fine wife."

Jakub did not know what to say, he sputtered: "Take another bride?"

"I am of the walking dead, Jakub. My honor has been tarnished, and I have no proof I took vengeance. I have no hold on you."

Was God punishing me for what I have done while at war? It doesn't matter. Only Agata matters now.

Jakub drew her close. ""You're my wife. I missed every deget of your face." Jakub kissed Agata's left cheek. Her brow. Her right cheek. He pressed his lips to hers.

"I've had other women: camp followers and laundresses. But I've only wanted one wife. I've dreamed of you a thousand times. I will never leave you."

*

Agata's body reacted to her husband as it always did, but this time, she had to focus on willing her fangs to remain in her gums. She had missed him so much. All of her anxiety had come home. She could hear his heartbeat. She smelled his sweat. She ran her fingers through Jakub's straggly black hair which had grown to his mid back, tied with a simple ribbon. The lines on his brow had grown deeper, and his skin had grown darker from the sun, however, his chiseled cheekbones and the same nose he gave to Irina were still sculpted to perfection. His blue eyes which he passed to both Irina and Petru had the same disquieting clarity as they always did.

He removed his clothing and stepped on a grated tray. A few new scars covered his body. She poured olive oil mixed with ash onto his shoulders. She scraped a strigil across his body to remove the dirt and excess oil.

He stepped into the warm rose bath. "Even though it will pain me, I want to know every detail of your adventure. Do not spare me, my love."

"I should air your clothes. Rest a moment and allow me to collect my thoughts."

Agata ran upstairs for his best embroidered cămaşa made linseed linen, sheepskin peiptar with the silver buttons, and white woolen pants decorated on the cuffs and pockets.

When she returned, crimson tears burned in her eyes. Yet, in a trembling voice, she told him everything.

*

Chapter 20

Jakub strode across Râuflor to the castle. The ancient red bricks made way to creamy stone as the castle progressed toward the sky. Though he was a boy there, it was not his home. The house he built with Agata was his home. Behind him, the peasants whispered, he felt their eyes on his back. They feared him too much to speak openly. His brother's manservant opened the door. Gavrilla stood behind him.

"Welcome to my home, the brother of my husband," Gavrilla said, inclining her head. She did not meet his eye, but her fingers twisted around a handkerchief.

"I'm glad to see you are well, but was surprised to see my house in its present state."

Gavrilla eyes brimmed with tears. They were clear, just water.

"You miss her?" Jakub asked.

"Yes," Gavrilla said softly. "I miss her jokes. She was clever."

"Is clever."

Gavrilla met his eyes. "You won't have her put aside?"

"I love her."

"Thank you."

"You're not thanking God?" Jakub asked.

"I'll thank Him later. You answered my prayers. Come, my husband has much to say to you."

Gavrilla led them into the hall where his brother, nephews, and eldest son sat. His old manservant, Florin, poured the wine. He wanted vengeance on existence. *How could life go on when Agata suffered?*

"Father, you've returned." Artur stood and inclined his head. He looked well, dressed in his uncle's livery, but his eyes betrayed his panic. "And Mother? Is she still unwell?"

Unwell? Unwell!

"Yes. I went to the house first," Jakub said, keeping his voice even. "And spoke to your sweet mother. Her concern for you, your brother, and sisters warmed my soul."

Mihai cleared his throat. "I might fear the voivode, but the Legatus of the Mountains is the true ruler of the county. He might burn Râuflor or our villages to the ground if he chooses or turn our children into slaves. Agata was a great lady, but she was lost as soon as he placed his eyes upon her."

Beside his uncle, Artur swigged a large gulp of wine.

Jakub wondered if Mihai would fear the Legatus as much if he knew he had been cast out of his fort by a group of angry concubines. However, Agata had warned, the vampire women would attack the county if their sacrifices did not keep coming. It had been months. They might have retained men.

Jakub did not speak of the other vampires; instead, he studied his weakling brother who did not protect his community while Jakub had ridden into battle in the name of Voivode Bogdan. The fur-lined coat did not hide his soft muscles. His embroidered collars did not cover his drooping double chin.

"Lost," Jakub snapped, "You were to protect her!" .

"I ... " Artur started, but his uncle interrupted him.

"She was a great lady," Mihai repeated, "But she is just a woman. With the land long at war, there are plenty of young widows. Such sorrow is known to all men."

"You claim to know my sorrow. My children's sorrow?" Jakub slammed his cup to the table, sloshing the wine. Florin quickly wiped it up.

"Agata was destroyed, brother. While it pains you, you must put her aside," Mihai said. "I am supposed to see the voivode next month. Our house must be in order. No one of substance will admit the Legatus attacked her. All the counts surrounding the mountains claim the Legatus as peasant stories—even though we all offer him a goat or sheep every month."

"Then pray, why did he attack Agata and her cow?" Jakub asked.

"I don't know. Perhaps he wanted beef, rather than mutton. Or perhaps he wanted another woman," Mihai stated.

Jakub turned toward Artur. "And you, my son, do you claim your mother without honor?"

Artur looked between his father and uncle. "We were attacked. I could not protect her. She had honor once, but the priest claims her curse is bestowed upon God or my sword arm would not have failed."

His voice quivered. Artur did not believe his own words, but Jakub had no pity.

"How convenient for you," Jakub said. "Very well. I will protect this family from scandal, but I will go with her. And I pray your bride is never set upon as your mother was."

"You live too much on Chivalric tales, Father. Even Lucretia committed suicide," Artur said.

Jakub stood up. He buried his fingernails into his palm before his hand flew. Those were Mihai's words. No wonder Agata tried to regain her honor. Why Gavrilla feared what Jakub would do more than any curse from God.

"I was once proud of my son. May one day you live to make me proud again, but I will not look upon the weakling boy who most likely would be dead if his mother had not also been in the barn."

"Father!" Artur cried.

"Your mother casts no blame. She has pride in her eldest son. I will never take it away from her, but I take no pride in a son who blames his mother for his failures.

"I will say goodbye to my other son and daughters. Then we will leave the county. Tell the nobility whatever you wish. That Agata was attacked or she fell ill." He slammed down a written account. "This is Daciana's dowry. Irina is in charge of it.

"Artur, the house is yours. We will vacate it in a week."

✳

Irina's home on merchant street was a fine wooden house, beside her in-laws' older but equally fine house. She and Agata had done well with her marriage.

"Father!" Petru yelled from a window. "Irina, Father has returned!"

Irina quickly came to the door and welcomed him into her home. She kissed his cheeks, took his coat, and set a chair for him by the fire. Petru embraced him. However, Daciana clung to Lexi's leg as he brought a bench to sit beside him.

"This is your father, Cia," he said kindly. "Go, kiss him."

The child looked at Jakub disbelieving, not hiding her emotions. "My father is a viteji!" she said. "Where's Mama? I want Mama!"

Jakub was not exactly surprised his youngest daughter did not know him, but it still hurt to see the little girl with Agata's eyes and black hair spurn him.

"I am a viteji and your father," he said. "Your mother is still ill. She's at home."

"Where's your armor if you're a viteji?" Daciana asked.

Lexi laughed. "Armor is only for battles, not visiting family."

Daciana pointed to the window.

"Where's Castor! Mama and Irina said you have a black warhorse with white socks named Castor. You walked here."

"It is a lovely day for a walk, sweetie. He is your father," Lexi said. "He has come home to set your house right."

Irina cringed but said nothing as she poured cups of spiced wine.

"When can I go home?" Daciana demanded.

"Not until Mama gets better," Petru said softly and took Jakub's hand. "I promise, Cia, this is our father."

Daciana let go of Lexi's leg. She hesitantly kissed Jakub's cheek and returned to Lexi's lap.

Jakub truly missed his elder children. Jakub loved Daciana, but he did not know her. She would not even remember him. Agata had provided for the children's future as well as she could.

"Cia is healthy." Irina handed Jakub a cup of wine. "And happy. Petru is doing well in his apprenticeship."

"And are you happy?" Jakub asked Irina.

"Yes, Father. Lexi is a good man." She glanced at her husband. "I'm with child." She crossed herself to protect the baby inside her.

"As Agata informed me." To Lexi, Jakub said, "No doubt, you wish for a son?"

"Boy or girl, I only hope he is healthy and if God is good to us, he will look like Irina," Lexi said.

Jakub opened a leather bag. "Agata bade me bring you these silver necklaces for you and this book of the truth about vampires. She has been conducting experiments upon herself. The ancient pact between the Legatus and the counties still holds, but if that changes, Agata wanted to give you and our descendants the knowledge to protect yourselves."

Jakub nodded. "I have left Artur the house. You two will keep Daciana until she is of marriageable age?"

Lexi took Jakub's hand. "My dearest wife's father, as I promised Agata: Irina's sister is my sister. I will find her a good husband when she is of age. Agata gave me the instructions for both Petru and Cia."

"Good. I care less for a noble name; I want Daciana's husband to be kind and industrious. Being the granddaughter of two counts means little when both parents are not heirs. Find her a man with a good head on his shoulders. Irina, you will be training her in the healer's art when she is older?"

"Yes, Father," Irina said.

"Excellent. This bag has her dowry. I have left receipts with the count."

"We will find the best husband for her," Lexi said.

"And Mother?" Irina said.

"Your mother and I will be going away, so the scandal doesn't harm the county."

"Uncle Mihai means well," Petru said.

Jakub was annoyed Petru felt compelled to protect his uncle. He would not say any cruel words to his younger son. As Agata said, casting blame would only hurt his sons. After all, for much of their lives, their uncle had been home, while Jakub had been on the battlefield. Their uncle would provide for them after he was gone. He should not blame them, any more than Agata did.

He felt a pang deep within his heart and regretted his final words to Artur.

"I'm sure Count Mihai believes he is doing the right thing. Let us not speak of scandals, but happy things. Petru, tell me all you have learned in your apprenticeship."

✻

Agata smiled as Jakub led a newly purchased calf and hogget into the kitchen. She already had built salt trays to dry the calf meat and mixed spices for sausages, but she felt a hollow sorrow. Everything was moving so fast.

"The children?"

"The children are well, my sweet wife," he said to Agata. "Daciana's dowry is safe. Petru is doing well in his apprenticeship. Gavrilla has found a match for Artur. Irina is happy and with child. We have been blessed."

"If you wish to leave me and stay with them, I will understand."

"You're worried about our children." Jakub kissed the top of her head. "Irina is married. Artur is grown. Petru has begun his apprenticeship. No little sister has ever been so loved as Cia.

"Still, I will regret leaving our children behind. I realized how much I did not know them. We are bound by blood, but we are strangers."

Her heart ached. She had prayed for Jakub to return from war and he had come home. She knew she must leave Râuflor, but if he went with her, he would be separated from the children once more.

"The vampires told me losing our children and grandchildren to eternity would cause us great pain. I would spare you from this pain if I could."

"You cannot spare me from anything," Jakub said. "I have done cruel things, profane things. Heaven has no place for me if you're not there. Like all men, I've had other women, but only one wife. I will become like you, and we will leave Râuflor."

"Must we leave immediately? Before Irina has her baby?"

"Listen well. We cannot stay here. Râuflor would eventually tire of living beside two vampires," he said. "And then our children will truly be in danger."

Agata lifted her chin to look at her husband. Her lips quivered, but she knew he was correct. She finally admitted the truth, which she had not wanted to face. That Sylvia Phillipa, Nicheloa, and Gaius warned her about. "I thought if I regained my honor, we could be a family again, but our existence won't ever be the same, will it?"

"No, it won't be," Jakub said. "Eternity will leave us with plenty of time to regret. Now we must think and plan. I will need your mind as you need my experience. You won't make our children pay for any folly of their parents. You're too kind of a mother. Now tell me how to travel under the sun?"

"What about your leather coat?" Agata said. "Over linen and wool, leather surely would block the sun."

"Indeed, my love."

"I could hide under coats for now. Where was it you wanted to go, my husband?"

"The Franks." Jakub's eyes seemed to glow with an inner light.

"Why to the Franks?"

"Because their cavalry officers believe in chivalry and their current king is called the Father of People. They are noble and kind. The language is similar to our own, but we must practice," Jakub said. "Perhaps, I can become landed by great deeds. We can start again. Though it pains me, you will need to sell off many of your treasures to finance this venture."

"You are my only treasure." Agata kissed her husband's lips.

*

Chapter 21

After their errands in Râuflor were complete, Jakub drove the horse and cart south along the main road to Bodeşti which edged the eastern side of the Carpathian Mountains. A long journey was in front of them on roads of questionable quality with an even more dubious map to the Black Sea. There, they would acquire passage on a ship to take them to the land of the Franks. He was not sure if he should go through the Principality of Wallachia or head north-west following the foothills which might be covered in snow. He feared crossing into the Ottoman Empire with his wife.

One horse easily pulled the small cart on narrow mountain roads. His warhorse, Castor, was tethered behind the wagon. Behind Castor was the freshly shorn yearling hogget for Jakub's transformation. The deep forest of spiraling and twisted pines cast the road in dappled golden shade. The canvas tent was lined with leather and tapestries to protect them from the sun and the rain. Agata was safe inside with oil sacks of earth from her garden. Besides, insulation, the tapestries they were light-weight and precious, hopefully, valuable enough to hire a ship.

Every hour, he found himself going over Agata's list again in his head. He wanted everything to go perfectly. If he were a younger man without a hint of gray in his black locks, he might have waited to arrive in France or at least a port city for the transformation, but the life of a soldier was a hard one. He did not want his body to age another night. Unless they turned around, the children—and the rest of the village—would be safe.

As the sun lowered, he came to a shallow creek. "We'll make camp here."

"Yes, my love," Agata said through the canvas.

Jakub pulled off the road into a somewhat smooth and level ground. He jumped from the cart to unhook and hobble the horses. His boots slipped under soft wet earth broken up by patches of grass. He watched the bugs skim lazily over it. Day birds quieted, and night birds and bats ruled the canopy of trees overhead. His last sunset.

At dusk, Agata emerged. As he helped her down, he noticed in the cart, she had spread rose petals and wolfsbane between their blankets where they made love. She opened her can of smoldering torchwood and let the sparks fall onto a few pieces of wood and moss. Her work was efficient as always.

"I am reminded of so many years ago when we left our bridal bed and ran out to the herdlands to make love under the stars," he said, watching as she poked sausages with sticks to hang over the fire.

"And we were caught by the servants," Agata said with a girlish giggle.

"Mihai was so angry. He was so worried we'd cause a scandal."

Agata smiled at him. "We did."

✳

Lying beside her husband, Agata listened to his rhythmic heartbeat and soft sounds of his body digesting dinner. He ran his fingers down the smooth skin of her inner arm.

"I will love you for eternity," she said.

Staring deep into his eyes, she lifted his wrist to her lips. She bit into it and sucked the blood from the wound.

He groaned as his heart fluttered. She bit open her own wrist and pressed it to his lips until he calmed.

Agata sliced open the flesh over his heart. He screamed loudly when she expanded her fangs and bit down, gulping the blood which poured into her mouth. His heart slowed. She listened for the moment his pulse shuddered.

She opened her breast and pressed his head to the wound. There was no hesitation as he swallowed her blood to be reborn into undeath.

Agata felt the infinity of the line of vampires into which she and Jakub were resurrected. Nicheloa. Gaius. A beautiful African woman. A tall man who stood in shadow. A hideous hunchback. A lad no older than Artur. All these souls and others were linked through blood.

She did not remember seeing these people during her change and wondered if Jakub could see them the way she did. The line of vampires disappeared as a hot rage overtook her vision. It was as if Gaius sensed Jakub and turned his eyes toward them. He would come for them. He desired revenge for what she had done.

Feeling the danger which Gaius posed, she wanted to flee with her husband, but his lips still sucked on her flesh, consuming her blood. She had no idea how much he needed to become a vampire, but if they stopped now, he might die.

All around them, the forest was full of deer and rabbits and insects buzzing, but she sensed no vampires. She said a quick prayer for God's guidance and protection and thanked Him for the bounty which they would consume.

Jakub fell to his back, clutching his left arm and pressing it to his chest. She could not shield him from the pain of death.

Agata silently moved into the glen where the hogget chewed on hay. After she tethered the hogget's legs, she opened the sheep's throat. She smiled as the blood streamed into a deep pan. The red liquid piqued her thirst, but she willed herself to remain in control.

Jakub shouted as he awoke from death.

"I am here, my love." She carried the pan to where he lie.

Using small wooden cups, they both feasted on the blood. They slurped and gulped the sheep's vital fluid like wine until their thirst slackened. Jakub licked the pan, not willing to waste a drop.

Jakub's stomach growled loudly. "There were days spent in battle where I didn't touch a morsel, yet I never remember a hunger such as this."

"It's our need for blood. It makes us hungrier. Take the heart."

With his knife, he cut out the sheep's heart. He plunged his teeth into the bloody muscle. Not willing to waste the carcass, she carved the flesh into steaks, rounds, and other pieces.

Still hungry, like the newly reborn monster he was, Jakub picked up the scraps and sucked the marrow from the bones. The meat was packed in an oilcloth before Jakub had his fill.

As if he were drunk or in a daze, Jakub stumbled to the creek and let the water spill over his body. With oil soap, Agata joined him in the icy water. They washed each other before climbing into the wagon for the coming day.

Agata let down her coil and let her raven hair tickle Jakub's chest. Finally, willing to speak of her fear, she whispered, "When I transformed you, did you see him, Gaius? The Legatus of the Mountains?"

"Yes, I saw him."

"He wants vengeance."

"Yes." He ran his fingers down her spine. "If I remember my war history, Gaius Lepidus Severus was a great general who won many wars until one day he disappeared. Great generals aren't known for taking their losses lightly — especially from a smaller foe he had underestimated."

"I would fear the sun if not for the cart, but perhaps we ought to sell it and tapestries? If I had my own leathers, we could travel twice as fast," she added.

He kissed her brow. "I would think the sanctuary from the sun is more important than speed. Moreover, the cart carries the earth from your garden. Even if Gaius knows where we camp tonight, he doesn't know which way we travel."

Agata nodded.

"I'm here now; there's nothing to fear."

Agata nodded again and squeezed his hand, but she was afraid. His chest rose and fell with a sigh. "So, this is the life of a monster? It's not quite what I expected if I'm honest."

*

Chivalry Among Vampires

1356

Prologue

In the war-torn Kingdom of France, there was not a château, fortress, house, or hut that did not know the Black Death. The winters were cold and dry; the land was barren and harsh. Crops failed. Bands of mercenaries roamed, bored, and unfruitful.

By order of the king, peasants were forced to rebuild châteaus for those destroyed in the war, which had already lasted nineteen years. This war would span over ninety years more.

At Poitiers, the English beat the French and King Jean II or Jean le Bon, was imprisoned. Starving, shamed peasants, called the Jacquerie, revolted against the nobility, acting in the name of their imprisoned king. While much of the violence was in northern France, there were sporadic terrible murders elsewhere.

Hundreds of knights, their ladies, and children were slain in the most gruesome of ways. The nobles' reprisals massacred thousands.

As another cold winter loomed, a mason seethed at a landed knight who rode his horse across their village but did not protect it from the mercenaries.

Each night, he prayed for vengeance. To other men, he

bitterly claimed to care that Jean le Bon rotted in an English prison, but his mind replayed the gasping deaths of his mother, followed by his wife. The Black Death had ravaged their bodies. Too poor to find a matron, nurse, or widow with milk, his child died of starvation. Her wails echoed into him. He would never be free of her cries.

One day, the mason woke to find egg-sized gavocciolos underneath his arms. He hid his disease. On the first day, he set his affairs in order. The next day, his thighs were covered in black spots.

He relished his spreading disease. Before the infection took over his lungs, he threw himself into the only clean year-round water source for the château.

The fall did not kill him, but as he lay broken and bleeding, he took comfort in the thought his death would murder the knight, his lady, children, and livestock.

The knight never even knew of the man's anger or, perhaps, did not care. The mason went to his reward; however, he did not succeed in killing his enemy. When a boy was lowered into the well to clear it of the rotting body, he saw the plague-ravaged corpse and begged to be pulled up.

Workers tossed stones down the well to bury the disease. The need for new wells stopped the rebuilding of the château. The mason's vengeance freed peasants and tradesmen from unpaid work.

Something else unexpected happened.

As workmen dug holes searching for clean water, an ancient creature stirred under the Earth.

Hibernation broken, it churned the dirt, pursuing

sustenance. The creature found nourishment in the mass graves of broken, decaying, putrid flesh. It cared not what the source: whether human, animal, plant, or fungus. It digested what it found.

In time, this creature of nightmares and legend would need something more.

The living made for delicious meat.

*

1510

Chapter 1

The vampire, Jakub Petruescu Christian, sensed the sun's movement toward the horizon. Only a few nights old, he ached for blood, but it would be another hour before sunset. The covered cart's layers of canvas lined with wool and silk tapestries protected him and his beloved wife from the immolating sun.

He ignored his thirst with dreams of the Kingdom of France. In his previous life as a cavalry officer of Christendom and vassal to both Stephen the Great and Bogdan, the One-Eyed, he had spent more time in battles than home, but he had never seen France. He remembered the drawings of the chapels in Toulon, Nice, Paris and the majestic Gothic castle at Boules. He thought of the praise he had heard from French crusaders and mercenaries for the beloved Louis the Twelfth. Jakub could serve the King of the People.

As a boy, he had read *Livre de chevalerie* by the knight, Geoffroi de Charny with great interest and vigor. Before their journey, he reread the treatise to prepare. Though the great knight was captured and killed in the great Battle of Poitiers in 1356 shortly after the book was released, it explained the ethos of the French fighting class. To be a Brother of the Sword with such great warriors was the highest honor Jakub could imagine.

"Did you hear that?" Agata Arturescue Vidraru whispered beside him.

It was strange to experience the road caring for his wife — or any respectable woman. De Charny advised knights to live an austere life and seek basic Spartan accommodation rather than sleep in a soft bed, however as a knight also must care for his lady, Jakub ensured the cart had some comforts for her.

He rolled over and looked her in the face. By the pronounced look of exhaustion, she had not slept again.

"I only hear Castor and Pollux, my love," he said, speaking of the horses, who were outside grazing.

"I am glad you are awake. I feel ... unsafe," she said.

He might only be a few nights old compared to her months of existence as a vampire, but he had familiarity with the road. She never criticized their newly-purchased wagon, but greener than the youngest squire, his poor wife had little experience on which to draw during this adventure. Agata's first fifteen years were spent in her father's town. After they married, she spent the next seventeen raising their five children, running the manor, her dairy, and performing midwifery. Jakub had believed his wife and family were safe in their thickly walled city. He had been wrong.

A dark, furious place in his mind whispered: *I fought for both God and princes. Yet, God allowed a vampire to rape my wife. His own representative murdered her. The nobility dared say I ought to set her aside.*

Away from me, Satan. I shall not dwell in these thoughts. We are leaving Moldavia so we may have a new existence.

In truth, they could not stay. Peasant stories claimed

vampires were evil and must be rooted out. However, as an important and beloved lady, their town had overlooked Agata's state as long as she remained quarantined, with their eldest bringing her weekly rabbits. She had only killed the man who killed her. No one else. Once Jakub returned home and decided to join her in death, they had to depart.

"Touch your earth, my love, and let it comfort you." He pushed the soft black locks away from her shoulders and kissed her bare neck.

Agata reached for a crock. She rubbed the earth from her garden between her fingers. She took a deep breath.

"Feel better?"

"Yes, the earth helps me see our children's faces."

The children again. Each dusk their four surviving children were first in her mind, and all five never left her heart.

Jakub thought of Job. *Is it God's will that my wife suffers the loss for eternity, and I suffer her sorrow?* "The children are fine. You gave them a bright future." He kissed her brow. She smiled without opening her eyes. Calmed, she cuddled up to him again, her raven hair spilling across them.

While he rubbed the small of her naked back, he reminded her how their eldest, Irina, was a grown and married woman, pregnant with her first child. She and her husband cared for their youngest, Daciana, who was left a generous dowry. Their two sons had their apprenticeships. The townhouse would go to Artur, and money was set aside for Petru to build a house.

He even mentioned Daniella. Out of his and Agata's five children, only Little Daniella did not make it past infancy. They were blessed; not even his elder brother had been so fortunate.

Mihai's wife suffered two miscarriages, and their firstborn died during infancy before his two sons and daughter came into the world.

"Do you think we might have children in this form?" Agata asked.

"My love, blood taints my seed, and have you had a phase as a vampire?"

She shook her head.

"And the other vampire women you met — had they?"

"I don't believe so. If Phillipa could have children, she would have."

"Then, no, my love."

She snuggled deeper. "That's what I assumed too, but my heart still aches."

She'd lost so much. It pained him he had not been home to defend her. To protect her now, Jakub followed his beloved wife willingly into undeath. There were unexpected benefits. At thirty-eight, his sword arm had begun to weaken, and his shield arm had an unceasing twinge. His back and shoulders ached. Yet since his transformation, he had not been bothered by any pain. He had a touch of gray in his temples, but Agata's raven hair would always be black as midnight.

"Perhaps, I can relax you," Jakub said.

She nodded and kissed his chest.

His fangs expanded, and he bit down on her flesh. She let him suck gently for a time. It cooled his hunger.

Time slowed as they became one. Time stopped as she bit into his wrist while he was inside her.

Chapter 2

After lovemaking, Jakub and Agata feasted upon blood sausage, salted meat, and water until the sky dimmed.

Calmed and satiated, his wife lay back on the tapestry. She closed her eyes and fell asleep. He kissed her on the temple and went to drive the cart.

He unhobbled Pollux and checked the sweet mare's hooves for rocks and other debris before connecting her to the driving shafts. He had just tied his warhorse's lead to the back of the cart and climbed onto the seat when he sensed something terrifying in the twilight. Something as dead as he.

It felt as if a million invisible insects crawled on his skin. He could not move. The mass of insects pulsed as one living thing. Their legs crawled, squirmed, writhed upon his flesh, then they burrowed through his eyes and attacked his brain.

A masked figure cloaked in ragged and torn leather emerged on horseback. Jakub had ridden horses his entire life, but he had never seen a horse with long fangs jutting over his thick lips. The gelding's teeth clattered in its muscular jaw in its elongated face. His black tail swished.

The vampire in human form could only be his wife's enemy: Gaius Lepidus Severus, the former Legatus of Carpathia during the Roman empire.

"Agata, run!" Jakub tried to raise his sword, but his arm could not strike against the progenitor of this bloodline. The insects burrowed deeper in his brain. "Agata!"

Agata scurried out of the back of the wagon.

"Remain still." Gaius took the sword out of Jakub's hand. "Remain still."

Jakub could not move a muscle. His eyes began to dry as he could no longer blink. In his chest, his heart and lungs began to ache.

"There's no need to fear me, my son. You will be my new Lictor. Stillness."

Even in rags of a bygone era, Gaius moved with the strength and purpose of a wolf. The lush long black hair had a rippling quality and moved as if it had a life of its own. The aquiline nose had once been broken but still balanced his prominent cheekbones and basalt chin covered in a short thick black beard. Like Jakub, he was dead but alive.

Gaius had created the vampire, Nicheloa, who, in the act of deranged cravings, raped Agata, drank her blood, and accidentally turned her into a vampire. Agata had bested Gaius in a battle of wits, and, in vengeance, she asked for Nicheloa's head as her prize. Gaius refused her. Unfortunately for Gaius, he had been a cruel master, unkind to his human servants and vampire women. They had risen against him. He had lost his home, his station, his women.

A man with nothing was always a dangerous foe.

Pollux reared up as Gaius bit into her throat. She had been such a happy pony who enjoyed pulling the cart. Jakub felt sad to see the pony bleed into Gaius's mouth. She stumbled under the vampire's grip. The thirst took hold of him as he watched blood trickle onto the ground. He ached for that trickle.

Castor, tethered to the back of the cart, reared as Gaius moved closer to him. His white socked hooves pattered the ground in panic.

Jakub's heart cried.

Castor was born for war and trained by Jakub's hand since he had been a foal. He had formidable muscles, able to easily spin past pikes, stop quickly, or sprint forward. The horse's strong profile, wide jaw, and deep brown eyes filled with terror in remembrance that horses were prey animals.

Jakub had been silent, because his mouth could make no sound, but as if Jakub had screamed, Gaius looked at him with a strange expression. He grimaced and let the warhorse be.

For a single moment, Jakub felt relief. Then Gaius turned toward him. Terror filled his heart as Gaius opened his linen cămaşa and sliced open his chest. The ancient vampire drank in his life essence until Jakub saw only darkness.

✳

Wet branches tore at Agata's skirts and roots grabbed at her legs as she dashed into the forest. Behind her, she heard a gurgle and the unmistakable sound of chains.

Twigs snapped with every footfall. She ducked down; she did not know which direction to go.

She might run into the horrid forest, or she might follow the road. But where would she go? No one would give her sanctuary. Villagers would kill a vampire.

Another shriek echoed through the wood.

She heard hoofbeats and ducked down behind a tree. A chill started at the base of her spine and worked through to her shoulders. Knees trembling, she clung to the pine, the moss on its bark drenched her shirt front.

Dear God, was that Castor? Or the dead horse, Nix? She tried to block the screams of terror from her mind. She had brought Jakub to this. *What would Gaius do to him?*

"I have to move," she whispered and rose to her feet. She hurried away from the scream. "Stupid woman, do what Jakub said. Move. You cannot help Jakub if you're dead."

The branches and underbrush grew thicker, reaching out and pulling on her loose hair and skirts. Sweat and bloody tears stung her eyes. She could barely see a few feet ahead of her. Yet, fear hastened her steps.

She glanced behind her and saw the silhouette of Gaius in the distance. She could not outrun a mounted man, but she would never surrender. She dashed into a grassy clearing and pushed herself on even faster. Pain began in her side. Her knees threatened to give. Sheaths of grass pulled on her skirts; a stick ripped at her flesh. She gasped through her throbbing lungs, unable to breathe.

A calloused, icy hand gripped her shoulder. The Legatus spun her around.

"Jakub," she cried. She threw punches and kicks. She might have been hitting a stone statue for all the good it did.

"Your husband can't save you," Gaius hissed in her face as he lifted her by her neck. He clamped an iron around her neck which was attached to a long silver chain. "I've taken most of his blood."

"Jakub!" She tried to grab the chain and run, but it burnt her bare hands.

As if she was no more than a rag doll, he threw her roughly to the ground.

"Jakub will be my new Lictor, and we shall retake my fort. Those harpies will regret raising a hand to me, as will you," Gaius said. By his tone, Agata could see Gaius believed Jakub would simply obey. Perhaps Jakub had no choice, but obedience, if Gaius dominated his mind.

He remounted Nix and urged his horse on to a gallop.

Agata tried to keep up. She tripped and was dragged along to the road. Dirt filled her mouth. Grit lodged itself between her teeth. Rocks and grasses ripped at her clothing, skin, and hair. Finally, he stopped at a wide crossroad. Her face was scratched; her neck was raw.

He pounded a silver stake into the ground and chained her to it. "The sun will rise, and you, and all the problems you caused me, will be gone."

"Jakub will save me!" Agata sobbed, bloody tears running down her cheeks.

Gaius raised his hand as if to strike her. She ducked.

The blow did not fall.

That was the strange thing about Gaius. He was an ogre, but he could not bear to be.

Perhaps if Agata had not loved her husband, she might have accepted him as a protector after her transformation. Then she wondered why she even considered it as she remembered that through the ages, he had murdered hundreds, if not thousands, of his concubines. Still, Phillipa survived. She was nearly as old as Gaius was.

"I warned you. Your great love is your downfall. You might have been one of my women. You might have been Nicheola's woman, but no. You had to have your husband."

"Jakub won't ever follow you!"

"Your man is a soldier first, just as I am a soldier. Not even after two thousand years did Phillipa and her harpies ever learn that. You chose your fate. Though Jakub and I shall burn with you, I'll rejoice and live on.

"Jakub will no doubt mourn, but he will forget you in the centuries to come. Once she is dead, no woman is unforgettable."

✻

Chapter 3

"Jakub!" Bloody tears streamed down Agata's face.

There was no answer except the night birds screaming somewhere deep in the woods. "Calm yourself," Agata hissed aloud. She had to focus on her situation. She was in the middle of the road. The chain was not long enough to allow her to find shelter in the nearby bushes and the sun would rise.

She clawed at the collar. She was not strong enough to bend the metal. She touched the silver chain; it burned her hands. Too soon, the sky grew pink and lightened. The sun peeked between the trees. Her protective shadow would soon be gone.

"Jakub!" No answer. "Jakub!" Still no answer. "Castor! Pollux!"

She cried, hoping one of the horses would hear. No sounds came. Her fangs bit her bottom lip.

She grabbed a handful of dirt and spit upon it. There was not enough saliva to make mud. She cut open her arm and added a little blood. It was enough to get a thick layer of dirt to stick to her hands. She carefully picked a single link and pulled it. Earth crumbled off her hands, and the silver touched her skin. She tried to readjust, but each time she brushed the silver with her flesh, her skin blistered. The nightbird's song faded as mourning doves began to coo, and songbirds began to twitter.

She yanked and tugged; her blisters popped and regrew. She screamed into the dawn.

A deep neigh sounded.

"Castor," she called with relief.

The black warhorse trotted toward her, the broken tether dragging behind him.

"Castor! Come here, boy!"

Castor neighed and reared up as she reached for him.

"Castor, help! Please come here."

Agata pulled the blanket from his back and, covering her hands, she tugged at the chain as hard as she could. She thought the link started to give.

She gave it a sharp yank. It remained solid.

The horse nudged her out of the way, he bit down on his blanket. At first, she feared the horse would nip her burnt fingers, but he tugged at the chain.

The stake broke free with a snap.

She tried to climb on Castor, but he reared. She hid her fear of the massive hooves as well as she could. Instead, she whistled and in a sing-song voice as if the horse was just a giant child, she said: "Come along, Castor, let us find Jakub."

Fortunately, the warhorse agreed and allowed her to hold his tether.

She hoped to follow the horse prints, but there were too many. Castor knew the way back to the cart. Pollux lay dead on the grass. She knelt down beside the pony. There was no pulse under her muscular frame.

Castor neighed and nudged the horse. He curled his lips over his teeth and grunted.

Agata tried to plan. She assumed Gaius had told her the truth, and he would take Jakub to the mountain fort. He had no reason to lie to her. She hoped she could catch up to them.

She covered the wagon with boughs and said a quick prayer for it to be there when she returned. She collected her jewelry, which she hid in her clothes. She wrapped herself first in her woolen traveling suman and then in the loose cow-skin coat with the hope the garments were thick enough to protect her.

Agata showed Castor a bag of oats. He neighed again and let her close to him. She did not know if she could lift the saddle, so she replaced the blanket on the horse. She tried to mount him again. This time he allowed it.

Agata pressed her thighs against Castor's sides, but Castor did not need her direction and would not have taken it anyway. She leaned forward as the horse galloped down the dirt road and let the horse take her where he was going.

The wind mottled her cheeks and found its way into the coat. She looked to the east as the sun topped the trees. She observed lines of red thread blowing in the wind, caught on trees, in the brush. That had to be a sign from Jakub. The horse's large, flexible nostrils flared. He lifted his head and widened his lips. Then snorted. She wondered if Castor could smell her husband. They were brothers-in-arms after all. They had seen violence together that she could not comprehend.

Her eyes darted along the tree line, searching for another thread. Castor found it first and pawed the ground.

"Calm yourself and think," Agata said. She had no idea how she would beat Gaius. He was stronger; he was ancient. If Gaius died, she wondered what would happen to Phillipa, Sylvia, and Julia. What would happen to Agata and Jakub? They know the agony, she had felt when Nicheloa died. Which meant Gaius and Jakub would have felt it when Agata died. They would not be able to travel. They must have some shelter.

She had beat Gaius once; he still thinks he could outmaneuver her with simple strength. *Maybe Jakub had already beaten him?*

As the sun crested the horizon, Agata found a series of large boulders that had rolled down the mountains. Some of the spaces between would offer shelter from the sun. She observed a north-facing cave on a cliff face, a red thread was caught between the rocks. Castor curled his thick lips over his teeth and pawed the gravel.

Knowing Castor could not climb such a steep, rocky incline, she patted him and left the horse to graze on the side of the road. She gently stepped on the rocks, trying not to make sound and scrambled to the rock shelter.

She peeked into the darkness.

Gaius slept heavily. Nix slept deeper in the cave. In Gaius's gloved hand was another chain and at the end of the chain, Jakub slept.

His pallor looked terrible for a vampire. His bare arm was covered in scratches and bruises. Agata had seen this before. Gaius was keeping him weak as he had done to his youngest concubine, Julia.

Agata wanted to hurt Gaius further, but she did not know

what would kill him except the sun or fire. She could not chance waking him. Escape was all that mattered.

Silent as most deaths, she crawled toward Jakub and pressed a hand to his shoulder.

His blue eyes fluttered open.

"Take my blood to heal you," she whispered.

Jakub shook his head and pointed at the opening. Holding the chain close to him and slowly wrapping it around his clothed arm, Jakub moved toward Gaius.

*

Jakub was proud to have such a brave and intelligent wife as Agata but felt self-loathing deep in his chest. *What kind of man, what kind of warrior, am I?* What would his brother, Count Mahai or the other soldiers think of a man who needed his wife to save him?

Holding his breath, Jakub cautiously stepped toward the ancient. Every time a rock shifted under his foot, he feared Gaius would open his eyes. The ancient vampire did not snore, but he did slumber. He slowly unwound the chain from Gaius's glove with each step, taking care that the chain did not clank. Nix's eyes opened and neighed.

Jakub did not move.

Gaius's fluttered open but closed again. The ancient vampire was either spent or overconfident. Good. Jakub craved killing the vampire who could debilitate them with only a word, he had been dreaming of ways since he had been incapacitated, but first steps first.

He took a step closer. Then another. Waiting to see if those

eyes would open, Jakub stretched out his hand and grabbed the keys off Gaius's belt.

Holding his breath, he joined Agata in the shade of a boulder. He glimpsed at their method of escape while shielding his eyes from the sun. "You brought the horses?"

"Pollux is dead, we just have Castor," she whispered.

Careful the silver did not touch his bare skin or Agata's, Jakub undid the chain and collar on his wife. While she rubbed her raw flesh, he unlocked his own.

As soon as he was freed, she murmured, "Come, we must escape."

Gripping her wrist, Jakub hissed in Agata's ear. "We can't just leave him here. He will come after us again. His demon horse moves faster than a cart."

"But we can't kill him. That's why Phillipa, Sylvia, and Julia threw him out. He has strength we don't even know, but I have an idea. We could run the chains across the entrance." Agata whispered.

Jakub did not know they could not kill him. It might only be that the women had not the strength to kill him. "Fear not. Leave me a gap, but finish your task and stay at the opening of the cave," he ordered.

Agata did not argue.

He returned to the ancient vampire. He unsheathed Gaius's pugio off his belt and plunged the dagger into his chest. Pugios were the weapon rumored to have killed Julius Ceaser and other Roman nobles; it felt right to thrust the leaf-shaped blade deep through Gaius's ribs to the bronze guard.

As the blade went through the ancient heart, Gaius's eyes

opened. He shrieked in agony.

Jakub gasped, choked, and coughed.

Nix screamed and bucked.

Agata rounded her body in a quivering, gasping ball among the rocks at the mouth of the cave.

Jakub's flesh moved through a field of razors wounding his skin. He squinted his burning eyes, and for a moment, he thought he was blind. No, not blind. Bloody sweat poured down his face.

The undead stallion kicked the walls of the cave, still screaming.

Fearing the worst, Jakub checked his chest. He was unwounded. *I can master the pain.* He pulled the blade from the vampire's wound and let it bleed out.

Jakub pressed his lips to the injury. The blood was ancient, he would have taken his fill and more, but he was in too much pain.

In his moment of triumph, he wanted to filch Gaius's spatha as his trophy, but it was hidden among the Legatus's gear. He needed to care for Agata, and they needed to escape.

"I know it hurts, but we are uninjured." Jakub lifted Agata off the ground and pressed her body to his chest. Her brow slick in a glaze of sweat, her blood stained his shirt.

He covered them both with the cow skin. Careful to remain out of the rising sun, Jakub carried Agata down the steppe. She leaned into his chest to help him keep the weight toward his center. Castor neighed and patted his feet to the ground as they approached.

"Where's my saddle?" he snapped.

Agata cringed and still trembling, whispered, "I couldn't lift the saddle, and I wasn't sure about all the straps, so I left it near the wagon."

He set Agata in the shade of a boulder. "Stay under the skin, my love."

Cursing under his breath about Agata's lack of riding experience and wary of every beam of immolating sunlight, Jakub's knuckles whitened as he adjusted the blanket on Castor.

The sun grew higher.

Jakub pushed Agata on the horse. He climbed up behind her and covered them both in the skin.

Agata whispered, "Don't be angry. I didn't want to hurt Castor."

Jakub patted her leg. "I'm not angry, just worried. If everything you think is true about vampires, Gaius lives, though that blow should've killed him if he were still a man."

"Yes, husband, I still sense him and his pain. And Nix didn't try to follow us or attack. I would think his horse will not leave his side as long as he exists." She explained how she was sure Castor came to get her to save Jakub once he realized he could not climb the steep hill.

"Which means Gaius may still take his vengeance. We must travel faster. We need to gather what we can and move."

"Yes, my love."

Suddenly she sobbed.

"Why are you weeping?" He wished his voice was more gentle, but he was still trying to master the pain.

She choked out: "I'm sorry for my weakness."

"My wife, you came after Gaius, I could ask for no more,"

Jakub said. "Cry if you must. Every squire cries after their first battle or when they realize all the stories about great battles are lies. God put us together, only God may separate us," he said with ferocity. "Not a vampire."

He might not have made a killing blow, but he felt virile, comforting his beloved and holding her to his chest.

Jakub was happy to see their wagon had not been vandalized even though they now had no way to move it. (Any good horsemen will tell you a warhorse does not pull a cart.)

After hobbling Castor in a nearby meadow to graze, the vampires ripped into sweet Pollux's decaying horseflesh. They sucked on the coagulated blood and ate her heart, lungs, and kidneys until they were satiated.

Jakub gently dabbed a salve upon Agata's palms and wrapped them to allow the silver burns to heal.

Strong with blood, Jakub tried to pull the wagon. It moved. Agata came up beside him to assist.

"My sweet lady, get on the wagon and call out directions and any obstacles in my way. Fear not, we still have time to cross the mountains and footlands before the winter snows. But I need more blood to keep our pace."

Over the dirt road, Jakub pulled the cart. He did not genuinely fear to tax his muscles. They would find another cart horse, ox, or sell some of their belongings in the next town. Perhaps they would find a lone traveler to feast upon.

Jakub was simply glad for the action. He did not understand why he felt so desolate. He remembered when Gaius allowed him to move, he unraveled the embroidery from his shirt so Agata might follow.

And she had followed.

My plan worked, why am I morose? Because I didn't meet a man in battle, I crept up on him unaware.

Does that matter?

It mattered to Jakub, even if it was more important he and his beloved were free.

Every step to the east was a step away from Gaius. The aching desolation in Jakub's heart grew more intense. Gaius was the only individual who could teach him how to be a vampire soldier.

Certainly, Agata could not. As a human, she was six years younger than he; as a vampire, she was only months older. As educated as she was in the maintenance of a manor, a herd and even womanly arts of healing, she was still a noblewoman with no knowledge of war.

*

1510

Chapter 4

They had made it. Deep in the night, they crossed into the border of the Ottoman Empire with Jakub pulling the wagon. They crossed without seeing Gaius and before the first frost. Yet Agata could not stop thinking he might be behind any tree, any building. If he hated her enough to come after her once, he might come again.

She reminded herself that Gaius had only found them after she had transformed Jakub. She reminded herself she had lived alone in their manor for months, learning what she could about her condition. She had created two copies of a journal — one for herself and one for Irina — of everything she had learned about the strengths and weaknesses of vampires. Gaius did not know which village her children lived, but if a vampire ever came for her children, Irina would be ready. And Irina would teach the other children who would pass the knowledge to their children. *I shall use my time on the ships to learn more and send the information to them.*

The border guard stopped the cart. He asked why Jakub was pulling the cart.

As planned, her husband answered in Arabic: "Horse limping a bit, that's also why we travel at night."

She heard and understood the word: *Masihiun.*
(Christian.) And later the word: "Chilia." Which was the port
where they were heading.

One of guards opened the flap to the cart. He did not seem
surprised she was inside. He ran his hands over the tapestries,
counting them, but did not speak to her. He spoke more Arabic
to Jakub.

Jakub told Agata: "Twenty *akche.*"

With a gloved hand, Agata counted out the 20 silver coins
for the duty. She handed it to her husband who handed it to the
guard. The other guard scribbled out a receipt and tied a tag to
the side of the cart.

They moved on. They traveled into the night and
throughout most of the next day. Jakub only stopping at midday
to rest for a few hours.

The sun had set, leaving the sky slashed with gold when
Jakub pulled the cart into Chilia. Ahead on smooth dirt streets,
the candle lighters ignited oil lamps.

Agata had never seen so many people in one place. The
mass of humanity beat with one giant pulse which rang in
her ears and made her mouth salivate. They moved past the
dockyards, warehouses, and customs houses. With every turn,
more humans, cows, goats, and sheep. Dogs and cats skulked
around the outside of buildings. Carts and stalls sold all types of
cuisines. The spices of the Turks, Greeks, Arabians, Italians, and
other cultures fill the air. She had thought that the town she had
married into was large, but it was a village compared to Chilia.

As they walked, Agata tightened her grip on Jakub's arm.
Jakub adjusted her, so she did not interfere with him, leading

Castor.

"What is wrong?" he asked her, his voice gentle.

"I've never seen so many people," she said. "Are all large cities like this?"

"Yes, Wife. I see nothing to fear here. Except us."

He had already told her in accordance with the law, Christians were not allowed to ride on horseback. He had also explained that in the Ottoman Empire, Christian women, especially with northern coloring, were valuable as slaves as were the black girls from Ethiopia and Nigeria. She did not have northern coloring, but her vampiric skin was fair.

"So many different peoples," she said. "Their clothing tells their country."

Around her, most women wore a loose, dark, modestly cut robe that buttoned all the way to the throat over their brightly colored salvar and robes. Their hair and face were covered with a pair of veils. Younger women, perhaps unmarried or the enslaved, wore shorter yelek over their layers of robes. The Ottoman men wore salvar and inner robes covered by longer yelek with decorative seams. On their heads, they wore conical woolen horasani and decorative turbans. However, the clothing was as varied as the multitude of cultures that spanned the streets. Some women wore embroidered le and fotã under thin shawls like Agata. Their hair covered by maramã if they were married or left free if not. Men freely donned the iţari, cămaşa, and pieptar with fur căciulă on their heads similar to the style Jakub wore.

She saw short dalmatica-style tunics on both men and women. The impoverished wore browns and yellows, while wealthier individuals wore brightly dyed long garments. A group of simply-dressed, thick-robed Christian monks and nuns crossed their path.

"Look, a Frank," Jakub said.

She saw the man Jakub mentioned. He wore hose under linen breeches. His linen shirt poked out from a bright, short tunic edged in fur. Beside him, a woman wore a long tunic under a long coat, closed in the front with multiple brooches and a belt. Her hair was braided and covered in a linen headdress of the same fabric as the man's tunic.

"What a strange way of dress," she said, referring to the man's hose and codpiece, which exposed the man's lower half so much, he might have been wearing nothing below his tunic.

They crossed an open market, which was now emptying under the fading twilight.

Jakub found the business he sought. "Stay with Castor," he said, though he had not needed to remind her.

Agata's gems were already on her person. Her clothing, the manuscript which she wrote upon, and her quills and inks and medical kit were in Castor's saddlebags. Jakub's clothing was packed in a heavy woven sack. Castor's riding saddle was on him but hidden by another blanket.

Jakub went inside. A man donned in salvar and an embroidered kaftcan, which showed the skill of the Ottoman weavers, came out and looked over the cart. He touched one of her tapestries and counted them. After a bit of bickering back and forth, Jakub went inside with the man again. Jakub returned with a bag of gold. They picked up their personal belongings and led Castor away.

"All these people makes me yearn for blood," Agata whispered. Her lips felt cracked and dry.

"As do I," Jakub said. "But soon, my love."

✳

Bright flags flew in the breeze, and Jakub could smell both the Danube and the Black Sea in the movement of the air. Though twilight had faded into the deep of night, many people were still on the streets. He wanted to escape the Ottoman Empire. Following the Muslim dhimmi system, under which Christians were a protected people with limited freedoms of worship. He kept his weapons packed safely away so no one might see he was armed. Castor was disguised as well as a charger could be as a pack animal. By the look in his eyes, Castor was not pleased.

France also had several sumptuary laws, but as a Catholic and a nobleman, he had better prospects there.

They had escaped Moldavia, and once they hired a ship, the Ottoman Empire. They would sail to Greece, around the Italian Peninsula and on to France. France — a land of music and art — had been at war with the English and had seen many losses. However, Jakub longed to serve a land with a great king worthy of his skills.

They sold the wagon for less than what they paid for it. No doubt they did not even get close to what it was worth to the buyer. However, that had been expected in the limited time at twilight in which they had to do business.

He wondered how Agata would feel trying to navigate the city during the day. In the thick kaftkans and veils, they might not be seen and protected from the sun. But dressed as Ottomans, someone might think they were spies.

Unlike the scent of animals, the aroma of humans stoked Jakub's hunger. Black, brown, ruddy, tan, white bodies hidden in rich embroidery or humble rags. Humans moved about as if they were fish in the sea, swimming about the froth. Not knowing or not wanting to know that two hungry sharks had come into their midst. He and Agata were still young vampires, but one night he would be ancient as Gaius was ancient. As old as the great serpents of the deep.

She pointed at a painted tower with the base form in a star. "Is that the church Stephen the Great and Holy built?"

"Yes, my wife, it is."

Stephen the Great and Holy was a merciless and great commander. He had won many wars; however, he had also lost Chilia. At the end of his life, Chilia remained in the hands of the Ottomans. His son, Bogdan, had other wars to fight.

The stable boy led Castor to a clean stall. Jakub inspected the half-bushel the stable provided for the charger. The mixed hay looked to be of good quality.

Jakub noticed how Agata's eyes counted the money he paid for Castor's care, but she did not speak. Stabling and maintaining Castor would be an expense, but a needed one, if Jakub were to gain a title. What were a few gifted tapestries when they had immortality to gain more? She still had her bridal jewels.

"Let us find a quiet inn to do our work," he said.

They moved past several noisy pubs until they found a respectable looking inn. Inside there were plenty of foreign merchants. They would blend in just fine until they could find a ship that would take them to safety.

Chapter 5

After securing Agata a private room, Jakub moved through the city until he came to a counting-house. He spoke to a group of merchants about selling more of her treasures to raise the money for passage. Assuming a powerful man like Gaius, or perhaps even his women, might have spies, he told them that he wanted passage to Constanța. Once deals were made, Jakub sought another type of wealth.

The man had a touch of Hercules in his stance. His thick black waves hung to the middle of his back. His eyes radiated energy and a joyous nature that only the young — or men who have never seen a battlefield — still know. Jakub typically did not want men, but he wanted his robust and regular heartbeat. And Agata would want him. She would welcome him into her room. Jealousy washed over Jakub.

Was this what it was to face eternity with a wife?

He watched the man. Was he or Agata the better bait?

The man whispered something to a serving woman. The woman scurried away with a smile that told Jakub she was being polite but hoped the man would forget the advance.

Jakub approached. "Do you seek company tonight? My wife and I have traveled long and are lonely for companionship."

He rose his eyes to the ceiling and gestured to upstairs.

"Your wife?"

"Is a passionate woman and needs more than any one man can give her."

"You spoil her. The good book says a man ought to beat his wife, so she knows who is the lord and master."

Jakub knew that was not true. Unlike this rich, ignorant wantwit, Jakub had actually read the Bible. Still, the man's words held a truth Jakub did not like. By law and tradition, a man had the power to break his wife's spirit. Her happiness was linked to his actions. Agata was made in the image of God as he was. He must treat her thusly.

However, since Jakub planned on killing the man anyway, he said, "She knows I am her lord. But you are not; if she cries out in anything other than pleasure, I'll be doing the same to you."

"I like to ... " The man made a lewd gesture.

Jakub had many experiences when he was at war, but he doubted Agata would have any idea what the gesture meant. He did not want her to know.

He would kill the ox quickly, before the man suggested such a thing to her.

The candlelight flickered as Jakub brought the man into the private room. Agata rose to pour the wine. Her black hair spilled freely down her back, her luminous skin had a haunting quality, but the man did not sense the danger. He looked enthralled with her.

His long dark hair spilled toward her as he bowed gallantly.

Holding a cup before their guest, Agata smiled. He stepped closer.

Agata handed him the cup and kissed the side of his neck.

His manhood rose, he did not seem to notice that her fangs had expanded. In a quick movement, she clamped down on his neck.

"What in hell?" their victim shouted.

She tore the flesh as he pushed her away. He clutched the side of his neck.

Through the haze of both yearning and repugnance,

Jakub stared at the blood spilling from the man's throat. His stomach growled loudly.

Faster and stronger than a human woman, Agata pushed the man against the wall. The sweet-salty smell filled the room, overtaking the stench of the fish and food and pipeweed and the other scents of the city.

The man fell to the floor; Jakub was upon him. He listened to the heartbeat growing fainter. In his mind, Jakub could only see the torrent of blood that this man's veins held.

"You chose well, my love," Agata said, her smiling lips coated with wet, gleaming crimson.

She bent over the man again to have her fill of the man's blood before it cooled.

Jakub stared at his wife's sparkling bloodlust-filled eyes. Her affection burned underneath her desire for blood, but Jakub wished he only saw her affection.

He missed the way she used to look at him, before they were vampires. The old Agata he could anticipate. He respected the old Agata, the other Agata as a mother, as a wife, as an estate manager and even as a midwife. He was not sure if he could respect this Agata. Yet, they were married and a man of chivalry would never abandon his wife.

Moreover, their victim's blood made Jakub feel alive. Human blood was better than sheep or horse blood; only Gaius had tasted sweeter.

Jakub licked the wound on his victim's wrist, not willing to waste a drop. He swallowed the man's vital fluid like wine until he felt free of the damnable craving.

This man who was alive was now dead. Jakub had killed

him not knowing his name, not knowing anything about him. He no longer required to eat. He desired to eat. As the man could not be hurt anymore and it wouldn't do to waste the body, Jakub sucked the marrow from his right femur and Agata his left.

With his knife, he cut out the man's heart and plunged his teeth into the bloody muscle. He cut Agata the sweetbreads. They shared the lungs. Chewing on the tough muscle, Jakub delighted in the pleasure of tearing flesh with his fangs.

They ate until they felt fat and sleepy

"We must not be caught with the room in this state," Agata said.

"It is too dangerous to sleep when there's so much work to be done," Jakub agreed.

Under Agata's direction, Jakub assisted in the carving of the flesh. As he aided her in the horrid work, he wondered if he and Agata were still made in the image of God.

The meat was packed in an oilcloth as if they were any other sailor's rations and tucked into a heavy wooden trunk between layers of salt and kelp to help it keep for the journey. Agata wiped the floor with a rag mop made from the chemise she had been wearing and cleaned the room in the nude.

In the dead of night, Jakub took the man's bones and the rag mop to the harbor. The rag mop was thrown on a trash heap.

"Perhaps, we are devils now," Jakub muttered to himself as he watched waves break on the shore. With a great splash, he dove into the water. His compassion for humans slipped to the bottom of the quay with the bones. He swam until his vampire eyes could no longer see traces of blood on his shirt.

Chapter 6

Jakub observed the one-masted trade-cog. The overlapping clinker planking, which he could see above the waterline, looked solidly built enough, but the keelplank, was only slightly thicker than the adjacent gardboards. It looked like it might snap in the first storm.

It was an older design, and the open hulled ship hardly seemed the place for Agata, who allowed a sailor to carry her aboard and set her under the canvas tent with their trunks for protection from the sun.

Jakub followed with Castor — who had some sailing experience — though he did not like it.

Inside, tarred moss clung to the carved grooves and wooden lathes, but tiny beams of light made their way through the hull. It did not give him anymore confidence about the ship.

Jakub brought over Castor's oats, brushed him, and spoke to him in sweet words.

At that moment, he remembered his old master, a great warrior who had taught Jakub with the same gentleness that he taught his hunting hounds and horses. He used to speak to the hunting hounds and his horses as he would any man. He always had time for Jakub's questions and encouraged learning.

He doubted if Gaius had such patience, but he did have answers. Jakub felt lost as the sea lapped against the side of the boat.

"What are you thinking, my love?" Agata asked.

"Gaius."

"I don't believe he is dead; I sense him now and again."

"Then we are well to be away from these shores." Jakub wished he felt the relief he indicated to Agata.

The men rowed the cog out of the harbor and then lifted the square-shaped sail.

The sailors' movements created sweat, which pervaded their clothing and the deck of the ship. He thought about taking one, just one, and drinking him dry. He and Agata would dine on his flesh. He must not fall prey to this lust. If he did, he would doom the ship and themselves. They had a trunk of salted flesh. One man died, so the crew could live. One man died, so two vampires could make it to France. Was this what being a vampire was?

To the blazes! I have killed hundreds of men, women, and boys on the battlefield, what is the life of one man? One adulterer? Jakub thought.

As the sun rose, he put on a large floppy hat and slid back deeper beside the crates. Agata had fallen asleep. In the shadows, she snored softly, her hand against the crock filled with earth from her garden.

She had a small smile on her lips. He wondered if she was dreaming of their children. She was and had been a wonderful mother.

There was more Agata had lost. She was used to being a

mistress of their home, keeping her herb garden, and herd of cattle. Agata missed his brother's wife, who had been her bosom companion and the other women of their village who she had been friendly due to her work as a midwife and healer. In their town, she was a beloved lady, an important lady. Now Agata was simply Jakub's wife, alone and wandering. Her losses pained him beyond measure.

"My wife is quite ill," he told a sailor.

"Vomit and feel better." The man gestured his hand.

"Already a bucketful, friend. She's sleeping now."

The sailor nodded and gestured for Jakub to stay. He hurried up to the captain, spoke a few words, and then returned.

"When your wife wakes, she chew on this," he said and passed him a small piece of licorice root.

*

Even the night air was warm in Constanţa, but Jakub felt insecure. The salt on his lips taunted his thirst and reminded him of blood. He wanted to move on quickly and get to Greece. Then to the Italian peninsula and on to France. "I feel someone watching," he whispered.

"But Gaius is back in Moldavia," Agata said.

"We ought not to believe he doesn't have his spies," Jakub said. "Or who knows another vampire might be watching. The Ottoman Empire has many great wizards in service to their sultans."

Agata nodded but said nothing. Jakub felt more despondent with each step on the roads of Constanţa in which he led Castor. This was the port where the poet Ovid spent the last eight years of his life. Ovid wrote the *Trista* and *Epistulae ex Ponto* in which he lamented in the knowledge he would never return home. Jakub was no poet, but he understood the sorrow of knowing he would never see his beloved Moldavia again.

The journey was so expensive. They would need to kill again in order to make it. Agata was forced to sell the ruby necklace that he had given her on the night of their wedding. Still, she did not speak a word of complaint.

With trunks filled with meat, they embarked on a single-masted, square-sail hulk. There were two castles, one at the bow, one at the stern. A smaller ship than the cog, it had better maneuverability.

The sailors made Agata a comfortable spot under the sterncastle.

Castor neighed uncomfortably, but as he had in journeys past, he did not succumb to seasickness. Agata was not so lucky.

Jakub grew used to walking on the moving ship. And he found comfort in the sounds of the water slapping the side of the hull.

Every morning, an hour before dawn, while the sailors were focused upon their own duties, Jakub did his exercises until the sun rose. In dark linen garments, so the sailors could not see he sweated blood, he practiced uppercuts, lower cuts, and back cuts. He lifted his saddle in the air and placed it down again. He was not sure if death would claim his muscles, but if it tried, he would refuse it.

Then, in the shade of the sterncastle, he massaged Castor's legs and brushed him as the sun rose. To pass the time, Agata asked questions in French while Jakub answered questions in the same. They practiced French courtly mannerisms and discussed French fashion.

Sometimes, Agata sang donias to Castor. The stallion seemed to be getting used to her ministrations though he preferred Jakub. He liked to rest his massive head on Jakub's shoulder while he listened to her songs.

Once the seasickness had passed, Agata returned to her studies. She recorded observable changes or the lack of change. She recorded their hunger and strange cravings.

Each night, she prayed to God for their children's safety and future. She wistfully spoke about the grandchild she would never see and wrote letters to Irina.

In Jakub's dour moments, he thought about how their universe was just the ship and the sailors moving around them. Only when he slept, he indulged in his monstrous cravings and undying thirst. Otherwise, he fantasied but dared not touch the sailors.

To give in would mean his, Agata, and Castor's death.

*

Chapter 7

The first crossing had been reasonably smooth, but deep in the Black Sea, the boat swayed to and fro. Agata did not want to complain about the rocking sea, but she was glad for the licorice root, which kept the vomiting at bay. Jakub had fallen asleep, leaning against Castor, who also slept nestled in the hay. But they both had been at sea before.

She peered out above the hull and saw black waves crested with white and gray mists. She could no longer see the land. Jakub told her such wondrous stories of the land of the Franks. She hoped the Kingdom of France would be all he believed it would be. But she had no hope for herself.

The boat pitched another way. She cried out and held tight to the railing. A sailor gestured at her and tried to speak, but it was in Arabic.

She bowed her head and showed him the licorice root.

He gestured to a bucket and moved his feet like he was slipping.

She guessed he meant the deck was slippery.

She nodded and pantomimed sleep.

He nodded back to her.

She returned to the sterncastle with an aching heart. She

tried to ignore the lump in her throat. The raindrops which fell on the deck mixed with her tears. She could never go home. The last time she embraced her daughters, the scent of their flesh made her want to bite their throats.

"We made the right choice for the children," Agata whispered to herself. *The children are safe from me. And Gaius. Phillipa is keeping the old truce between the vampires and human villages,* she thought to her crock of earth for comfort.

When she touched her earth, the voices of her children came to her. Their songs, their donias, their games. She regretted every time she scolded or switched them. She rejoiced in the memories of playing peek-a-boo, teaching them to read and write, or when she kissed their troubled brows.

She thought of Irina's wedding, how she now wore her hair in a married woman's coil, and had a child on the way. Artur, a vassal of Count Mihai, followed in the footsteps of his courageous father. Petru apprenticed under Irina's husband. Daniella buried in the family plot. And little Daciana lived with Irina.

She thought of Jakub's family, especially Gavrilla. She missed her with an intensity she had not imagined. *Away foul spirit. They are not lost to heaven, they live on. Safe. Perhaps once we are settled in France, I might even correspond with them.*

The ship seemed to pitch more furiously as she lay awake thinking about the children, her sister-in-law, and all the babies (human, cow, dog, and the occasional sheep) that she had helped bring into the world. She did not regret killing her rapist, Nicheloa, or the priest, Bogdan, who murdered her. She realized she did not even mind killing the young man in Chilia, so Jakub and she might make this journey.

Jakub had tried to keep the man's brutality from her, but she had sensed the man had been an ox. She had not exactly known what he wanted, but she knew if he had found a girl without protection, he would have shamed her and abandoned her to the fates.

It was right to kill such men.

Holding her cloak tight, she peeked out again. Storm clouds covered the sky, blocking the light.

The crew scrambled to action in a frantic pace as rain poured furiously down upon them. In every direction were swells of hideous gray and white.

Agata heard another cry in Arabic. A sailor ran over with thick bindings and babbled to Jakub, who threw on his coat.

Jakub tried to smile as the sailor tied them to the mast.

She felt flayed by each droplet of water, but as her skin grew numb and cold, the spray lost it sting. Her maramă was ripped away in the wind. She clutched at her cloak tighter.

Jakub's eyes looked at her with a coldness as if Agata was a stranger. The thought warped her mind as she stared at her hideous and hungry, undead beloved.

"Do you think we will succeed? Will we make it to France?" Agata asked.

"Why ask such questions? God put us together and only God could tear us apart. Do you fear, perhaps, God controls this storm? There's nothing I can do. I know about horses, not ships."

Yet the cold nothingness lifted from his eyes. "I hate being powerless against the sea. Sailors are no more powerful, but ride with Neptune's blessings."

A wave poured over them. Another wave pummeled them from the other direction.

"I would pray to Neptune if I thought it would do any good, but I doubt Neptune's mercy as much as I doubt Jehovah's." He shouted over the sound of the waves.

"Perhaps Salacia!" Agata said in jest. (Neptune's wife, Salacia, is the personification of the calm and sunlit sea.)

Jakub invoked her name, but it did not calm the sea.

Agata choked on seawater. Were they sinking? She could not see. Jakub appeared as the boat pitched again. A crack of lightning brightened the sky. Agata clasped Jakub's closer arm and wept. She vomited on the deck, but another surge splashed the bloody vomit away. "I love you," she said.

"What?" he shouted.

"I love you," Agata raised her voice over the sound of the waves.

With his free hand, he stroked her wet white cheek until it was over. The wind died. And the sea calmed as if the storm had never been.

Once the sailor undid the binding, Agata collapsed into Jakub's arms. He carried her back to their space under the sterncastle. Castor was soaked and annoyed but survived. So had most of their trunks.

A fish flopped on the deck. A sailor cut it open and gave the flesh to Agata and gestured for her to eat.

Jakub said, "He said, 'For the little mother's strength.'"

Agata accepted it with a bow of her head. Jakub thanked

the sailor in Arabic.

When they were alone, Agata and Jakub sucked the flesh from the spiny bones.

*

Dearest Irina,

Your father and I hope this missive finds you well. I pray nightly for the health of you, your husband, your brothers, sister and your newborn infant. Did you have a boy or a girl? What name have you christened him?

Though there have been some dangers crossing the mountains, and we rode many ships, we see the coast of France.

Your noble father is greatly pleased as am I. Castor cannot speak of course, but I am sure the horse longs for solid earth under his hooves as we both do.

Enclosed are two more recipes, one which your father and I tried in Moldavia and one which I gathered in the Italian Peninsula.

With all my love,
Mother

On the next page, written carefully in code and disguised as ways to salt fish were descriptions of how to trap a vampire with silver chains.

*

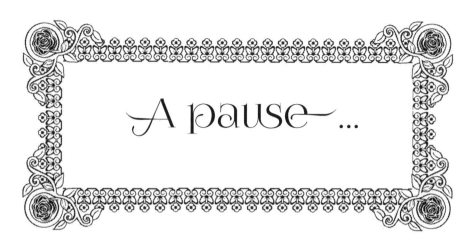

A pause ...

In the Kingdom of France in a tiny forgotten village, a boy of seven called for his family's missing goat. His voice carried in the darkness. He could hear his elder sister in the distance, also calling. The pen had not been left open, but the goat was gone. It was not his fault—or hers. Still, they feared returning home without the animal.

In his worries, he did not notice the tentacle writhing along the ground, feeling the tremors of earth. It had found other tasty prey in the area and searched for more. The boy hardly had a chance to scream when it slithered up his leg and grabbed him around the chest. He was fortunate, the thing which squeezed him crushed his bones. He was dead before he was dragged under the earth.

His sister was not so lucky. It grasped her ankle and squeezed. While her bones were crushed, she hit the ground alive. She pressed her eyes shut trying to stop the ripping of her flesh. Earth pressed in on her, smothering. Her mouth and nostrils filled with gravel and dirt, she sputtered. Her lungs ached to breath, but filled with viscous, slimy mud.

✳

Chapter 8

With five legs of the journey completed, the ship sailed from the Mediterranean in between two large stone towers to a bay and the royal port of Toulon. Jakub's heart soared. Brushing his horse, he spoke happily to Castor: "I must fulfill military service, but the French nobility has explicit lawful and financial privileges. We'll have the right to hunt, and my beloved wife will dine on venison each night.

"More importantly, I can wear a sword and ride you instead of leading you."

Castor neighed and nodded as if in agreement. A warhorse should not have to disguise his natural poise. Plus, the horse was no doubt glad to be getting off the ship.

Jakub was pleased that his first glimpse of the Kingdom of France looked precisely as it had in his dreams.

He held his breath and checked his wide-brimmed hat as the sun peeked out from behind the clouds. Even with his limited view, he saw the white towered manor surrounded by gardens. Behind the towers, mountains rose even higher. Below, a fishing village surrounded by a stone wall with a large chapel reaching to the sky. Gulls cried their haunting songs as they ascended on the funnels of sea-wind and dove into the water.

Under her veils, Agata got on her toes and clasped Jakub's hand.

"You did it. We are in France!" she whispered excitedly. She embraced him around the neck and kissed him. "Look, isn't the chapel beautiful?"

Jakub's attention was on the expansive manor house, but Agata would want to give thanks to God and pray for the children.

Jakub tried to plan as the ship approached the harbor, but he was not sure how to proceed. He did not want Agata to worry. He had letters of introduction and recommendation written by his brother and Voivode Bogdan III. However, he must connect with the French nobility in order to ensure his success at court.

He quickly wrote two letters: one to the count and on to the mayor of Toulon petitioning for their assistance.

He found the captain and asked if the cabin boy might run an errand for him.

"What errand?"

"Bring this letter to the Count of Provence. I will pay you both a franc for your trouble." As soon as the ship brushed the side of the dock, the boy dashed off.

With Agata wearing layers of veils and Jakub in a wide-brimmed hat, they traversed a labyrinth of docks and buildings. Other than fashions and color of the heraldry, the French port of Toulon was not much different than the Moorish ports. Longshoremen buzzed around the docks unloading and loading ships. Passengers hurriedly embarked or disembarked ships. Sailors swaggered drunkenly. Families embraced. Beyond, brothels and cardrooms lined the docks.

After the stop at the customs house, where they paid a sizable duty, Jakub observed the old Roman aqueducts were in ruins. He suggested Agata ride Castor and met Castor's eyes. The man and his warhorse had a moment of understanding as they had when Jakub had ridden into battle. Agata was safer if she was astride the horse.

Garbage and human feces lined the streets. Dogs and cats roamed, hunting for scraps.

They passed a series of warehouses and an open market which was still bustling in the twilight. Someone coughed nearby. Jakub scanned the crowd for weakened prey. They would need blood if they were to meet the count. Two men pushed a cart piled high with bags of flour past them. A group of women carried bundles on their heads and children on their backs. Men with sacks slung over the shoulders. Older children played in the shadow of the tower. Wealthy individuals rode on horses or in carriages in their delicate embroidered fabrics, but what surprised Jakub was the small black patches of silk or velvet in contrast to their full face of ivory cosmetics. One or two were pretty enough, but some faces were sprinkled with them.

They drew near to the church. He helped Agata off Castor's saddle. They went inside the stone building where an elaborately carved and painted wooden retable surrounded the alter.

Agata bowed her head as she crossed herself.

Jakub crossed himself out of habit and to please his wife.

When he did not speak, Agata began: "Father, Son, and Holy Spirit, Holy Trinity of love, we praise you for keeping us safe during our journey and bless you for calling us to be your holy people. Remain in our hearts. Guide us in our love and service. We praise you now and forever. Amen!"

"Amen," Jakub repeated.

Jakub escorted Agata to the candles where she lit a flame for the children.

He gestured at a priest. "My lady seeks communion."

"Just your wife?"

He was not sure if he ever believed in God. Not how deeply Agata believed anyway, but he said, "Both of us."

The priest listened to Agata's confession first. They spoke a few minutes in private, and she left the confessional with a downcast look upon her face.

Jakub went into the confessional. He spoke of being short-tempered with his wife for her ignorance. The priest's heart skipped a beat which inflamed Jakub's bloodlust.

Jakub spoke of missing his men and not knowing where God led them.

The priest's eyes never left Jakub's face as he spoke of sin and repentance. His lips glistened as he told Jakub his penalty.

Jakub nodded but stopped listening as he would not wear sackcloth beneath his clothes or fast in prayer. In their former town, the town gate was carved with the words: "God is love."

Jakub was not sure if God was love in France, he hoped it was only this particular God's representative who was simply a wantwit. The last priest who thought to come between Agata and the ones she loved wound up dead.

He salivated at the thought of killing the man. His fangs pressed against his gums. Fearing the other people in and near the cathedral, he took his wife's arm and hurried out of the church without violence to the idiot.

"Whatever he said to you, I want you to forget. He was a bumbler who mangled the truth with his own ideas," Jakub said gruffly and kissed her hand.

"I am ready to meet the administrator of the county," Agata whispered from behind her veils.

"Before we eat?" Jakub asked.

"After, but I believe it's best if we go as soon as possible. We don't want to accidentally insult them," Agata said. "I fear this place. The patches on the faces and other customs seem so strange."

They found a butcher, bought two thick steaks from a cow's loin. Hidden in an alley, they consumed the meat raw.

✳

Chapter 9

Agata was careful not to step into the sunbeam as she removed her veils. Jakub appeared to be walking with less care, but she did not speak a word against him. He had a plan, and they must see it through.

Lit candles flickered about the parlor and were reflected in polished mirrors. Agata hoped no one would notice that only their clothing was reflected in the brass, not their bodies. The curtains were open. The smell of the sea, humanity, and animals drifted inside, but her nose was tickled by the sweet orange perfume, tallow, and burning paper.

"Welcome to Provence, my foreign friends," Estienne Hamon the Count of Provence said in a deep bass voice which seemed younger the rest of the man.

Jakub bowed and replied a few general kindnesses toward the countess — a woman who looked to be a decade senior to Agata, but a decade younger than her husband. Her hair was covered with a wimple and veil. As was common in French fashion, her conical gown artificially widened her hips while exposing more of the breast than what is modest in Moldavia. *Soon, I must learn to dress in such a way.*

Agata curtsied.

The Count of Provence might have once been dashing. A Roman nose and high forehead sat above loose jowls. His round brown eyes were lined with heavy lines, but Roman features did not surprise Agata. Who knew? This man might even share a bond by the blood of the same ancient ancestor to Jakub or Agata.

Estienne Hamon waddled slightly in his heavy garments, which covered his burly frame. His wide-necked satin blue doublet strained against his stomach as he sat down. Thick strips of alternating colors in red, blue, and gold ran up his arms. His shirt bore a large frill edged in black at the neck and wide ruffles at the wrist. On a heavy golden chain, he wore a gold amulet with a deep blue sapphire to match his doublet.

She had learned from Jakub this part of the Kingdom of France shared much history with their own Moldavia— which before the Roman occupation in 106 AD was the Kingdom of Dacia. She knew during the 2nd century BC, the people of this area appealed to Rome for help against the Ligures who invaded them from north-western Italy. The Roman legions entered the area now called Provence three times.

Beside her, Jakub's muscles tensed as the count kissed her hand.

The countess claimed to be glad to meet the daughter of a foreign count.

"So, how may I help you, honorable son of Peter?" the count said.

"I have come to join my French brothers-in-arms. There are many wars. Your king is magnanimous. Louis XII is a king of the people, they say."

"He is, but as of late, he is more concerned with the lack of a son. His first queen was sterile. His second queen had several miscarriages, stillborn son, and two daughters," the count sighed. "Many a son has died in the wars ... now it seems more are on the horizon. Ah, well, cest la vie."

"What of the daughter?" Agata asked.

"What of her?" The countess asked.

"Will she inherit?"

"In France, daughters do not inherit the throne. Our majesty will ensure his family's inheritance through betrothal," the count said.

"I hope she will be happy in her marriage." Agata crossed herself to bless the girl she had never met.

"What hope is there for that?" the countess whispered drolly to Agata, but loud enough, the men could hear.

Agata spoke to the countess on marriages, of her children and theirs, and other womanly matters. The countess's children were safe with their nurse, but many other children of France were starving. Through the spoken word and unspoken look, she learned many of France's counties were reeling from unending wars and famine.

✳

The count exchanged a knowing look with Jakub that said one thing: *Women*. It was apparent the nobles did not have a happy marriage. Nor did the count care. Jakub chuckled, but he was wary of a man who did not love his wife and children. He was even more suspicious of a man who dressed in luxurious silks and jewels while wearing a slender gold-handled rapier on his belt and a black velvet star over his eye.

The count was not what Jakub expected from the nobility of France. French law required the count to see military service. In *Livre de chevalerie,* de Charny guided knights to be reasonable and measured in their eating, keep their bodies healthy, and avoid luxurious clothing. De Charny would have hated the layers of silk.

Jakub thought of his brother, Count Mihai, who because of their birth order, never ventured from the safety of their town. He was a competent administer, but he had not, nor ever had been, a warrior. Though Count Estienne wore a sword, perhaps he was not a warrior either, but had a younger brother who served in his stead.

The gem Count Estienne wore danced in the firelight and hypnotized Jakub. He dreamed of tearing out the count's fat throat and drinking his blood dry. He would bestow the gem on Agata. He envisaged the gem hanging between Agata's naked breasts and pushed the thought away.

Agata asked, "Do you enjoy the ongoing of the court?"

"Unfortunately, Blois is too far for my husband to travel," the countess said with marked bitterness.

The count cleared his throat. "Madame, this port has only been part of the Kingdom since 1486 when Provence joined the empire. Have you seen much of Provence?"

"We came directly after we gave thanks for our safe journey in the chapel. We wished to be right with God as well as man," Jakub said.

"Indeed," the count said. "Our chapel is lovely, isn't it? The present building was begun in 1096 by Gilbert, Count of

Provence in gratitude for his safe return from the Crusades."

Jakub must have missed something in the count's words or behavior because the count stopped talking. "Perhaps I offended you."

"No. I love history, Count, at times listen quite intently. Forgive me for it," Jakub said. "Perhaps, you might enlighten me of your magnificent community, if it pleases you."

By the glimmer in the count's eye, nothing would please him more. "Oh, how I wish my son was as interested in our history as you, Sir Jakub. Perhaps you, a knight of Moldavia, would be a good example to him.

"Stay tonight, and experience our table."

Jakub learned, even decades later, France's counties tottered from shortages of everything but war. And he learned Count Estienne did not consider Provence part of the Kingdom.

*

Chapter 10

With the Count of Provence's letter of introduction to King Louis XII, they rode toward a series of wooden and thatched huts.

"The poor ought to have some sick and I need to hunt now," Jakub whispered, lightheaded with the lack of fresh blood. He only had minimal amounts of cooked animal flesh with vegetables and stewed fruits for several days. The old pains moved through his joints. His neck ached. "If only we could find a lost servant or better yet a brigand."

"As do I," Agata replied. "My head aches terribly."

"Have you learned why the count and countess wore those small black velvet patches?" Jakub asked, hoping to distract his wife from her pain.

"To cover mars in their complexion so each one can resemble a beautiful porcelain doll."

"You will do this?"

"I shall do what is necessary, my love, but our skin is pale enough without paint."

Out of the corner of his eye, he observed three forms dressed in rags slink out of a window. They moved too quick to be human.

"Vampires," Agata whispered beside him.

He did not know if they would be friends or foes. They did not wear swords, so they must be commoners.

"Hail, I am Jakub Petrescu, Son of Count Petru. This is my wife, Agata, the daughter of Count Artur."

The largest man did not reply with his name, but said, "We are Jacquerie. She is your lady?"

Jakub did not feel the slightest fear though he knew who the Jacquerie were. He tasted Agata's distress in the sound of her pulse.

The two men, who had not spoken, lunged at Agata and caught hold of her skirt and yanked her off Castor. Jakub's heart cried at the ghastly expression of wide-eyed horror on his wife's face as she screamed. Her vulnerability and fear of ravishment overwhelmed him.

Agata tried to swing a fist at her assailants, but she did not have any power in her blows. She collapsed as a punch struck the side of her head.

As Jakub expected, it threw the man who held her weight off balance.

Jakub barreled into him, his second blade drawn.

They tumbled onto the dirt road. The man released Agata as Jakub's knife entered the attacker's chest, crashing against his ribs. Jakub retracted his blade and slashed the man across the throat. Blood bubbled to the surface and splattered against his lips, mesmerizing him. His fangs expanded in want of blood, but as it had on the battlefield, Jakub's mind achieved a strange mental state of calmness. He was aware of each moment of this battle. They were commoners with their hands and cudgels. He had a dagger and a sword. Two opponents came at him. He took a leg. An arm. Another arm.

Agata screamed.

He leaped to his feet. He sized up the next two thugs. So had Castor.

The warhorse got between Agata and the man pursuing her. He kicked him squarely in the chest. The man fell back, but then sprang onto Castor's back.

The final man, the one who spoke, swung his cudgel at Jakub's head. He parried each blow. He struck out when appropriate.

Out of the corner of his eye, Jakub saw Agata haul his shield in the air and dash it against the man who held Castor. The pointed end of his shield entered the attacker's flesh. He fell to the ground.

Castor reared up and pummeled the man on the ground with his iron shoes.

The vampire screamed as Castor's hooves rained down.

Jakub slashed his sword down in front of his foe, forcing him to stop short. And in this hesitation, the next blow decapitated him.

The third vampire had escaped Castor's hooves and tried to jump upon him. Jakub threw him off his back and cracked his skull with his pommel. He wanted him to feel the pain that his sweet wife felt. His sword cut through flesh and bone.

Once the vampires were wailing, incapacitated, he carved the three vampires into pieces. He knew they still lived; still felt the agony from his blade. Somewhere an older vampire felt the loss of his children. He told himself these common vampires were nothing to him and each time his blade dug into their still living flesh, he felt a strange gladness. If only they had been worthy opponents, rather than commoners, he might have felt joy.

"Drink of them and become strong, my beloved," he said.

Agata knelt down and sucked from the bloody remains. The vampires whose heads were more or less intact opened their mouths in agony. He gorged on the most tender organs. He popped an eye into his mouth and crushed it with his teeth. He bit into the kidneys and devoured their sweetness. He felt stronger than he had in days.

He cut out another set of kidneys for Agata. After they had their fill, Jakub spread out the body parts in a glade.

"We might have been allies, but now you will burn in the coming day," Jakub said, his mind suddenly went to Gaius. The ancient vampire was laughing.

Jakub found the vampires' trail and followed it to a low stone grotto. They had to duck to go inside, but the room opened up. Massive boulders lined the gravel floor, which the vampires had used as makeshift tables or bunks. Leather bags and clothing rotted hanging from a line that crossed two natural pillars.

A statue of the Virgin looked down upon them.

Water had carved out the limestone cave. A small creek ran through the bottom. Agata tested it and told Jakub it was fresh. Castor guzzled the clean water. Jakub went out and harvested leaves and grasses.

She built a fire in the fire ring and went through the vampire's belongings. She found a few coins within the rags but little else of value. The cloths fueled their fire.

A cave filled with bugs is no place for Agata. I failed my wife again. He almost wished she would complain and nag at him, but no word of grievance or criticism came from her lips as she moved back toward the opening of the grotto.

He wanted to pull her back deeper inside, but the sky was still dark, and rain had begun to fall.

"What are you doing?" he asked, trying to shake away the feeling of claustrophobia working its way through his humors.

"Watching the raindrops," Agata said slowly. "Would you like to join me?"

"No."

"Once we get settled," she said.

Settled.

"I shall be returning to my former profession."

He did not answer her. *She once asked for my permission,*

now she dictates.

"Do you still love me, Jakub?" Agata asked, breaking the silence.

"You are my wife," he said, with the hope that would be the final word. It was not.

"But we are vampires, and eternity is a long time," Agata said.

"We make our own heaven and hell. Apparently, your heaven is looking after pregnant women."

"And building things that grow. Perhaps I'd even like to take in children someday."

Jakub scowled. "Child vampires?"

Perhaps the old stories were true. *Had Agata become like Lamia, destined to destroy all who loved her? After all, they left Moldavia to ensure their children would be safe. But what of France's children?*

"No, my love, orphans whom we might raise. Though I fear Gaius finding us if we do, we might make them into vampires as adults if they wish."

"Sounds like hell." Jakub said.

"What is your idea of heaven?" Agata asked so softly her voice was barely audible over the rain.

"Having something to fight for, something to protect."

"Besides me?"

"Something bigger than you. I miss being an officer ... I was a good officer. If you hadn't been attacked ... why were you in that barn? That's what we paid Robert for."

"I ... "

"What's a cow and a calf to our lives? To a herdsman's

life. Robert is dead and is at rest. We are dead, but we walk! Perhaps Mihai was right. I should have put you away."

A bloody tear slipped down Agata's cheek, and she clutched at the cross she wore at her neck. "I offered you freedom once. I won't stay with you if I pain you so. I have no need for eternal misery."

The idea of losing Agata terrified him. It was not only that he loved his wife. She was the mother of his children. She created their home with thoughtfulness, and until the attack, it had been a place of joy. However, he felt a more profound fear. If she was lost to him, despair and bitterness would defeat his better nature.

"You are my wife. I swore to protect and provide for you. You swore to obey me."

"We swore till death. We have both died. We can make our own rules now. Stay with me in love or leave me."

Her words created an icy spot in Jakub's soul. He felt like a raindrop cascading from the clouds to the earth, not knowing where he would end up. Worse, though he was snapping at her for her foolishness, he thought *I should have been there*.

"And if I leave you to your fate? Then what?"

"I don't know where God will lead us. I suppose I shall find a village and try to midwife again. You can find a war to fight in," Agata said in an unwavering tone. "But it is not my fault that France is not the place you dreamed it to be."

"No, it is not," Jakub admitted.

"You knew what he meant when he called themselves Jacquerie," Agata demanded.

"Jacquerie were peasants who revolted against the nobility

over a century ago during the French and English conflicts. They killed knights and their ladies because mercenaries were attacking and raping commoners. The nobility were stuck fighting a war over who was king of France and could not help them."

"If you hadn't killed them ... "

It annoyed Jakub that Agata was asking questions to which she knew the answer, but he said, "The vampires planned to kill and rob me, they would have raped and killed you. Evil men are the same as evil men everywhere."

"Then it is good that we ate them," she said. "I felt guilt, but no longer."

*

Chapter 11

Jakub and Agata barely spoke, though he felt her sweet breath on the back of his neck as they rode Castor. They traveled at night when most humans, except a patrol or a drunk farmer, were in bed.

The French countryside had regressed to an antediluvian state. Former Roman roads had degenerated to bumpy, potholed, and furrowed dirt paths barely large enough for two carts to pass side by side. Jakub worried about Castor twisting an ankle or throwing a shoe.

"It would be better if Castor had our eyesight," Jakub muttered. "This must be why Gaius changed his horses."

"Undeniably, my love, it might be," Agata said thoughtfully. "But we will need meat and blood for one more and may not be able to stable him if he is a vampire."

What does Agata know of stabling a horse and his care? She had never ridden a horse before she became a vampire. His thoughts were broken by a young buck in a clearing.

"But I'll help you transform him, if ... ," she said quickly as if she suspected she had angered him.

"Shhh. Hold."

He put his hand up and pointed at the buck. He glanced

around and drew his crossbow. Knowing they could not chance being caught poaching, he carefully aimed. The bolt flew through the air.

The shot penetrated the buck's hide.

The deer took two steps and fell.

Surveying the area, Jakub lifted the carcass to his shoulders and carried it deeper into the forest before he cleaned it.

Agata made a fire.

Once the animal was cleaned, Jakub carved the meat. Agata put a shoulder onto a spit and cooked it over a fire. It smelled heavenly. They hung the skin and rest of the flesh to dry over the smoke.

At first, the sound was no more than a faint murmur, shuffling leaves by the wind, a broken branch. Yet Jakub's senses, honed in battle, detected that undead approached. Noxious rage built inside him as he thought of the vampire who had grabbed Agata.

"Someone's coming," he told her.

He and Agata gulped the deer's blood deeply, quickly to prepare for the vampires.

"I have a sword," he shouted.

Agata dashed toward Castor.

A female wearing ripped green and white fabrics approached first. Behind her, twenty vampires in rags skulked at the edge of the clearing. Perhaps the first had been a lady, but the rest were simple peasants who had the unfortunate experience of being turned into vampires.

"We have no quarrel, but there are more of us, and we are

hungry. The winter has been hard," the woman said in French. "If you wish to keep your horse, leave."

Jakub raised his sword.

Laughter and whoops answered them. Sounds of hideous starving mania.

The horde of filthy monsters crept closer. The vampires wanted nothing to do with them. Behind them, more vampires gathered and pushed them away from their bloody prey. Jakub lifted Agata on Castor. As quickly as he dared, Jakub led his horse into the darkness. *Were all vampires in France so low?*

✳

Agata could see the pines and underbrush and blackness beyond. Her stomach growled; her lips and tongue felt like sand. She tried to think of the sweet taste of deer blood, but the few sips had not satiated her. She thought of the vampire flesh she had eaten weeks before.

Agata felt the French vampires' presence in every breeze and movement in the underbrush. She feared they would follow. Mile after mile, they slowly moved northwest farther from the pack of hungry vampires who may or may not be their enemy.

Jakub plastered a wane smile on his face, each time he looked back at her. Agata knew that smile was for her benefit. He was worried and hungry too.

Their silk tapestries were gone; only a few of her precious jewels remained. They had bits of gold and silver from their victims, but not enough to buy a place at court. Hopefully, the last of their wealth might buy them an appropriate wardrobe.

They found a farming hamlet which had been erected

beside a fast-moving river. They stopped to water Castor and fill their skins. They rode past stone and earth cottages and wooden barns. Before the sun rose, Jakub hid Agata in a hollow of a tree and hobbled Castor beside it so he might graze.

She worried as she waited. Every second the sun moved closer to the horizon. He returned with a man's corpse who smelled of foul wine and a bundle of hay. With an attentive expression, Agata clutched her cross. Her stomach turned by the smell of dirty flesh, but she desired his blood. Her fangs expanded.

She waited until Jakub saw to Castor's needs. Then she and her husband gorged on the drunk farmer's blood. Once finished, they left the corpse to rot.

*

Chapter 12

Castor carried them over broken roads and through small hamlets where they found shelter and prey. Three weeks later, Jakub and Agata rode into the city of Blois in the twilight and found lodging and stabling. From their window, they could see toward the castle. Built over several centuries, the Château Royal de Blois was comprised of several buildings with different architectural styles. Beneath the stone moldings and lobed arches was an older fortress. The new, Gothic-style entry and main castle featured a large statue of the mounted king above the entrance.

It was hard not to be carried away by exciting thoughts. King Louis XII was a knight, as Jakub was. A warrior king, a king of the people, Louis XII would understand his needs.

With the last of her jewelry, save her wedding ring and rosary, they found a suitable tailor to meet with them.

With the need for blood, but unable to chance poaching a deer, Jakub went hunting for someone who would not be missed. He found a tiny street urchin, hiding against the elements under the eaves of a building. Though he would have preferred a grown hunter or a washerwoman, her pulsing heart was like a song in his ears. It created an agonizing thirst in his soul.

However, he was supposed to be temperate with his eating habits. Was it against the code of Chivalry to harm her?

Before he could decide to let her go, he snatched the child and broke her neck. Whether or not he would eat the child or just give her to Agata, there was no reason to make a child suffer.

Agata said nothing of their meal. With a slack expression and wet eyes, Agata clutched her cross. She plastered a quivery smile on her lips and then bent down to take a bite out of the dead child. He felt a sharp pain in the back of his throat as he swallowed his remorse.

However, upon seeing Agata drink, Jakub could no longer contain his hunger.

He let his fangs expand and drank her blood. Her flesh was tender — more tender than anything else he had eaten at a vampire. He was a beast, not a knight. This proved it. This was why the vampires roamed, starving in France. They could not quell their hunger.

Agata had her fill and began to weep.

Jakub quickly grew tired of her crying.

How can I love such a woman? Jakub thought without warning. Surprised, he felt lost; his existence was in disarray. *The man I had been is dead. And Agata has become Lamia.* He thought of striking his wife down, cutting off her head and then killing himself and laying them both in the sun.

Forcing his voice to remain low, Jakub growled, "We are reveling in our sins. We are away from God, killing children."

She trembled as his voice rose, but she replied, "I never told you to get a child."

With a bitter smile, he said, "No, but I must hunt while

you are safely inside."

"Then, I shall hunt."

"You! You!" Jakub roared. "You are a woman, my wife, and you will not be hunting."

"I could find ... " Agata began.

He cut her off. "I know how you would do it. You would pretend to be a strumpet in order to entice the dogs."

"You pretended I was a strumpet to find our prey in Chilia," Agata snapped.

Exasperation increased in his regret. His hand clenched into a fist. He feared he would strike her, Jakub slammed out of the rented room.

"Where are you going?" Agata asked at the door.

"I need to walk the bear," he snapped and went down the stairs. Thankfully, she did not follow.

He walked to the stables on a pretend task. Every apprentice scooping horse shit, or running errands reminded him of all he had lost. He once knew his place in the world. He once owned an elegant house. He was a father of five— though his children did not know him the way they had known their mother. He once was a noble citizen of Moldovia, but now he had killed an innocent child. He should drop the Christian from his name, but his papers referred to him thus. Perhaps he was not even the child of Petru any longer. His father was dead. And Jakub was a vampire.

But all that had happened because he left Agata alone to be raped by a vampire and murdered by a priest. If he had been there, he might have protected her. He had failed his lady, his family. He did not deserve to be a knight.

He walked until the sky lightened and returned to their lodging. Thankfully what was edible on the child had been carved into steaks and what was not had been disposed of. He wanted to apologize to his wife, he wanted to share his pain with her, but he could not find the words.

The only words he was able to amass into a semblance of a thought was: "I know you are not a strumpet."

*

Chapter 13

Jakub asked Agata to clip his hair to his shoulders as other men — including Louis XII — typically wore. French fashion also dictated he shave off his beard. He had worn a beard and mustache as long as he could grow them. Clean-shaven, he felt even more lost, as if the man he was had drifted even farther away.

He pulled a linen shirt over his head and ensured perfect symmetrical gathers at the gold ornamented neckband. Then donned a red velvet collarless doublet cut square and low. His skirted jerkins were tied over the doublet and to that bright satin sleeves. His loose, fur-lined gown opened down the front, with a large turned back collar that broadened over the shoulders. His legs were covered in multiple colored hose, supported by garters.

Jakub did not like the thick French velvets and satin. If de Charny had been alive, Jakub doubted he would like them either. Without seeing his face, studying his clothing in the polished mirror was unsatisfying. Jakub feared something might be used against him: his accent, his Moldavian mannerisms. Agata's accent nearly disappeared under the French, his was always present. And though he understood words when he heard them, speaking was much harder.

He planned for obstacles and strategized ways to overcome them, but he had not ever been this afraid in battle. He would suffer at his task if it meant Agata was safe. Then onto whatever war, the king needed him.

And Agata would have a place in society as his wife.

"The carriage is here," Agata said softly.

His beloved wore a round hood over a linen cap and a silk square-necked gown over a kirtle in the French style. The gown had a narrow row of red and black floral embroidery at the neck but was otherwise unadorned. Rubies and diamonds should be set about her throat, but the only jewelry she had left was the amber crucifix and rosary.

Jakub held Agata's hand as they descended the stairs. "My love, I have been fighting wars my entire life, but for this battle, I wish I had Mihai's education."

"Fear not, we shall learn this together." Agata squeezed his hand.

Did that touch mean she had forgiven me my outburst? Jakub hoped so.

With his assistance, she settled into the far cushion of the hired carriage; Jakub sat beside her. The footman pushed the door shut behind them with an irritated squeak of the hinges and the thud of wood hitting wood. The leather smelled like moldy bread — no doubt from France's incessant rain.

The carriage carried them up the hill to the Château Royal de Blois's main entrance. Jakub smiled at the statue again.

As they climbed the grand stone staircase, Jakub rubbed his sweaty hands on his clothes. He was glad they chose the red velvet to hide any drips of blood.

The courtiers seem to have a dance in the way that they moved. Yet the dance was unknown to Jakub. He felt clumsy and unsure of himself. Their unending pulses might have driven him mad, if they had not fed on the child.

I am making excuses for my misdeeds, Jakub thought. *I must learn control.*

The soft-spoken French ladies wore heavy skirts of beautiful, brilliant colors. They covered their long hair with French hoods and decorated their caps and billaments with embroidery in a thousand colorful patterns. Their plentiful endowments were hidden by jeweled shawls and exposed by square-cut necklines. While Agata's gray silk seemed plain against the taffeta gowns with embroidered pearls, she was more beautiful than he had ever seen her.

While they waited until their turn to seek an audience with the king, Jakub studied everything. Nothing was as de Charny described, not even the knights. Of course, this was a different court.

Jakub was slightly covetous, though the king was a man of forty-eight, there was not a touch of gray in the smooth brown hair that he wore to his shoulders. Steely, intelligent eyes sat above his falcon's nose. His high cheekbones gave his face a noble bearing.

Jakub noticed how, when Louis stood, he limped ever so slightly. The man had seen several wars. Jakub remembered how before Agata transformed him into a vampire, he too had pains in his back and knees. Yet, in the back of Jakub's mind, he had a strong inclination the king suffered from gout.

Hours went by. The sun moved higher. Jakub's feet and knees ached.

Listening to the petitioners, Jakub tried not to be disappointed. The Franks he had met as allies and enemies seemed eloquent and noble. He had thought France would be a magical, wondrous place, but in many ways, it was more backward than Moldavia. There were wars, women in bondage, and starvation among the people, whether they be vampires or humans.

Finally, the herald called out his name.

Jakub and Agata approached the throne.

"Majesty. May I present my wife, Agata, the daughter of Count Artur of the House Vidraru to your queen."

"My lady," the King said with hardly a glance.

The Queen said, "Lady Agata."

Agata did not say anything as she curtsied as the French women. He knew she was listening both to Jakub's conversation with the King and the discussions around the court.

"And how may I assist you?" the King asked.

"You are a man of peace, and you have dealt with your enemies in kind fashion and policy. Your knights, many whom I met on the battlefields in the east, speak of your graciousness." Jakub named a few of the noble knights he worked with during the wars with the Ottoman Empire and Poland, but his words felt clumsy in his mouth. "And I have come to request sanctuary in your lands for my beloved wife and myself. I would forgo hope to join the nobles of the sword."

Jakub passed his references from Voivode Bogdan, his brother, and his letters of introduction from the Count of

Provence.

"The deputies representing the Second Estate want foreigners to be prohibited from command positions in the military," the king said.

Jakub's dead heart went cold at the new policy. *Did I make a mistake? Will Agata die because I can't protect her.* His face did not leave the King's, but he felt a longing to tear out this King's throat and see his royal blood. Instead, he said, "If not a command position, I heard you require noble horseman in the gendarmerie in the Italian Peninsula. My horse and I have both seen battle."

"Indeed," King Louis said. "Are you Catholic?"

"Yes, Majesty," Jakub said.

"Then I bid you to remain at court, my servants will see to your wife's comfort. I may have something for a man of your talents."

"Thank you, Majesty."

Jakub and Agata backed away to their places in the room.

Then the king spoke to another petitioner who needed help with collecting taxes.

They stood silently in the back of the room listening to the gossip and requests, Jakub learned the rumors he heard from the Count of Providence was correct. The courtiers were preoccupied with budgetary concerns and reduced pensions. However, Louis XII was more concerned with the lack of a male heir and holding France's hard-won colonies and French expansion into the Italian peninsula. His first queen had been sterile, and rumored disfigured though no one could quite say how.

His second queen had several miscarriages, a stillborn son, and two daughters. King Louis was seeking another queen, but that had nothing to do with Jakub, so he remained silent on the matter and hoped Agata would remain silent on such matters as well.

When the Queen rose to attend the chapel, Agata left with the other women.

Sunlight gleamed against the windows. The glare hurt his eyes. Although, he ached for sleep, Jakub's mind wandered. He wondered if their ancestor was still in the cave, trapped, and hungry. Gaius is alone with no one but his demon horse to offer him comfort. But if all that were so, why had he saw him laughing?

Not knowing how or why, he drifted away from his body. He felt as if he could see through the cells of his own blood. He saw Agata with the other women, then a dark space of falling ash, and found Gaius astride Nix, both hiding under layers of cloth and armor.

"You went with her, stay with her. Let immortality destroy your love," Gaius said to the air.

Jakub tried to back away but found himself stuck, seemingly flying alongside Gaius and Nix.

"I apologize," Jakub whispered, with the hope his body was not doing anything strange in the French courtroom and Gaius would release him from this new bondage quickly. "But I couldn't stay."

"You aren't the first ungrateful offspring, nor will you be the last," Gaius said. "Go to your wife, Jakub, I have an occupation I have set my mind to."

Still not able to return, Jakub asked, "And what is that?"

"Like you, I seek a king."

"To what end?"

"Kings have wars. Wars are good for profit."

"But why am I with you?" Jakub whispered.

Gaius gave him a knowing look and shook his head. "You are my offspring and gifted with the ability to travel through the bloodline." He chuckled. "When you learn to control your gifts, you can find anything you seek better than most. As you dreamed of me, dream of Agata, or better yet yourself, you will find your home again."

Gaius did not lead him astray. Though he put a dagger through Gaius's chest, the ancient vampire had just helped him. He merely called him an ungrateful offspring. It made him think of his elder son, Artur, who had been with Agata when she was attacked in the barn. He had tried to protect her from Nicheola and failed. Jakub regretted that their last conversation was one of casting blame and anger.

In the courtroom, no one was looking at Jakub or whispering his way. He continued to stand, unmoving. Trying to listen, hoping being surrounded by French accents would help him learn better diction.

＊

The gravel path to the castle's chapel was damp from an earlier storm, but the ladies followed their queen without complaint. Agata wondered if Jakub felt the ache in his feet the way she did. Court was exhausting. At least the layers of clothing and veils protected her from the sun.

Her throat parched, Agata found her bloodlust growing. The queen and ladies' perfumes mixed with sour breath, sweat, menstrual blood, and the smell of food cooking in the nearby kitchen. Even the jingle of coin, jewelry, and purses under clothing and dresses piqued her hunger.

However, every movement, every gesture she made was watched. She was careful to remain with women of her own rank: countesses and count's daughters. Ahead, the higher-ranking women laughed when one made a joke but quieted as they drew closer to the church. Agata caught the distinct sound of the dragging of a rake.

A gardener shoved a rake against the dirty path collecting leaves. His body was covered in a light sweat due to his exertions. She smelled him and heard his regular heartbeat.

The other women's laughter and words fell away. The gardener was the only person in the world. Her prey. She might be able to rush him and take him as he fell to the ground. She would bring the dead man's body to Jakub and show him she could also hunt. She was strong now. She was a vampire.

She shook the thought away and forced herself to remember their shared mission. As a foreigner, some minor missteps in etiquette might be tolerated, but not murdering a gardener. And most certainly, not drinking a dying man's blood in front of the queen.

Agata dipped the fingertips of her right hand in the font of Holy Water beside the entrance to the church and made the sign of the Cross.

She placed her right knee, lightly and briefly on the ground as she faced the tabernacle. Then she entered the pew beside the other ladies of her rank.

Agata focused on the Holy Mother and said a prayer for her children in broken French so the women would know what she prayed for.

She wished she could help Jakub in some way, but if he was to become a knight of France, this path was the only way. Agata would not speak of her past as a midwife.

Though she wanted to help the queen, but could not chance becoming embroiled in scandal if this king divorced her or died without a male heir. Moreover, France's sumptuary laws held the nobility to a strict standard of behavior and dress. Agata had learned laws even prevented them from plowing their own fields under penalty of losing their titles and lands. Who knew if the titled were allowed to be midwives and healers?

It was of utmost importance, Jakub and Agata prove that they were good Catholics and though they were foreigners understood, accepted, and would assimilate to French culture.

✽

Chapter 14

For days, Jakub stood as still as he could, dressed in French court fashion in place, listening to rumors. Each night he fell into bed and rested in Agata's arms, but neither of them slept well. When they woke, they always found his hair and beard had grown long, and Agata would cut his hair and shave him. They hungered for blood and found it in pigeons and cattle, which held back their thirst, but did not satisfy them. They would not chance killing courtiers or any more commoners — even those who would not be missed.

He feared the waiting would never end. He wondered about Gaius's words: "I seek a king."

One morning after a fortnight, the king's advisor sought him out and asked him to come into the king's bedchamber — a true honor.

Jakub bowed as he entered the bedchamber.

A nobleman shaved the king's face, careful not to nick the royal throat with the razor. Another count brushed off a doublet, nearby.

"At times, I look back with gratification at the expulsion of the English from French soil, but now it is time to expand French interests," Louis said. "As you mentioned, I look to the

Italian peninsula."

"Yes, Majesty," Jakub said, forcing excitement back into his stomach.

"However, the Second Estate denies foreigners, no matter how capable, to oversee our men. Still, I might have an occupation for a man of your talents."

"I shall not fail you, Majesty."

"As you say. My queen tells me your wife is a devout," the King said.

"Indeed, Majesty."

"Yet, she travels beside you."

"My beloved longed to see your beautiful cities and cathedrals. She has a gift with languages; however, my wife has never gone to war with me, nor will she. If you set me upon the Italian Penisula, I ask for her protection."

The king raised an eyebrow. "Is she your beloved? This is the second time you have called her thus."

"Yes, Majesty. It was a match between my father and hers to open a trade agreement, but I happily found I love her and have come to rely upon her good sense."

"A rare gift."

"Thank you, Majesty." Jakub was not sure if he spoke of love or a wife with good sense.

"Tell me, why did you come to France? The real reason. You have five children, or so I am told."

At this moment, Jakub knew he must speak plainly. "I was away in battle. My lady was raped by a man who came to steal our cows. Our elder son tried to stop him and suffered injuries. He is, but a lad of fourteen. The priests claimed his sword arm failed according to God's will, but what do priests know of battle?

"My son was outmatched by a full-grown man. Only by God's mercy, my elder daughter is already married, and my youngest was safe with her nurse. Afterward, my brother told me to set my lady aside and hide the shame of our house."

The noblemen seemed aghast, but the king continued his grooming.

Jakub waited. So far, he had not been dismissed. "I love her. And my lady is worthy of my devotion."

The king's face was wiped with a towel. "I see. Thank you for your honesty."

"Honesty is a trait which your famed Geoffroi de Charny attributed to all knights, Majesty."

"You know of de Charny?" Louis XII asked.

"Yes, I read his works when I was a lad. He is why I came to France."

"Indeed, de Charny was a great knight. But do you betray your people, your king, for the love of a woman?"

Moldovia did not have kings, but this was not the time to make the comparison.

"I would have never gone to Moldavia's enemies. As my viovode gave me a recommendation and his blessings to go to France, I do not think he feels betrayed. My brother also understood. My younger nephew fights in the name of our family and my son has taken up my mantle for Viovode Bogdan."

"The same son who failed your lady?"

"The same. But every knight knows the truth, Majesty."

"Which is?" the king asked.

"My son will face many battles in his life. He will win some days, and he will lose others. One day, he will die as any soldier. His scars carry insight, just as mine do."

Louis XII made a short nod. "As we expand our interests, the Kingdom has some problematic roads along the countryside which require assistance. Please speak to my Minister of Internal Affairs."

He gestured toward a letter.

One of Louis XII's advisors took the missive with a deep bow. He backed toward Jakub. The men backed out of the chamber together and bowed once more before leaving the room. The advisor escorted Jakub to the office of the Minister of Internal Affairs.

The minister took the letter, wrote a few words on it, stamped it with the royal seal, and handed it to Jakub along with copies of three letters from Oliver Cosson Banquier, Count of Limousin.

"Your wife rides beside you?" The advisor said.

"Yes."

"Take care. Count Oliver has one wife in the grave, one wife living, and three mistresses, but not a single son or daughter."

"Not even bastards?" Jakub asked.

"Not even one," the advisor whispered. "And his holdings are large. As our King looks for a wife who can give him a son, so does Count of Limousin."

"Thank you, Sir," Jakub said.

*

Chapter 15

The ancient road to Limousin was pitted and holed as other country roads were. Between towns, they passed a few merchant carts, but most had become captives of the cold winter weather. They ate animals that would not be missed: rodents, cats, dogs. They ate the stray human when they could find one alone.

Raindrops fell, incessantly pelting and penetrating the long wool cloaks that covered the vampires and protected them from the cold and occasional sunbreak. Icy air stabbed through layers of wet wool and linen. The undead flesh of Agata's hands, wrapped around his waist and protected by his cloak, felt even colder. The entire countryside smelled damp and musty. The smell of mold, the smell of death. Jakub dreamed of a hot bath, preferably in front of a hearth. He was sure Agata felt the same.

Fearless Castor, his constant friend, slowly walked with his head hung down, his mane dripped from the icy rain. Mud covered his white socks, he looked black from head to hoof. He occasionally snorted, shook his head and slowed to graze at a stray strand of grass near the road. Jakub did not press the horse on. It was better they moved safely and assuredly through the countryside rather than rush and throw a shoe or twist an ankle.

To distract himself from his discomfort, Jakub thought of the letters that Count Limousin sent to the Crown begging for assistance. They were strangely reticent in detail of the problems plaguing his county. For the last three years, livestock and children around the manor disappeared without a trace. Their people were poor. The loss made collecting taxes near impossible.

Jakub's mission was to discover what was happening to the people of the county seat of Limousin and bring in the taxes which had been lost.

Though the task was not as Jakub hoped, he found himself with the desire to enjoy this moment. He had found employment in service of the King and Count Limousin. Even though he was freezing, he briefly closed his eyes and drew a deep breath in his nose to allow in some sweet relief, but in the back of his mind, he worried.

They rode past the patchwork of fields, somewhere farmers harvested the late crops while others lay fallow. Oxen and sheep grazed the common land. No doubt, all in line with the common plans of the manor.

Jakub rode passed open windows filled with humanity and animal alike. A breadmaker and her cat, probably a hard-working mouser. A chandelier. A sculptor and his faithful dog. A stable filled with horses, oxen, mules, and beside it a pen of goats. In another enclosure, chickens clucked, gathering the last few grains before night.

Deeper in town, the blacksmiths were closing shop, tapers, and potters zigzag through the streets carrying their

256

deliveries. A woman leading an ale cart walked up the road to the church, a French Gothic structure rising to the heavens.

Outside the town, lay the sprawling manor lands. They rode past an old crumbled château, it's stone returning to Earth. As they drew closer, the ground was littered with broken weapons and rocks.

Jakub wondered why. Many great châteaus were rebuilt after the wars with the English. Perhaps, though Count Limousin's holdings were extensive, over 1200 acres, he had fallen out of the King's favor. After all, a foreign knight was coming to assist him.

"The old Château looks almost idyllic, but it must have been under siege," Agata whispered.

"France has fought in many wars, Sweet Wife. If the Count's family has held the land for generations, no doubt he will tell us the story."

Agata murmured a sound of assent, then she pointed, "Look there!"

Above the treeline, a tower rose in red brick with white stonework built in the newer Gothic style.

✱

Chapter 16

The new manor was smaller than the old one, and though also in the newer style, seemed heavier and squatter than the royal château. It had two towers which rose to heaven, but fewer windows.

"Good, that should protect us from the sun," Jakub said.

"Well it will if this rain ever relents," Agata replied,

Two manservants rushed out to meet them. "We heard word, you and your ladyship were coming, Monsieur," The first one said.

Another man came out to take Castor to the stables

Jakub and Agata were brought before Oliver Cosson Banquier, Count of Limousin, a slender man who must be nearing sixty. He had a swirling, mane of silver hair tied with a satin ribbon. Bushy white eyebrows and a dashing well-groomed mustache sprouted from the old man's face.

He swam in his wide-necked satin red doublet under gold jerkin. Thick golden leaves ran up his arms, creating contrasting stripes on his oversized scarlet sleeves. His shirt bore a large frill edged in black at the neck and wide ruffles at the wrist.

On a golden chain, he wore a gold amulet embossed with a large swirling letter B, which danced in the firelight.

Jakub removed his hat and cloak before bowed at the count and then the countess.

"And may I present my wife, the Lady Agata, Daughter of Count Artur Vidraru."

Though she did not speak or rise from her bench, Marie Banquier, Countess of Limousin, a woman who looked to be near the same age as Agata, seemed to overpower the room in her conical gown in black edged with white and gold flowers. Her hips artificially widened for fashion. As beautiful as she was, Jakub sensed a sadness.

If she was as wise as Agata, he would be a fool not to acknowledge her. Jakub bowed and offered a few general kindnesses.

She replied in kind and then welcomed Agata to her bench. Agata took her hand. What the ladies spoke about after that Jakub could not hear.

Count Limousin poured Jakub a glass of wine and spoke of business. "I feared the King would send no one. I am thankful you have come though you are a foreign knight, Honorable Petrescu."

"I was pleased with the opportunity, Count Limousin."

"The manor charges a fair banalite for the use of our mills, but instead of the cens tax, this year, I demanded a portion of ten percent of my vassals' harvests in return for permission to use the land I own. This will be sent to help the war effort on the Italian Peninsula. King Louis is pleased with this arrangement which is why you were sent. However, this county's land and road are not important to the King — his wars abroad are his focus. I am so unimportant that he sends a foreign knight to battle my adversaries."

"What adversaries, Count Limousin?"

The count sighed and looked at his hands. They were soft and manicured.

Nobles in France are not allowed to plow their own fields. Perhaps that is why they were so soft, Jakub thought.

"Once I was a great knight as you are now, somehow I became old. Don't become old, it is quite inconvenient to the laws of Chivalry! You are in your prime, but soon you too will whither."

"Not even the fastest horse can outrun death, Count."

"Indeed." The count said, "Between my great grandfather's service and money, my family became administrators of this land. Long ago, I was injured in battle. I am a man with no son."

Jakub nodded in understanding, but he knew the man did not want him to speak.

"I can't work the land and keep my title, but the land withers. You are a chevalier without land, without title in this country. She has given you children?"

"Yes. Five. The eldest shall be a mother herself soon."

"Sons?"

"Two."

He nodded and sighed again.

"Who are your enemies, my Count?"

"My township and lands wither due to three witches that live in a glen. They have a legion on brigands who hunt along our trade road. I have a gendarmery at my command, they are not true warriors.

"They are not battle-tested and have no stomach for it.

I, myself, am old. Kill them for me and I shall call you son. As my son you will inherit this land in perpetuity for your sons and their sons, better than my damned nephew who haven't seen so much as a winter's chill. He would squander the inheritance."

Jakub's heart felt as if it skipped a beat, then froze solid. He had seen too often inconvenient women called witches. It was one thing to need to eat people, it was quite another to kill three innocent women for political gain. Trying to stall he said, "That is beyond generous, but I am still a foreigner."

The count said, "If the King denies this, then we can buy an office from the King. I must be generous because the task at hand is most vile — and many others have failed."

"Buy an office?" Jakub asked, growing more disillusioned by France with every word.

"The new generation are vastly different than those who lived previously. Our culture has moved toward the secular. The crown has noble titles for sale, even though merchants and their ilk care not for the divine right of the King. They care for money and comforts," the count said.

"I think we all care for comforts to a certain degree," Jakub said. "Not for ourselves, but for our wives. How will I find these witches?"

"They are led by Deifrida Millet, the other two are Adelina and Iuletta. One of them has had a babe. That's why my men didn't kill them before. They live in the glade near a moss-covered carved megalith. It is there they sacrifice children to Satan."

"They sacrifice children to Satan?" Jakub was sure now the women weren't witches, but he could not show his internal conflict.

"How else can we explain all those we lost?" the count said. It was not a question.

"And Agata will be safe here 'til I return?"

"Of course, she's in my hospitality and protection."

"Thank you, Count Limousin."

"Now you must be hungry and tired from your journey, my wife has already seen to your comfort.

Your rooms are ready, and there is water to bathe yourselves."

✳

Jakub entered Agata's bedchamber with a determination in his step. Seeing the maid, a young girl of fifteen or sixteen, who ran a comb through her tumbling waves of hair. He said in Moldavian: "Tell her to leave."

"Leave us," Agata told the girl, who curtsied and left. Yet he did not doubt the maid would listen at the door and report what was said to the count or countess. He gestured for her to continue in Moldavian.

Agata untied the lashings, which held the layers of fabric in place until she wore only a chemise.

Jakub sharpened his sword. "The count has asked me to kill witches. You know as well as I, the chances are these witches are just midwives or someone else otherwise inconvenient. Did you tell anyone here you practice midwifery?"

"No, my love. We spoke of our journey to France that I got quite seasick and we missed our children and hope to be reunited one day, though our eldest son lives well and runs our estate."

"Good. Take care of your words until I return. You must not be inconvenient to the count or his wife. These people are not what I expected."

"Why do you fret so?" she asked.

"These people are backward. So, speak of nothing unless you want to be burned at the stake or strung up to a tree."

"Perhaps, I might come with you. You will be dealing with women and my conversational French is cleaner than yours."

Jakub collected his thoughts as he moved precisely and organized his gear. He scabbarded his newly sharpened blade. After fighting for princes who changed allies even in the middle of wars, Jakub learned long ago, he must be flexible with the rules of engagement. Unorthodox thinking and humility above all else were one of the reasons he walked away from battles that others had not.

"Very well, my lady, you will walk beside me, but you must do what I say and retreat when I tell you to retreat."

"Yes, my husband."

"And if our foes grow too numerous, I wish for you to return to this place. It is not a perfect sanctuary, but does offer some protections and comforts," Jakub said.

*

Chapter 17

Agata clutched Jakub around the waist as they rode through the formal garden with its neat hedgerows. The stone path became a sunken dirt trail as they passed the beehives, and the fruit orchard became a wild forest of oak, beech, and ash trees. With every step, civilization seemed farther away. She hoped these witches were just wise women as she once had been. Happy he agreed to take her, Agata refused to whine. She wanted to be brave for her husband, but it was logical that if vampires existed, then witches existed as well.

Whether they be witches or just wise women, perhaps I might learn French remedies and become a beloved lady again. This thought soothed her nerves.

Three miles from town, they passed the carved, moss-covered megalith and found a small wooden lean-to hut, just where the count had told Jakub it would be.

An elderly woman and two young girls — the older one looked to be twelve or thirteen and younger five or six — cleaned and shelled beans. A woman in her prime chopped firewood with a small hatchet.

The women wore their wool tunics to mid-calf over a longer tunic which was most likely made from hemp. The younger had her tunic tucked into her belt. Their feet were clad in loose leather. Like other married women of France, their hair was covered with a veil held by a ribbon of the same wool as their tunics. The older woman had a simple shawl made of what looked like goatskin. The younger woman wore no outer garment. Sweat stained her undertunic.

The children's tunics were slightly shorter, and their feet were bare. The younger looked up, her light brown hair floating in the breeze. Agata pined for Daciana. She would have had her fifth birthday by now.

Deifrida snapped, "Iuletta, take Joia inside."

That was Iuletta? A girl? Agata felt a pain in the back of her throat. Witch or not, she did not want to see Jakub murder another child.

The elder picked up the bucket of beans and tried to take her sister's hand.

The little one tried to protest, but, ahead of her grandmother's swat, the younger girl ran into the cabin.

"Who's there?" the older woman called. "Show yourself, Devil, or my daughter-in-law will send you to meet your maker."

Jakub led Castor before the women. The women glanced at him and then up at Agata. *Dear God, let Jakub be merciful ...*

*

Jakub saw Agata glance toward the heavens and press her hands to her breastbone. He did not need his wife to speak to see the girls' presence had upset her. Jakub sensed the younger woman tense her small hands around her ax.

"You are the witch, Deifrida?" Jakub asked the old

woman, but he did not draw his sword or make any move toward violence. He kept his hands in front of him.

"I am Deifrida, pilgrim. But I am no witch, who in God's name, are you, foreigner, and your lady?" The old woman replied.

"I am Sir Jakub, Son of the late Count Petru, brother to Count Mihai, this is my wife, the Lady Agata, daughter of Count Artur, brother to Count Artur the second."

The two women glanced at each other.

The younger one curtsied. The older one only inclined her head.

"We were told witches roamed the land and caused mischief; Jakub was told to find you," Agata said in French.

"What's it to you, foreigner? Are you one of the damned inquisitors? We swear on the good book, we are Catholics."

"No, I am not an inquisitor. I was charged to clean the road of its troubles to bring trade to the village by the king's orders," Jakub switched to Moldavian. Agata translated.

"I am sure our great king knows nothing of us — though I gave my husband and son to his war. My daughter-in-law, Adelina, gave her husband, the girls gave their father. Haven't we paid enough?"

"We came ... "

Deifrida was not finished. Her voice took on a scolding tone "Joia never even met her father. Poor Iuettta weeps for him to come home."

Even before Agata translated, Jakub felt a slight tremble in his hand. He had killed women before. All on the battlefield died from the sword, but he did not want to hurt four women in a little hovel. His heart ached for the little girl who never knew her father. His youngest had not really known him either.

"Are you midwives?" Agata asked from Castor's back. Jakub sensed she was careful that her voice did not crack in pain or fear.

"No, milady. We make soap from the moss in the forest," Deifrida said. "And the slime of the beast."

"Why would someone call you a witch?" Jakub asked.

"Because people don't like widows and fatherless babes, no matter how we try to protect them from the beast."

"Protect them?" Agata asked.

"Milady and Milord, there is a beast in the wood."

"We don't like to speak of it, lest you think we are mad. But we are not mad. The creature exists. I swear it on your good lady's holy cross, milord," Deifrida said.

"What is the beast?" Agata asked.

"We don't know exactly, perhaps some giant snake. It lives under the ground , deep in the caverns to the south, and snatches children and livestock caught unaware." Adelina called into the house. "Iuletta, bring us a jar of slime."

The elder girl did as her mother bade.

"But it makes this slime which we put in our soap," Iuletta said. The story that the witches told Agata seemed so fantastic, Jakub was not sure if Agata's broken French was sufficient, but he chose to trust the women. He knew they were telling the truth at least as they knew it.

"We can't catch it on our own, but we can tell you to avoid being detected by the beast. That is paramount when surviving with it," Deifrida said.

"We smell like it, so it doesn't smell us. That is how we survive living in the wood," the younger girl, Joia, said from the window.

"If people weren't so ignorant, they'd survive too, but they don't want to smell like our soap," Adelina said.

"We were chased out of the village when we thought to rub the slime on the door frames so it would pass over us, just like the blood and the angels in the Good Book."

"Why don't you leave?"

"And go where? At least here, we are left unravaged, but what of my daughters? The road is dangerous and expensive."

Jakub nodded. He did not know if the creature the Millet women described had a nose, but like other large game, the greatest obstacle to cornering and defeating the beast would be deactivating its nose or other smelling apparatus.

"I have no wish to kill innocent women, so I shall seek this beast out. I hope for your sake you speak the truth.

"Come, my lady, I'll take you home."

Deifrida pressed a large bar of soap into Jakub's gloved hands. "Take the soap, it will protect you. And you lady? Take the soap and wipe it on you and your house."

Jakub glanced up at Agata. Her brow had risen to a concerned point. He fished in his saddlebag for payment. He gave them a single gold coin, a loaf of bread, and dried mutton for their time and the soap.

"If Jakub falls, then you must run for your daughters' sake," Agata warned them.

✳

Dear Irina,

I hope this missive finds you well.

Your honored father and I might have found a home. There is a great evil here that he must vanquish. I pray to God for his victory and the health of you and your newborn child.

We are staying with the kind Count and his gentle wife of Limousin.

Please write to me and tell me how you fare and if the child is a boy or a girl. And tell me how Daciana, Artur, and Petru fare.

With all my love,
Mother

On the next page was another recipe. This one called Sun-Preserved Venison was a coded description of how Jakub carved the vampires and left them to burn in the daylight.

*

Chapter 18

The Count Limousin had a lightness to his steps as he and a servant met Jakub and Agata. Jakub liked him less for it. Even if they were witches, there was no need to enjoy the killing of four helpless women.

"The witches have met their doom?" the count said.

"No. There may be a bigger problem than witches," Jakub said dismounting.

Count Oliver's expression went hard. "A bigger problem? So, you will fail me?"

Jakub helped Agata off Castor's back as he spoke: "The women are merely poor widows, uncouth and unkempt, yes, but women who lost their husbands in the King's war in the Italian Peninsula."

"They are trying to protect the town with their remedies, not cause suffering," Agata said.

Jakub noticed how careful she was to not use the word witches.

"Perhaps, Lady, you think you ought to give them comfort," the count said. "But we burn heretics in France."

Agata looked to the ground. "Forgive me, Count Oliver."

Jakub could see Agata was already playing the part of a

dutiful and obedient daughter-in-law to Oliver, wife to Jakub.

"Before I kill any women, I must see the truth in their crimes. I will see your magistrate," Jakub said.

"You put the lives of three witches above a chance to be a knight?"

"A noble name is nothing without a noble purpose," Jakub said.

"Young people!" the count said. "Very well, off with you."

✳

Jakub let Castor run down the dirt road between the manor and the town. Agata held on tightly to his waist. As the horse galloped, Jakub felt young. Free. He had made the right decision in not killing the Millet women. Now he just needed to make the powers-that-be understand that.

The horse slowed as they entered the town and passed two monks walked side by side. Jakub scowled at their dirty clothes and lice-filled hair.

"God be with you," they called out. "But shouldn't ... "

Jakub ignored them. Castor snorted.

In Moldavia, it was considered a wickedness not to marry and have children even among most priests, but here in France many men lived in solitude with other men as monks.

That was not a life of adventure and daring. He cared not what they claimed was a sin: especially in regard to Agata.

They stopped at the town hall and went inside.

The mayor and the magistrate welcomed Agata and Jakub into the town hall with their words. Their eyes held suspicion, but their wrinkled faces exposed that these men wanted what the count wanted. It was good for all of them.

"When did the town first notice the disappearance?" Jakub asked the magistrate.

Well, let's see," The magistrate took out a large tome. He blew a cloud of dust off the old volume before opening it. His offhand fingers turned the vellum carefully as he ran a finger along a column of dates.

"Now, these attacks always start in the spring and end after the first frost..."

1508:

21/04: Missing goat reported

05/05: Missing goat reported

09/06: Missing goat reported

12/07: Missing goat reported

19/07: Brigands were seen on the road. Three men,

one woman.

18/08: Missing pig reported in the summer pasture.

19/08: Iean Val reported missing while searching for loss pig

17/09: Missing goat reported

3/10: Missing goat reported

26/10: Missing cow

Jakub looked up from the page. "This does not say anyone was attacked by the brigands?"

"No, it doesn't." He turned the page.

"Or at least not very masterful brigands," Agata said. "Was anyone brought in?"

"No, they seem to have disappeared or moved on to more profitable roads, but of course, no one would report that," the magistrate said.

"Then why does the Count believe the brigands still disturb the road?" Jakub asked.

"Because we have no better answer," the magistrate said in exasperation.

"Even if the Millet women were stealing all this livestock, certainly they couldn't use it all," Jakub said.

"At least for no Christian purpose," the magistrate said.

They examined the reports for 1509. They were similar. Starting in the spring and ending in the fall, several goats, cows, and children were reported missing. In 1510, more of the same, but after two children disappeared, there was a "public disturbance."

"What does that mean?" Jakub asked.

"Well, the public blamed the witches and chased them

from the town."

Agata flipped the book back ten years. "But look here, two children, six goats, and a cow go missing..."

She flipped back to the beginning of the book: more disappearances.

"I want the previous volume."

The magistrate fetched it for her.

Agata's voice had begun to raise in irritation as she moved back from year to year. "Defrida Millet is an old woman, but these disappearances go back much longer than she might have even lived. Look."

The magistrate looked at the pages where Agata pointed.

"What could have done this? Made people disappear?" Agata asked.

No one answered her. The magistrate looked at Jakub to settle his lady.

Jakub growled out: "Answer the lady's question."

The magistrate muttered some unintelligible words.

"At least we might discover how long this has been going on," Agata said.

The magistrate opened an even older book and continued to read. With Agata peering over his shoulder, he took out another volume.

Finally, he said, "According to this, it looks like right after the town built the new well."

"How deep is the well?" Jakub asked.

"Near a hundred feet. We had to go deep. Our former well was tainted with the plague. The English." He spat out the word English.

"So, it may be a beast that lives in the Earth," Agata said thoughtfully. "Do you have a bestiary at your disposal?"

"No, my lady, but I'll call on the mayor. His brother is a man of great learning. Boy!" the magistrate shouted. "Get this to the mayor."

"What is it that you seek, my lady?" Jakub asked.

Agata smiled at Jakub. "Some creatures can only be killed by poison. Some can only be destroyed by fire. Perhaps I cannot ride into battle with you, but I shall help any way I can."

The boy returned with a youngish man — the mayor's brother — holding his book as if it was a sacred treasure.

"I wasn't sure you could read." the mayor's brother said.

"French is not our first language, so I accept any help you give, Good sir," Agata said.

Jakub might have laughed for soon, she had pushed the mayor's brother away from his book as she poured through the bestiary. She sought serpents, giant worms, and other creatures of the underground.

To distract the other men from his wife's task, Jakub asked for more information about the area and the well.

*

Agata had been sitting in one position for a few hours when she noticed the men were speaking softly by the fire. She turned the final page and went back to each scrap of paper in which she marked pages and reread each description.

Basilisks were a possibility, as they lived in deep caves. However, they turned their victims to stone. Statues of children and livestock, suddenly appearing and dotting the countryside, would have been remembered.

Giant worms plowed with gaping maws through solid rock for prey and some are known to have stingers on their tails, but those were more often seen in the mountains. La Guivere were serpents with horns sprouting from its forehead known to attack without provocation. Lou Carcolh was a giant mollusk with tentacles that burrowed through the ground to strike prey. They were known to leave trails of slime.

This must be it!

"Jakub, I believe you may be facing Lou Carcolh," Agata said. "Unfortunately, my love, there is no known way to kill the beast."

"Lou Carcolh has not been seen for an age in these parts!" the mayor's brother said.

"I also wondered about La Guivere, but they don't leave a trail of slime," Agata said. "Logic dictates a beast so large, but unseen is wise and more deliberate in their actions."

"I should say just the fact it existed for centuries, tells us that," the mayor's brother said with a huff.

✳

"I need a cart and a man at arms to drive it," Jakub said to the Count's company of men. This was no job for Castor. He would not be charging into battle, but exterminating a beast.

For a moment, the men just looked at each other. There were grumbles about working for a strange foreigner.

"Milord, I would volunteer if it pleases you." a young man, perhaps of nineteen or twenty, said quickly. Timothé de Caron was a dark-haired man who, even between shaves, did not have a full beard. His frame still held the lankiness of youth under his leathers, but his eyes looked upon Jakub as if he saw something sacred.

"Your rank, good sir?"

"Gendarme. I am capable with both the lance and the bow, my lord." Timothé paused, "And I am the younger son, my lord."

He was the younger, more expendable, son of a landed knight. As Jakub was the younger, more expendable, son of a count, he understood Timothé's wish to prove himself. The lad's eyes shined with a desire for glory rather than to stand guard in this small, quiet corner of France.

"And your captain gives his blessings?" Jakub asked.

"He will if you request me, my lord."

"Can you drive a cart as well as ride?"

"Yes, my lord."

"Are you married, sir?" Jakub asked. He did not want a man to see his doom before he lived at least a little.

"Yes."

"And your wife?"

"Is here in the castle with our babe and pregnant with our second," Timothé said.

"Excellent. Timothé de Caron walk with me," Jakub said.

The younger man fell into step, and the two moved to the armory.

"Are we going to kill the witches, milord?" Timothé asked.

"We are going to kill a bigger beast than that," Jakub said. "Killing women is nothing; do you want fake glory or your name to live on forever?"

Timothé's young face lit up in excitement. "What are we going to do first?"

"First, I need a strong ox or cart horse and a cart. Then we both need armaments. And slabs of venison. See to it."

"Yes, milord," Timothé said.

Watching the younger man scurry to his tasks, Jakub rubbed the back of his neck and stretched though the routine soreness had disappeared and went to the stables.

"This is no place for a charger, Castor, you will be remain here," he said, giving his horse a pat. "But Agata or the stable boy will ride you once a day for exercise and brush you. We'll be reunited soon."

If Banquier would name him son, then he would be Jakub Banquier and would inherit Limonsin. It was not what he hoped for, but it would give them a place.

✳

Chapter 19

"Be well, and be safe, my love." Agata tied an embroidered ribbon to his arm as the French ladies were known to do. "This quest will take all of your senses to succeed, but I believe you will."

Though the Count and Countess watched, she kissed him on the lips. Not a nobleman in several countries could claim a wife like Agata.

Emboldened, Timothé's wife, a girl no older than Irina, said goodbye in the same manner.

Agata and Madame de Caron waved goodbye with tears in their eyes. Driving the cart pulled by a brown mare named Buttercup, Jakub and Timothé rode away from the village. Timothé stretched his back and took a deep breath. Jakub noticed how the mist leaving the gendarme's mouth was more substantial than his own, he would have to be careful.

"Tired?"

"Yes, my lord. Apologies. But I am ready for action."

Jakub got an inkling the other man was happy to be leaving the château.

"And your family is well?"

"Baby was up all night with the colic. My good wife was up

pacing with her all the while our son was kicking her. A strong boy will be a nice change."

"My firstborn was a daughter, too," Jakub said. "Then a boy, then a girl, then another boy and another girl. They all cried.And they all favored my lady when they were small. As a babe's needs defeat that of any warrior, I must say I also looked toward battle at times. However, you and I, Timothé, look toward a battle we can win." Jakub took a skin of watered wine and handed it to the man at arms. "To your lady's health and the health of your two babes."

"Thank you, my lord."

Buttercup neighed as if in agreement.

✳

Jakub rode beside Timothé on the cart back to Deifrida's hovel. Timothé held his breath and crossed himself once he spotted the Millet women who, like before, shuffled the girls back into their hovel. Jakub jumped down from the cart and said, "Hail, good women."

"You've returned," Deifrida said.

"I, along with my beloved wife, have gotten the community to believe in the beast," he told the two women. "Now, this man and I hunt it. First, we wish you to anoint our cart and horse and us with your soap. And tell us anything you know."

The women did what was asked and then gestured to the men to follow them deeper into the wood.

"The one thing we know for sure is that this spiraling trail exposes the path where the beast has traveled," Deifrida said. She pushed branches out of the way until she showed them a spiraling pattern in the dirt which ended in a hole which spanned the width of Jakub's hand.

"Good we didn't bring the horse, likely to break a leg," Timothé said.

"These deep holes are a sign the trail is fresh," Adelia said. "When they are older they fill in with worms, dirt, and leaves from the trees."

"Big, old beasts learn and adjust. You must do the same," Deifrida said.

That all seems simple, doesn't it? Jakub thought. *Track the beast, become a childless man's son, and get Agata a place in society.*

"It would be best all-around if you traveled under cover of darkness, Sir," Deifrida said.

Suddenly Jakub wondered if the wise old woman was not more than a woman. *As long as she lived by the laws of the land, it doesn't matter if she's a witch.*

With the Millet womens' advice, he and Timothé tracked the beast for two nights deeper into the weir. As the trees grew thick; the men found more slimy holes filled with worms. Then Jakub discovered a swirling track broken by several holes on the end of a long finger of woods.

Timothé remained with the cart and Buttercup.

Fearing to leave his scent too close, Jakub walked two paces beside the trail to see where it led. He found a wetland with thick cover. The signs disappeared under the murky water, but there was a high ground that looked to be the perfect vantage point. Except Jakub had hunted both man and beast too often to know ideal vantage points, do not guarantee success.

He returned to Timothé.

They gathered their gear and, holding it above their heads, waded out to the small patch of ground.

The men set up a makeshift camp. They hung a tarp and covered it with moss to create a blind limiting the beast's knowledge of their movements. Flies buzzed about and bit Timothé, who slapped them away. Occasionally, Jakub pretended to slap them away from himself.

He worried they caused too much commotion with their movements and he wondered if Timothé's pulse was as loud to the beast as it was to him.

*

Chapter 20

Agata was in a deep sleep when she was summoned to the parlor. Though the sun was up, she knew better to keep the countess waiting. She dressed as formally as her limited wardrobe would allow. Meeting her hostess in the parlor was undesirable. If Countess Banquier wanted to be bosom companions or even friends, she would have met Agata in her bedroom.

Marie, Countess Banquier, was no doubt adored by the male sex for her flowing golden hair, which lay braided and covered. Her imperious nose and angular cheekbones might look masculine, except they tapered down to her soft jaw. Her brown eyes darted toward the door, agleam with emotion. "You often sleep during the day." Her crescent moon eyebrows rose as if her statement was a question, but it was an accusation.

"Yes, I find myself exhausted from our recent excursions," Agata replied.

"Perhaps I ought to call a midwife?" Marie handed Agata a flagon of wine.

Agata wanted to say: "I am a midwife," instead she said, "There is no need, Countess, though I thank you for your concern."

Marie took a large gulp of wine. This was also a bad sign.

"Would you steal my home from me?" Her perfectly manicured nails tapped on the wooden top of the small table on which she set her cup.

"No, Countess," Agata said.

Agata sensed Marie's heart beat faster. The elevated pulse clouded Agata's vision of the woman in front of her.

"You think you might be the mistress of this estate and cast me out? You. The foreign wife of a foreign knight errant will never be mistress of this estate."

"No, Countess," Agata said.

Marie rose to her feet and grabbed Agata's wrist. She squeezed tightly. This close, Agata could see the pulse under her throat. She longed to open that delicate throat and drink.

"You wrote your daughter this letter!" The unsent letter sat on Countess Banquier's table.

Thankfully, there was nothing of their condition in it, even in code, but Agata hoped Irina was well.

Marie's eyes grew wider. "Are you with child? Do not mock me!"

Agata now knew Marie meant to kill anyone who stood in her way. She cried, "No. But I promise you this. If Jakub succeeds, you will not be cast out. You shall be his stepmother after all."

Marie's face grew ugly as fury twisted her lips into a sneer. She lifted a small knife from under her skirt and dashed toward Agata.

Agata sidestepped away from the blade.

Agata wished she knew more vampire powers. Perhaps she should have stayed in Moldavia to learn them

"Countess, if Jakub succeeds, we were going to ask for the old château. We wanted to rebuild it." She hoped she was dominating Marie's mind, but she was not sure.

Marie dropped the knife. It clattered on the wooden floor. She sank down into a chair and began to weep into her hands.

Agata kicked the knife across the room.

"Did you marry for love?" Marie whispered between sobs.

"No, our fathers wanted to solidify a contract."

"You are so lucky to have not been married to an old man. I have been married for fifteen years and have not carried a child to term. It is his seed. I know it is."

"Has he ever had a bastard?"

"No. Not a one."

"Yet, still, the women are always blamed," Agata said. "It is the same everywhere."

Marie nodded dully. Agata's confidence increased. *Have I dominated her?*

Agata took Marie's slender arm and walked into the countess's private chamber. The carved bed looked snug enough, but Agata was shocked to see the lack of comforts. Her own room had a woven rug on the floor, but Marie's was simply bare wood.

"We might be sisters, you and I," Agata said softly and drew closer.

Marie's eyes were bloodshot from crying, but she raised her head. "I'll call the guards if you don't leave."

Not entirely dominated then.

"No, you will protect my husband, your only son," Agata said.

"Why?"

"Because, if you follow your end of this bargain, he and I shall care for you greater than any natural-born son. You will remain mistress of this house and advisor to the new count, Good Countess. Unlike your husband, Jakub will never deny you any liberty. If you wish to remarry, for love, you may do so."

"What are the promises of his wife?"

"I am noble-born. I give my oath upon my noble blood. Look into my eyes and see I speak the truth."

Agata tried to push the vision into Marie's mind. She did not know if she was succeeding. Seconds ticked by in silence. There was no answer, but Marie had not screamed either.

Agata gently embraced her and sunk her teeth into the countess's throat. Careful not to take too much, she sipped the blood. Marie's skin grew paler, but her heart remained strong. Agata pressed a handkerchief onto the wound, kissed her, and tucked her under her blankets.

"I will protect my new son," Marie said in a deadened voice.

And we shall protect you and offer you every comfort after your husband passes from this world, she thought to Marie.

"Let it be quick," Marie prayed before she fell asleep.

"You will have only sweet dreams of me and Jakub, of friends and of comfort in your dotage," Agata whispered.

Exhausted, she left the countess and went into the count's study. "Hail, my lady, Agata."

"Hello, Count Oliver. I ask you to mail this letter to my child in Moldavia. Apparently, it was waylaid. You may read it if you so desire. You will find it speaks highly of you and your dear wife."

The count pressed Agata toward the fireplace. No matter what he claimed, he was never a knight. Not like Jakub.

"Will you not go to your wife's room tonight?"

"For what purpose?"

"You seem to still want a natural-born son rather than an embraced one," Agata said.

"I might try for a bastard," he said with a lecherous smile.

"Then, my count, you ought to sleep and regain your strength."

The count yawned.

It was working! And this time much faster.

"Perhaps I might call for wine?" Agata said.

"Wine would be good." He yawned again.

She rang the bell and told the steward. "The count called for his most potent wine."

"Yes, the most potent," the count repeated.

She also ensured this time the count told the steward to mail the letter at the inn.

*

Chapter 21

A coldness passed over Jakub as he sat in the muck, waiting for a sign of the beast. He listened to the heartbeat of his man at arms and the cart horse, Buttercup, who was back on the road. Each beat steady. Each beat reminded him he was a vampire.

He thought of Gaius bleeding in the cave, his pugio sticking out of his chest. *The great general who made a covenant with the nobility that lasted a thousand years at least. The great warrior who my wife defeated. And I didn't even make a killing blow.*

Jakub wondered if this regret would ever pass or if it was eternal as he was eternal.

Perhaps that is why the legends speak of vampires existing away from God. We live with the regret of many lifetimes, rather than just one.

A glimmering light caught Jakub's eye. There it was. Coated in a shimmering slime, a giant serpent, its underbelly covered in suckers, and slithered through the underbrush. Searching, it pressed blades of grass and branches out of its way. Occasionally it broke a twig.

"Look there!" Jakub whispered.

"My lord, it is as large as we assumed," Timothé said softly in awe.

Watching the creature's movement, Jakub was sure all of its weight was not on its limb. That must mean there is more of the beast, somewhere. Just as Agata's description had said.

"And that's just the limb?" Jakub said.

"A limb?" Timothé repeated, rather dumbly. Then his face paled with understanding.

Jakub threw a deer shank toward the slithering limb. When it hit the grass, the tentacle hastened toward the vibration. Jakub could still not see where the tentacle ended. It wrapped itself around the deer shank and swung it side to side as if trying to snap the neck of its prey.

Jakub leaped from his blind with a saber in his right hand, a dagger in his left. He stabbed the tentacle who pulled at the bloody meat. The smell of rancid algae rotting on a scorching day filled Jakub's nostrils. The appendage jerked backward and circled around the meat again. It grabbed hold and retracted into the wet earth.

Jakub and Timothé hunted for the creature, watching movement under the ground until they came to a wet grotto. Inside they could hear shifting and slithering. They had found its lair.

*

Chapter 22

Agata spread the witches' soap onto her clothing in the hope that it worked as they claimed and climbed out the window.

The garden paths, divided into four separate walks, were designed to be enjoy vistas in each direction. The western route passed the main pastures and stables, quiet now with the horses and cows in the barn for the night. She crossed under a large shrub of blooming blackthorn as three does dashed away across the meadow, now a blanket of spring flowers: violets, bleeding hearts, and lily-of-the-valley. She walked on to the forest glade, full of deep-rooted oaks, beech, and ash trees which bore witness to times past. *It's so beautiful, and one night, I shall be its mistress.*

Agata traced the path through the grove to the ancient megaliths. Chamomile, dill, rosemary, and other herbs trembled in the night breeze concealing, yet drawing attention, to the small lean-to. Inside, the child, Joia, argued about going to bed.

Agata's heart ached for her own children, but her eyes alighted upon two rabbit carcasses draining into a trough. Resisting the urge to feast upon their blood, she knocked on the heavy red door.

The old witch peeked out of the small window.

"Hello, Madame. Do you remember me?" Agata asked.

"How may we serve you, undead lady?"

"You know me?" Agata asked.

The old witch smiled and gestured toward the rabbits. "And we knew you would come. For your refreshment, my lady."

The old witch passed her a cup. Once, Agata had her fill, the old woman opened the door and motioned for her to enter.

Inside, the room was clean, Agata, immediately, felt the oppressive nature of the small cabin. Ample wooden cupboards filled with ceramic jars of organs, eyeballs. Empty beakers, scales, and ceramics of all shapes and sizes lined the east wall.

She forced a smile and sat in the chair which the woman offered. "Why do you pretend you aren't a witch?"

"Why do you pretend you aren't a vampire?" Deifrida said.

"Society deems us evil."

"They deem us evil as well."

Deifrida set out bread studded with currants and put a pot of herbal tea over the fire. Agata did not partake of the bread but did take a sip of chamomile tea.

"Like you, I know the healing arts — I would like to offer a trade-your knowledge of local plants for the healing arts of Moldavia?" Agata suggested.

A shadow of desolation drifted onto the younger witch's face, but it disappeared quickly when her mother-in-law turned to her.

"We need your society more than knowledge," the old witch said.

Agata would have never guessed the witches might be

lonely. "I, too, walk alone with only Jakub as my companion."

"And the countess?"

"Believes I want to kick her out of her house."

"If she would invite us — even to a fate — we would be reinstated in the village."

"I shall do what I can, but I can't guarantee an invitation. ... It might be many years until I am mistress of the house, perhaps, in the mean time, I could hire your elder daughter as my maid. It will also put her near the townsfolk. Then, at Easter, I could invite you all. The count could not deny my maid's family at the spring party."

A look passed between the two women.

"Then we'll share our knowledge with you, Lady Agata," Deifrida said.

✱

Viscous slime covered the opening of the cave. The entrance was smaller than a man, and Jakub could barely squeeze inside with a bag of chunks of deer carcass. Timothé entered behind with his own bag, opening the hole slightly more.

"A foul place, Milord," the gendarme whispered.

Dawn's light spilled inside revealing mucky soil and vegetable debris littering the floor and a deep void. Sheltered in the earth and enveloped by darkness, Jakub felt at home for the first time since landing in France. He removed his glove and scooped a handful of dirt into a bag which he set on his belt. He felt the earth between his fingers and knew the comfort that Agata knew from her crock of garden soil.

Timothé's heartbeat echoed in Jakub's ears, but otherwise,

the lack of sound reminded Jakub of the silence after a battle. He enjoyed such moments.

They lit the first candle and stuck it into the dirt wall, high enough that they would not knock into it.

As they moved deeper, Jakub's nostrils filled with a musty, brackish smell. Beyond the next turn, he heard water dripping and hitting a small pond.

The tunnel curved; darkness became complete. Jackub took a step into icy water. Thankfully, it was not deep. He feared washing away the soap.

"We dare not go much further, Milord," Timothé said. He heaved the bag of deer carcass into the mud. He lit another candle and stuck it in the dirt. The candlelight bounced off the glittering, slime-covered walls. "I can barely see even with the candles, Milord?"

Jakub saw outlines of boulders and rocks along the muddy walls and roots hang from the ceiling. "Agreed. Let us begin the baiting of the beast here," Jakub ordered. "But I wish to save the torches. We might need the heat to drive the beast."

"Very good, Milord." Timothé opened his bag and pulled out a skinned loin of venison. He hammered a stake into the cave and tied it tight.

The men moved twenty feet deeper into the tunnel and repeated the process to lure the beast. Jakub's heart sank as he pondered his mood. Smaller holes and hidden entrances for Lou Carcolh or its appendages might be anywhere. He was not afraid, though he could smell Timothé's body break out in sweat.

As a man, I have been a viteji, one of the brave, but could I ever be a knight with such thoughts running through my head? If a man would fall, because only a vampire might kill this beast... If that was the case, then did God give me the opportunity to be a vampire to slay this beast? Jakub did not like the thought because its logical conclusion was God allowed Agata to be raped and murdered. *And if God could be that cruel, then I would kill Him too if I get the chance.*

Jakub's foot stepped on something, which snapped. He knew it was not a stick. He looked down and found the bones of animals and humans. Fractured fence posts, hewn boards, and bundles of straw littered the floor of the cave.

Something slithered by their feet.

"Light the torches."

The firelight fell upon the slithering part of the creature which went past them for the deer meat. A tentacle grasped the venison, tugged the meat free with little effort, and quickly retracted into the darkness.

"Oh, dear God," Timothé breathed as he shoved the torch into the cave wall and lit a second.

More tentacles snaked towards them.

"Oh, dear God," Timothé repeated.

"Indeed," Jakub said. "Perhaps, once such a massive terror such as Lou Carcolh would have been venerated as a God."

Timothé crossed himself against the blasphemy and lit the third torch, revealing the monster.

Peering out of a spiraling shell of brilliant spirals of indigo, violet, and magenta was a mass of globular flesh with two eyes and a large pointed beak. When it opened its mouth to taste the bloody wound at the end of the tentacle, the creature's gut-wrenching breath smelled like rotten eggs and algae.

Jakub and Timothé threw pieces of deer toward it.

It took the bait. As it pulled the flesh of the deer toward its mouth, Jakub witnessed how viscous saliva pooled between its rows of teeth and spilled onto the earth upon the ground among its own glutinous slime. As Agata had warned, the creature's gaping mouth was surrounded by several long, hairy, and slime-covered tentacles that extended outward, though not for miles. These appendages stretched out from the cave it inhabited for a long distance and dragged victims back to its abode.

Rows of hard teeth scraped the flesh off the carcass before clamping its gigantic mouth shut on the entire thing. On its head, it bore four retractile tentacles. The lower pair was shorter and the upper longer; on its chest were even longer tentacles. And only one was injured.

Fleshy folds of skin, like the smaller snails Jakub had seen, Lou Carcolh moved on one foot.

Jakub felt both excited and horrified by the grotesque scourge. Its very existence meant something. He was no longer just a cavalry officer in a battle against men. This was his moment to become who he had always wanted to be: a knight sent on a quest to defeat a mighty beast. And yet, he felt sad. He wondered if Saint George felt this way when he first saw the dragon.

A healthy tentacle reached for him, but he stepped back toward the wall with a celerity he never knew in life. It reached for Timothé, who shouted and jumped back to his torch.

Timothé reached for fire and struck the beast with it. The tentacle withdrew from the heat for a moment, but only as if a fly had bit him.

There was no more waiting and no way around the beast. Jakub unsheathed his sword. "Ready yourself. We may not get

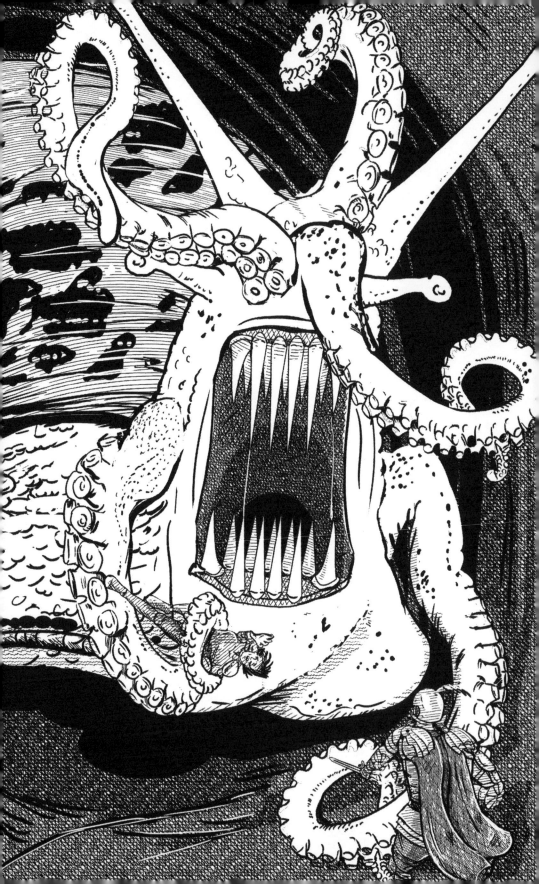

another chance to weaken it."

Timothé did so.

Both men raised their swords and chopped at the sinewy mucus-filled flesh of the nearest tentacle. A roar came from deeper in the cave. Most of the tentacle retreated into the deep blackness.

Amid this horrific numbness of spirit, Lou Carcolh roared again. It was a sound that could shake the foundations of the earth if there was such a thing.

Faster than Jakub could see, another tentacle squirmed toward them.

Timothe's saber blade sliced through the slimy flesh.

A second tentacle came from above. Jakub's own saber quickly divided the slimy flesh from its stalk.

Another appendage turned in time to back away from his swing. It parried and swung wildly. This must be a somewhat intelligent creature. Agata had been correct about that, too.

Unfeelingness, coldness surrounded him. He heard splashing, drips from the ceiling, and below it all, a dull clamor of a waterfall, maybe. Perhaps, it was the beast. Two tentacles took hold of his legs. They pulled him through a darkened mist.

His body was contracted and stretched by the tentacles.

Spots formed before his eyes. They morphed into hellish demons just beyond his field of vision. Enthralled by his imminent death, Jakub laughed as reckless abandon overcame him.

Another tentacle grasped Jakub by the sword arm. It ripped his weapon away. Another tentacle squeezed Jakub around the waist. He felt his armor crack under pressure. Seconds expanded out into eternity. *Could I give up?* He could decide to die to be defeated by Lou Carcolh; what did it matter if his body was slowly digested? He had lost everything by becoming a vampire. All he had left was Agata.

Agata. He had promised his wife they would make a home in France together.

De Charny said a knight's lady could inspire great deeds. Jakub could not bear the thought of Agata weeping over his death.

Timothé screamed. Jakub heard the gendarme's bones cracking under the squeezing tentacle. He hacked. His face purpled. He was dying.

Fighting as if he were a lad in his first battle, Jakub reached for the half-dead but still screaming Timothé and caught his flailing arm. He pulled himself closer.

Timothé's eyes alighted as Jakub neared. Perhaps the young gendarme thought Jakub was trying to save him. Then, his face became a mask of sheer terror.

Jakub's fangs expanded. He ripped into the gendarme's flesh. The man shrieked louder. Timothé's fear made his blood bitter, but Jakub needed his strength. He wanted to feel the softness of Agata's long black hair spilling across him once more. A mouthful of blood was swallowed, then another and another. The young man's strength surged through Jakub's body as they were pulled toward the beast's gaping maw.

The stomach will likely be acid. There are better ways

inside.

Grunting in pain, Jakub pulled a second saber from its scabbard and stabbed the tentacle that squeezed him. It loosened.

Dazed, he swung the saber toward the fourth tentacle. Jakub felt the give of flesh. He shook his head to clear it as he scrambled to his feet. He rolled to the cave wall, hoping to flank the beast.

Grappling with the mounds of loose flopping flesh, Jakub shouted in fury. He had no idea how to find the vital organs.

Like a flea on a dog, Jakub bit into the flesh. Slime raced into open mouth and nose, choking him. He spat it out and bit down again. Jakub cut and tore as he fought through thick mucus. Lou Carcolh roared. *Was it in pain?*

Not seeing any other option, Jakub scabbarded his second saber. Dagger in hand, he cut until his arm muscles cramped. He took large bites, ripping with his fangs. At times, he was able to spit out the putrid things. At times, he swallowed. His jaw threatened to give out when he tasted not mucous and slippery tissues but blood.

Blood.

He must find Lou Carcolh's heart.

With his blade, he dug deeper until he found a visceral mass of organs coiled around one another. He cut through a sticky transparent membrane. Waste and offal spilled outward toward him.

All around him, the monster started thrashing and trembling. Muscles contracted around him, squeezing.

He could not breathe. The stench was overwhelming. He

pinched his mouth shut. His lungs shrieked from the exertion. It did not matter because Jakub did not need to breathe, but his body cried out in agony as airspace was taken by liquid. He dug deeper, hacking through the unending liquid and thicker mass until he found the beast's heart.

He bit into the two-chambered mass. Blood flowed into his mouth. He slurped it up until he believed he had drowned.

Jakub lost his grip on the heart and fell back into the viscous liquid. He swam through the dark blood and bit down into the muscle again.

When his stomach screamed that it was unable to take in more, he used his saber again. He slashed and pierced the organ until it shuddered. The torrent of gore slowed and ultimately stopped.

Jakub turned and half-swam, half-climbed, half-shambled his way free from the mass of stagnant blood and dead flesh.

*

Destroying the creature, Jakub felt the same sense of loss he had felt when his uncle had died. He felt even lonelier when his father died and his brother had inherited the county.

Sitting in the darkness, he said, "I might have learned what Gaius could teach me." However, he was a grown man. He did not need a mentor any longer, and he had no tears for Gaius.

Jakub grunted as he pulled the beast by the tentacles. Slowly, inch by inch, he shifted it out of the cave, tearing its once majestic flesh. A strange thought overwhelmed him.

For the first time, he felt he understood Gaius as an old

general who had created a home in that old Carpathian fort. He had made peace with all the surrounding counts. For better or worse, Agata destroyed that peace. "That's why he hates her. That's why he came for me. He believes her malevolent, but I never believed you were malevolent; you were a monster who frightened men, and for that, you needed to perish. I am sorry."

Once outside, using the swamp's slick mud and vampiric strength, Jakub was able to haul it on the cart. While grumbling at the hard labor of lifting the cumbersome beast alone, he remembered he had killed Timothé.

He had tears for the young gendarme.

"I am more of a beast than the dreaded Lou Carcolh," he said to the mare.

The sound of his voice felt deadened by the swamp. "And no one but you, Buttercup, will ever know of my sin of eating Timothé. For this, you will be housed with honor in my own stables."

After preparing the Buttercup, he hooked the draft poles to her padded leather yoke. Knowing the mare could not haul such a heavy load on her own, especially on such uneven, wet ground, he yoked himself as well.

They slowly pulled the wagon first to the road, then the château.

As he grew closer to civilization, a bitter, sour taste grew in his mouth. His victory felt hollow. He had to kill a man to kill the monster. He was no knight.

*

Chapter 23

Agata's eyes sparkled.

Would they sparkle if she knew what he had done?
She rushed out of the keep and threw herself in Jakub's filthy,
slime-covered arms.

"My love, take care, don't spoil your fine gown," he said.

She threw her head back and laughed so hard that Jakub
saw her fangs poking out of her gums in front of her other teeth.
Her complexion grew ruddy and more alive. She had been
feeding.

Jakub felt a lightness in his chest. He hoped she had not
done anything ill-advised.

"Where is Gendarme de Caron?" she asked.

"The beast ate him."

"Sacrificed so you might defeat Lou Carcolh?" she
whispered.

Jakub stared at her for a moment.

*How did she know? I guess Buttercup isn't the only one
who would keep his secret.*

Agata did not pull away from him. Her eyes sparkled
though sadness faded their light. Still, she was mesmerizingly

vampiric. *Is she the evil entity that Gaius saw or is she my wife?*

"Fear not, a beauty such as Madame de Caron won't be a widow for long." Agata said. "And her babies will still have a father. I am only sorry, because she did love him."

She pulled his head to her lips and whispered in his ear. "Your stepmother wishes for her own son to inherit his father's wealth. I had to protect you."

"Is the countess pregnant?"

"Of course not. She has an old man for a husband who has never fathered a child."

"Then why worry?"

"Because if the count realizes our true existence, we are in danger. He has many wants," Agata whispered.

"Danger?"

"If he understood what we are, he might choose the stake for us and eternity for him rather than have a son. I dominated her to protect us with the promise you will take care of her in her dotage or see her married if she finds love. I dominated him and told him to rest."

"You, sweet wife, are wise beyond any woman or man, but now we are together again there is no need to fear anymore." Though he did not feel clean enough to touch her lips, Jakub kissed her. He needed to bathe.

His soon-to-be-father and stepmother exited the door, both were glaring at the scene. "And how did your adventure fare?" the countess asked softly.

"Countess." Jakub bowed and gestured toward Buttercup and the cart filled with masses of flesh and shell. "If you would come to the cart, I shall present to you, Lou Carcolh."

The countess left her husband's arm. She kissed Jakub on the cheek and then the other cheek. Then repeated the routine with Agata. "I am pleased to see our family finally grow. It seems to me, husband, that your son ought to have a statue raised in his honor."

Something was wrong. The woman he remembered would not speak so slowly. *Was this what domination looked like on the outside?*

"But Jakub did not defeat the task I asked him to accomplish," the count said. "Perhaps it is folly to make this man my son."

"You promised, husband," Countess Marie reminded him.

Count Oliver did not like to be reminded. He pinched his wife's arm. Her eyes screamed in pain, but she did not whimper.

Jakub stood taller. His hand went to his sword. "Father, the Millet women are not witches, just widows."

"In fact, when our own home is completed, I mean to invite the young Iuetta to work for us. The daughter is a bright hard-work girl, too young to live a life of solitude in the forest," Agata said.

"Careful there, Lady Agata," Count Oliver warned. "The village still despises them. I would hate to see such a clever lady, especially one attached to my son, burned as a heretic because she made senseless decisions."

Agata lowered her eyes. "Did you know, Count Oliver, the inside of mussels create an expensive purple dye. I assisted your countess in the research."

"We wonder if this shell would also produce a specialty

dye," Countess Marie said in the same slow, steady voice. "That might bring money back into the village, pay for the back taxes and secure Jakub's place as your son."

"What do women know of such things?" Count Oliver snapped.

"Lady Agata and I researched this problem," Countess Marie's voice wavered. "There was no folly in your son's slaying of this beast, rather than the Millet women."

"He is not my son, yet," Count Oliver replied.

Agata's eyes flashed to the countess. Jakub knew the other woman was not exactly under Agata's will. Indeed, it was as if the other woman was taking Agata's voice and inner strength. Yet, she was not a vampire. She was a human woman, outwardly frail.

"Husband, many are without employment," Countess Marie said. "We might use the giant shell to create our own unique pigment. With French court fashions, we might bring suitable trade here. Men who feed their families don't revolt.

"Just like in the days of old, the dyers keep the secret. The ancient Romans claimed the brew stunk, but since we have only one monstrous shell, we thought perhaps, dear husband, the townsfolk could create vats of dye and sell it slowly over an age to the crown."

"I shall think on it," Count Oliver said with a huff, but Jakub could see the old man's mind turning toward the suggestion.

"It is quite clever of my new mother to come up with such a plan," Jakub said.

"Yes, a godly woman can make the difference," the Count

said, with marked bitterness in his voice. "As my wife cannot bring me a legitimate son, as promised, I will claim you as my legitimate son. Let us call the priest and the magistrate and be done with it."

Watching Count Oliver's retreating frame, Jakub knew he would lose his new father before long. He was an old man, hopefully he would die soon. Yet, if Death did not come, Agata would kill him for his ignoble actions toward the Countess.

Jakub found it was hard to care about a man who accepted a noble's name and benefits, but not his responsibility to his vassals.

"Promise her, Jakub," Agata whispered.

De Charny gave a lady permission to leave her husband if he did not accomplish great deeds, but the Church did not. The King did not. Countess Marie was stuck in this rural corner of France without protection, no wonder she accepted Agata's strength.

Jakub knelt. "I swear I will act as if you were my mother and you will be cared for as if I were your natural-born son. Better even."

*

Chapter 24

Jakub did not watch the marble statue being formed in the town's square. It seemed uncouth somehow to expose oneself to one's own victories, especially when they had come at such a cost. He saw Timothé's face again and again in his mind.

The *Bible* offered him no comfort, nor did *Livre de chevalerie*.

He pretended to be human. He refused to eat the flesh of a human and kept to the beef and lamb. Before dawn, he rose — even before the stable boy — to brush and bath his horse. As if he was a human, under heavy cloaks and a brimmed hat, he rode his horse through the village at dusk, took a night watch with the gendarmes, and rode again early in the morning.

During Lent, he fasted with the rest of the populace, which made his hunger more intense. He heard the villagers' heartbeats and would only dream of ripping into their bodies. Instead, he drank clear water. Jakub knew he was dangerous, more perilous to the populace than any wild animal in the forest. He was even more dangerous than Lou Carcolh, because he walked among them as a man in the image of God.

While meat was forbidden for Lent, every morning he sipped the blood which Agata brought him. As he knew the taste of their flesh, he learned to taste the differences in the blood of cows, lambs, goats, and pigs. He grew gaunt and his complexion paled further.

He knew he did not deserve the accolade, but by conquering the monster, his destiny became certain. Though he wished to leave, he remained.

On the days approaching Easter festivities, one of the King's knights, Monsieur Michael De Paul, was welcomed into the manor. He was an older man whose scarred body and face showed his many battles. Jakub appreciated how he treated his squire, a boy of fifteen, and their horses.

When the sun rose on Saturday, Monsieur Michael went with Jakub to the family's chapel to make a confession in order to help purify Jakub for the coming ceremony.

Since Jakub could not mention he was a vampire or even Oliver's adopted son, he simply said, "I feel unworthy. Timothé's sacrifice is the only way I was able to defeat the monster."

"All who battle feel guilty for surviving when their gendarme does not," the old knight said and put his arm about his shoulders.

Jakub stifled a tear, he wanted to cry out a confession if he had not killed Timothé for his blood, he would not have the strength to kill Lou Carcolh. He knew if he told these people that, he and his beloved would most likely be burned at the stake as sorcerers. He wisely stifled the urge.

"Is there anything else?"

"I spoke with harshness to my valet," Jakub said.

Monsieur Michael and the priest seemed disappointed.

"Several times. I ought to be a better master," Jakub said.

"The poor man has served my father before me, but I've been more short-tempered in my hunger during this Lent."

"Indeed, you should be a better master," the priest said.

"There is more, I think. You must be pure to be a knight," Monsieur Michael said with a knowing air that made Jakub think about ripping out his throat and tasting his warrior's blood.

"I've killed women and children."

"Battles are never clean, no matter what the populace wants to believe." Monsieur Michael nodded and encouraged Jakub to confess more.

"I lust after my wife, near constantly," Jakub said.

"God gave you a wife to bring forth children, not Earthly pleasures. Contemplate upon this during your vigil," the priest said.

"Only your wife?" the knight said.

"My wife is both beautiful and clever. Only while at war have I taken other women," Jakub said. "When I was a gendarme." He thought sadly, *I was not a gendarme, but a general of men, but that past is no more. Every moment, I become someone else, and even those who know don't care.*

"You must confess your sins," the priest said.

Monsieur Michael had been to war. He knew what soldiers did when away from their families. Though Jakub felt no shame, he confessed his infidelities. Since he could not confess his true sins without harming his wife, he did not profess the iniquity which soaked his entire being. He could not tell the priest or knight that Agata was left alone to be raped by a vampire and murdered by a priest. If he had been there, he might have protected her. He had failed his lady, but God nor the King could ever give him pardon.

However, after hearing about the several times, Jakub made love to his laundress; finally, the priest gave him absolution.

Confession was followed by a long steaming bath. Jakub must keep his body pure until he was knighted, but he wished Agata bathed him rather than Monsieur Michael. Once he was bathed and rested, the other knight dressed him in new white linens, followed by a finely woven red tunic, black hose, bound by a white belt of rope. Finally, he laid a scarlet cloak upon his shoulders.

Jakub returned to the chapel and kept vigil until the following morning. He did not pray, though many knights spent their vigil that way. Instead, he dreamed of the glory Gaius might find as a mercenary. And he thought of the demon horse, Nix. Though he knew death would part them, he decided it was a crime to give Castor the same fate. Castor deserved eternal rest in Paradise.

On Easter morning, church bells filled the air announcing the Resurrection of Christ.

He turned as the family filed into the chapel, but did not rise. The priest performed a mass. At the appropriate time, Jakub received Communion. The Host tasted like ash in his mouth, but Jakub swallowed it without fail. He half-hoped by the mounting doubt in his chest, the wafer would poison him. It did not.

Once the service ended, Monsieur Michael kissed Jakub's cheeks and began the Accolade. He bestowed upon Jakub gilded spurs. He slapped his shoulders lightly with a double-edged sword, dubbing him "Monsieur Jakub," after which he presented the sword to him.

The sword's golden pummel and guard shined liked the sun. The fullered double-sided blade was lighter than his Moldavian sidearm. The lump in his throat implied not worthy to wield such a blade. Jakub dream of becoming a knight of the Kingdom of France should be the greatest moment of his existence, yet it reminded him when he was a boy and played soldiers with his brother and cousin. He was not the son of Count Oliver. He was not even human any longer.

He did not speak as he followed Monsieur Michael to the unveiling of his statue. He watched the populace devouring eggs — a treat which had been forbidden during Lent — as they cheered. The thick tarp cracked and the peerless, translucent, polished stone was uncovered.

Jakub's image held a sword over a massive cockle shell with swirling, twisting tendrils surrounding him. His steely likeness was set in determination. Timothé's expression was one of horror and pain as he tried to fight the beast's other spiraling tentacles.

The village cheered his name: "Monsieur Jakub." Instead of their voices, he only heard their thundering pulses. He longed he had felt deserving of such an honor, but the evil within his soul lurked just behind his eyes.

He only found solace that the embossed copper plaque under the statue read: Monsieur Jakub de Banquier, son of Count Oliver, defeated Lou Carcolh by the sacrifice of his loyal and noble gendarme, Timothé de Caron.

Timothé would be known forever.

"It is a great likeness," Agata said to the artist. "You have captured my handsome husband very well. Don't you think so, Countess Marie?"

The Countess murmured in agreement.

Jakub dutifully went to receive the honor from his new father and thank the young artist who created such a masterpiece. He had fought the battle to give Agata had a place in society. As long as their secret was safe, their problems were over, at least for now. But who knew what the centuries would bring? The thought of centuries without Castor brought tears to his eyes, but the thought of forcing Castor into eternity as a demon-horse, like poor Nix, made him weep.

Suddenly Monsieur Micheal had his arm. "Wipe your face, Monsieur. The cloak hides tears well enough, even when your eyes are injured," he whispered. Aloud to the crowd, Michael exclaimed: "It is good to weep for the fallen gendarme."

Jakub did not know what was happening. Only that they were walking away from the crowds. Agata was on the other side of him.

"Don't fret so, my love," Agata whispered in Moldavian. "No doubt, God will send birds to shit on your statue."

Monsieur Michael must have understood at least part of Agata's words because he chuckled.

For a moment, Jakub was irritated, then he laughed.

"Your lady is clever. I feared you'd never crack a smile on this of all days," Monsieur Michael said.

"I take joy in the Resurrection, but the rest feels like theater," Jakub said to his mentor knight.

Monsieur Michael put his arm around Jakub's shoulders. "That ceremony is for the people. You and I know the battlefield.

We know what lies out there. By that look in her eyes, your lady has seen some sights that would make most ladies faint.

"The secret of your parentage is safe with me. I don't care, nor does the King, you are a bastard. That is why I am here and not some lesser man who was knighted after he was just a squire.

"God's Blessings, Monsieur Jakub. See you at the feast."

"God's Blessings, Monsieur Michael."

And Jakub was alone with Agata again.

"Come," she said, "I've a shoulder of lamb for you. Lean on me if you need to, love."

Jakub felt guilty that his wife supported him. He ought to be strong enough to carry her across this village, but he was not. "How is it ... "

"I never gave up meat this Lent," Agata said. "I feared I might not have your strength."

"You ate meat during Lent? You?" Jakub was becoming more annoyed at his wife.

"I gave up eating meat in God's likeness," Agata whispered. "Just animals."

He pushed her away from him. "I can make it on my own. Go back to the puppets," he hissed.

Confused by his rush of anger, he stormed to the manor's kitchens, where he found a shoulder of lamb waiting for him bubbling in its own juices and fat. He tore into the flesh without a word of thanks to the cook, not caring that he stained his knightly tunic.

As he ate, he remembered Gaius's prediction that immortality would kill their love. *Who knew what they would face in the coming centuries? What if Gaius had been right?*

Chapter 25

Agata did not try to hide her joy and delight to see Irina's hand. Curious, yet fearing the news of her children, she scanned the letter quickly, knowing she could savor the sweet words again and again.

Dear Mamă and Tă,

Congratulations, you are bunici! The baby is a boy. He is a happy baby, and Lexi is quite a proud tă.

Since Lexi's tă is also an Alexander, as is his cousin, we didn't feel the need to name our firstborn after Lexi. Instead, we christened him Jakub.

Daciana is doing well. She has started reading the Proverbs aloud. Fortunately and unfortunately, she has taken some of it quite literally and will remind Petru of any minor misdeeds or mishaps. She also knows all of the herbs and their uses. She does visit Artur quite often and still follows him around. She rides her cousin's palfrey each day and speaks to it as you, Tă, speak to Castor. She has claimed she might become a sworn virgin so she might ride into battle with our brother.

Whether this is a phase or to be her life only time

will tell. For now, we appease her by asking her to practice herbary beside swordsmanship since if her fate is to become a soldier, then she ought to know healing for the good of her regiment.

Petru continues to do well under Lexi and Alexander. He has started to eye Fredrica Alexescue. He often sits with her family at church, and I saw them dancing at Easter. She is blossoming into a pretty girl and apprenticing to be an alewife. She has a good head on her shoulders, Mamă, and though she is a common girl, her family is reputable and kind. Neither her family or we have said much until we are sure this is not puppy love.

Artur has seen war, Tǎ, yet he remains as kind and gracious as ever. He has not forgiven himself for Mamă's injuries or that you and he parted in anger. He wishes for your blessing to marry Elena Julescue upon his eighteenth year. She is a fine girl, a year younger than he, from a family of furniture makers. Due to their craftsmanship and reputation, they are well established themselves in the merchant class. Her family sent Elena to Aunt Gavrilla for finishing. Uncle has already blessed him, but he needs your blessings too and your forgiveness.

To answer your questions: we haven't seen any fish in the village, except when Uncle puts out the good bait on the seventh day after the full moon, but I keep your recipes if they begin biting again. The old trade agreements still stand for the good of all the Carpathian counties.

Please write again soon,
All my love, Irina

*

Agata thanked God that it was overall good news. She wanted to find Jakub and share her pleasure, but her maid had questions and she was a lady of the French court now, the wife of a knight.

*

Jakub stared at the fire and fiddled with his elaborate oversized cuffs, which French fashion dictated were necessary. Since he became a knight, he had not slept, haunted by Gaius's words and de Charny's expectations.

There had been no word from the King.

With his new father's permission, Jakub and Agata had moved into the old château and hired workmen to rebuild it. Once the dye trade had come to their county, the old man became pliable toward his wife's suggestions. He saw her in a more favorable light which in turn made him see Agata more favorably as well.

Thus he still lived.

Outside, masons slapped mortar onto bricks and stones, while workman hammered scaffolding. Further away, out in the workman's hut, he could hear bickering over a game. The workmen were paid and fed, but gambling and drinking would always be a problem.

Though this chamber had been cleaned and furnished, old dust filled his nostrils. Jakub ran his hand along the stone walls. The mortar between the stones was made of mud that held ancient blood spilled in battle. Jakub sensed the dead's presence. *Perhaps, war would come to France again. One could only hope.*

The only other two rooms that functioned were the corridor to the kitchen and the kitchen itself. It would be a decade at least until this house was restored.

Did our home in Moldavia feel so claustrophobic?

In the corridor, Agata's excited voice directed their two servants: a cook and a maid.

The maid — the older Millet girl, Iuletta, — asked a question about her duties. Her high-pitched voice drilled into Jakub's brain, he imagined biting into her slender throat and drinking her dry. Outside, Agata answered with patience and kindness.

It is my duty to protect the commoners. I will not take my vassals' blood. I will not give my people any reason to doubt me. I must know how to fight this senseless deterioration.

Perhaps, my body no longer decays, but my mind and morals must return to the vows I once made for myself.

Why do I need war to endure?

Wishing for a true enemy, he obsessed about Gaius and wondered if the ancient vampire ever found his king or if he was a sword for hire. He speculated about the other vampires that he and Agata met on the road. None had been warriors, but that did not mean no other vampire warriors existed. If vampires attacked humans in his county, they must fall to his sword. He smiled at that thought.

Perhaps there are even other monsters who need culling.

Agata came into the chamber, followed by her maid. Quiet as a mouse, Iuletta went to her seat in the corner to do some mending. He heard the girl's heartbeat and thought about the monster, which was hidden inside his own body.

"My love, look! A letter from Irina! You must read it."

He looked up at his wife. Agata's gown could be of any French lady of the Court. Blackwork embroidered flowers that lined the edges of her square-necked chemise peeked out of her boldly patterned silk brocade. A gold lattice-work partlet, studded with pearls caught the light as she moved through the sitting room.

"What is wrong, my love?"

"This place seems empty and full at the same time," he said.

"Do you miss the children?" she asked.

"Of course," he answered, but he did not know if that was true in the moment.

"I wished our children could have come with us to France," Agata said.

He glanced over her pearl covered shoulders and whispered in Moldavian, "Why do you believe in a God Who separated you from your children?"

Agata gestured toward her maid. The girl curtsied and hurried out. "I believe in Him because the world is rich — far richer than we ever thought possible."

"And for this, these people would judge you as a heretic. So if this God came to you, right now?" Jakub asked.

"I would bow to Him, because no matter His other crimes, we exist together."

"And if I do not bow?"

"I would beg for your soul to remain beside mine," Agata said.

"The priests believe ... " Jakub trailed off.

Agata sat for a moment ensuring he was done before answering. "I do not care what men believe. They may be God's representatives, but they are not Gods. They are fallible."

Jakub was incensed by Agata's calm judgment. "My new father is right, my wife is a heretic."

"And you are an apostate, but I love you just the same," she said.

Infuriated, he stormed out of the small room, but remembered he had nowhere to go other than the kitchens. Outside, the sun was high. The maid trembled by the door but curtsied at him again. She kept her eyes to the floor. Around her neck, a silver chain sparkled. Agata had told him the girl knew of vampires.

"Bring us some wine," he growled at the girl. Bare feet slapping against the tile, she ran off toward the kitchens.

He turned back toward their only room.

"Do you wish to walk beside me for eternity?" Agata asked him in Moldavian. "I have a safe home again, a place in society. If you wish to go on knightly quests, I shall understand that a vassalage to protect is not the same as fighting for the honor of God."

"If He exists, I will not fight for His honor."

"The King then?"

"I don't know. When called, I must ride or send someone in my stead."

"And you fear this?"

"No. I doubt he will call unless another monster rears itself. Perhaps the next will call for Jakub's son, Jakub."

"Do you still love me, Jakub?" Agata asked.

"Why ask that? You are my wife."

"But do you love me?" Her voice trembled with terrible anguish.

"I long for a war to fight," He paused and collected his thoughts. "Gaius became a mercenary. I think he may be in Prussia. I see him in my dreams from time to time, but that is no life for a man with an honorable woman beside him."

She gently guided his chin and met his eye. "Do you wish to join him?"

"Yes," he said.

"Then, I set you free," Agata's voice cracked. She turned away, so he did not see her eyes. "But before you go, read Irina's letter and answer it.

"Artur needs your blessing in marriage and you must forgive him for what happened."

"I don't blame the boy."

"Then you must tell him that — in your own hand. It is the words he must hear from you," Agata said.

He looked at his sword, hanging on the weapons rack.

For a moment he felt free of the eternal responsibility of a wife. A sudden manifestation of the essential nature of reality ripped through his heart. Gaius could teach him to be a warrior vampire, but there would be no love or chivalry or any other tenet upon which he had built his life in that existence. He had killed countless people on the battlefield. It was never magnificent. It had only been one bloody mess after another.

If Jakub truly believed in chivalry, his new battle was how to remain a knight and a husband while being a vampire. He needed to confess the sin on his heart which slowly picked away at their love. Not to the priests. They did not matter.

"I don't blame our son or you," he said, "I blame myself for what happened to you."

"You weren't there," Agata said. It was not a rebuke. She never carried blame in her heart.

"I should have been. There was always another war to fight, a prince to serve. I fought for a God who betrayed my goodwill and left my lady alone for years!"

He met his wife's beautiful eyes. "For now, I must remain here and protect you and this county. There is no path to glory except by conquering the monster inside me. I confront it each time a living heart moves near me."

"Then why pine for what you cannot have?"

"For the same reason, you pine for the children."

Jakub wrapped his arms around Agata. He kissed her brow, each cheek, and her soft quivering lips.

"I miss our previous existence. I might grieve, but I will not be one of the vampires wandering the countryside in rags. And I'll not have you be one either. Or Castor. And Gaius would transform Castor. There is something evil in that."

"Moreover, I conquered Lou Carcolh so our love would have a place in this world, but I was only able to succeed by killing an innocent. To survive as a vampire, I must grow to become a man of peace and protect those in my vassalage."

Jakub knelt in front of his wife and clasped her hands in his. "Eternity will be long, but love is rare and precious, and I swear to protect our love above all else."

Agata bestowed kisses upon his brow, his cheeks, his lips.

His heart filled with joy. Unlike his public accolade, this one mattered. He no longer believed in a benevolent King or the Church, only his lady's generous love was eternal.

And they existed in love and relative happiness forever after.

*If you enjoyed this book, please leave a kind
review at your favorite book site
or simply tell all your friends!*

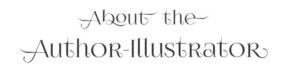

About the Author-Illustrator

Much to her chagrin, Elizabeth Guizzetti discovered she was not a cyborg and growing up to be an otter would be impractical, so began writing stories at age twelve. Three decades later, Guizzetti is an illustrator and author best known for her demon-poodle based comics, *Out for Souls & Cookies* and *Legends of Walnut Razorfang.* She is also an author who loves vampires, especially their everyday lives!

Guizzetti lives in Seattle with her husband and dog. When not writing or illustrating, she loves hiking and birdwatching.

Follow her work on:

Web: http://www .elizabethguizzetti.com
Instagram: @elizabeth_guizzetti
Facebook: Elizabeth.Guizzetti.Author

Enjoy other stories told in the

Paper Flower Consortium Universe.

Accident Among Vampires or What Would Dracula Do? *(Set in USA, 1951)*

Norma's Cleaning Service Mysteries
(Set in USA)
Death Pulls a Stake Out
Death Hears a Siren
Death Sticks a Pixie

Immortal House: A Nightmarish Tale of Vampires and Real Estate, 2018
(Set in USA)

Vampires of the Paper Flower Consortium Podcast

And more novels to come...
Loyalty Among Vampires
(Set in Brandenburg and France, 1683-86)
Intrigue Among Vampires
(Set in France, 1685-92)
A Situation Among Vampires
(Set in England, Oregon Trail, US Territories, 1841-51)

*

Elizabeth's Other Works

Comics

For Blood, Bones, & Biscuits:
The Legend of Walnut Razorfang
Faminelands
Out For Souls & Cookies!
Lure

Novels and Novellas

Other Systems
The Light Side of the Moon
The Grove
Chronicles of the Martlet
The War Ender's Apprentice: Book 1
The Morality of a Necromancer: Book 2
The Assassin's Twisted Path: Book 3

Illustration Projects

A is for Apex written by Jennifer Brozek

The Prince of Artemis V written by Jennifer Brozek

Made in the USA
Monee, IL
29 September 2023

e313a5b7-4bdb-4d06-aaa9-dbae4fb4fd6aR01